WITCH'S REIGN

The Desert Cursed Series, Book 1

SHANNON MAYER

HIJINKS

WITCH'S REIGN

The Desert Cursed Trilogy Book 1

Shannon Mayer

ACKNOWLEDGMENTS

For the readers who hang with me.
For the dreamers who fly on the wings of the
dragons, and harpies.
For the believers in magic.
You are my tribe, you are my people, you are
my pride.
This one is for you.

HiJinks Ink Pubishing
www.shannonmayer.com

.

This is a work of fiction. Names, characters, places and incidents are either the product of the author's imagination or are used fictitiously, and any resemblance to actual persons living or dead, business establishments, events or locales is entirely coincidental.

Original illustrations by Ravven
Photography by With Love Photography
Models: Bayley Russell and "Parker"
Mayer, Shannon

ISBN-13: 978-1983486395
ISBN-10: 1983486396

CHAPTER ONE

The thing about giants is that while they *are* dumb as a bag of rocks, they're fast and mean, and don't like giving up on prey. Especially prey that is running flat out, prey who just stole a prized possession from them that they believed kept their power at its peak, prey that may or may not have flipped them off as it ran away.

I smiled to myself and dropped my hands. What could I say? The giants deserved at least a one-finger salute.

I bent low over my horse's neck, urging him to greater speed, even though the ground was rock hard, covered in a thin sheen of ice in some places, and bubbling toxic waste in others. No problem.

A pool spewed to my left and we veered to the

right to avoid splash back from the stinking green fluid that could burn through flesh and bone if so much as a drop landed on us. I glanced over my shoulder, then let out a low growl at the big-ass creatures charging down the gorge after us.

Weighing in at five tons per giant, they literally thundered along behind, their feet slamming mini craters with each step.

"Nasty shit eaters," I grumbled, doing what I could to squash the fear. Really, it was nothing new. Steal the jewel, run from those we stole from. Simple, yet not really. The giants let out a cacophony of roars that made the hair on the back of my neck stand. The sound was like a wicked choir singing for our destruction.

"Zam, distract them!" Steve shouted from ahead of me, panic lacing his words.

I turned my attention to doing just that. Balder, my horse, could outrun Steve's bigger war horse, no problem, but I couldn't leave him behind. My job was to get the idiot, and the jewel he carried, back to the Stockyards—preferably in one piece.

I glanced back again at the giants. "Shit." I whispered the word and Balder tried to turn on the speed, picking up on the tension that raced through me, but the ice below us made traction for that kind of speed impossible and dangerous. If we fell, that would be bad, worse if we tumbled into one of the toxic pits. Even my shifter healing metabolism wouldn't save me then.

I held Balder back even as the giants closed in around us. He fought and shook his head, knowing as well as I that we were very much the prey of the day.

Seven giants drove us from behind, and that would have been bad enough. But the gorge we galloped through had fifty-foot-high sides blocking any easy escape. But wait, it got better.

On those walls were five more giants, two on the left, three on the right. They used their clawed toes and fingers as if they were enormous, maw-gaping spiders, leaping and working their way toward us on all fours, horizontal. As in sideways. Like gravity somehow no longer existed for the oversized dumbs that they were. Then again, they weren't so dumb that we'd been able to slip in and out without being noticed.

"Steve," I growled. He'd just had to try and get all the glory of the theft.

Now, though, I had work to do. I dropped the reins, giving Balder his head despite the danger of added speed. I needed both hands for dealing with our retreat. I reached for the weapon tucked behind my leg. An over-under shotgun with a grenade launcher, one of the few toys of my father's I still had.

And one that I used sparingly. Coming by ammunition was not a small task.

"Please work," I whispered to the weapon. It was finicky at the best of times in perfect conditions. Of which we were not in, with the cold and ice frosting every damn thing around us.

I pulled my feet out of the stirrups and twisted so I sat backward in the saddle, facing the oncoming horde. Goddess of the desert and all she held holy, they were ugly creatures. You'd think they'd be just upsized versions of the average human. But not so much.

Some of them had two heads or multiple arms. Or two arms on one side, and no arms on the other. They all had disfigured faces thick with teeth, noses, and eyes. Like everything was just larger in terms of their senses to make up for their lack of brains, but nothing was really in the traditional place. Like a mouth on the forehead, eyes on the chin, and that sort of shit.

The giant in the middle was the queen, or what passed for their queen. She was the biggest of the brutes and had three tits that hung almost to her waist. As I watched, two of them swung so hard that they hit the giant next to her, knocking him backward onto his ass.

For once, I was grateful I hadn't been so blessed

in the boob department. A smile twitched over my lips as I lifted the gun. "Steady, Balder, this is going to be loud."

I aimed for the wall to my right, tucked the butt of the gun against my shoulder as I tightened my legs on my horse, drew a breath and slowly let it out as I pulled the trigger for the grenade launcher.

It blew out with a roar that echoed through the canyon. Before it hit, I spun around to the front of the saddle and jammed the gun into its holster under my leg. Behind me, the explosion of the grenade hitting rocked the air, sending out a shockwave that rumbled through my back.

The reverberation continued through the stones and the ground under our feet. That shouldn't be happening. What the hell had gone wrong now? I had to dare a look back.

The air was filled with dust and shards of rock, and for just a moment, I thought we'd escaped the big assholes—check that, *I'd* gotten us clear of them. Steve, as always, was too busy saving himself to bother thinking about anyone else. I frowned as I stared in the direction we'd come. Something was off, my senses twitched and I turned to face the direction we were running.

The scrabble of rocks ahead of me was the only warning we had and Balder saved us both. A giant leapt off the side wall—how the fuck he'd gotten so far ahead in stealth mode was beyond me—and came at us with a wide mouth and three grasping hands.

Balder zigged to the right, turning on the speed, slipping only once as his iron shoes somehow miraculously took hold on the ice. The giant landed where we'd been only a second before, a three-fingered hand that would engulf us both snaking toward us, closing the gap Balder had created. I grabbed the shotgun, yanked it out and twisted around, shooting before I even sighted properly. I pulled the trigger and the gun bucked against my shoulder, unbalancing me. I hit the giant's middle finger, blowing the tip off. He roared and snapped his hand back but I knew it wouldn't stop him.

Basically, I'd just pissed him off and given him even more reason to come after me long beyond the edge of his territory.

Good fucking job, Zamira.

I straightened and tucked the gun away, looking for Steve.

His horse was a black bay and stood out against the browns of the gorge walls, which meant I should have spotted him right away.

"STEVE?" I yelled for him. Where was that camel's asshole anyway?

There was a low roll of laughter from behind me

and my heart sank. I spun Balder around and he slid and slipped to a stop.

Behind us was the queen of the giants and at her feet were Steve and his horse. The horse—Batman by name—seemed stunned, but was still standing, if shaking like a leaf. One of the spiderlike giants grinned back at us, preening. They'd gotten ahead of me in the mess and snagged Steve.

The giant I'd just blown a hole in scurried back to his queen, whimpering and whining, holding up his bleeding finger. She grabbed it and shoved it in her mouth, biting the whole hand off. He howled as she chewed as if she'd gotten a wad of tobacco and then spit the mangled limb to the side.

Steve was alive, his eyes about as big as I'd ever seen them, and I'd seen him caught red-handed cheating on his wife. No small thing that was either. I suspected he'd preferred being caught by the giants than by his now ex-wife.

The queen held him up by one leg, dangling him as though she would bring him to her mouth and bite his head off. I sighed. I should probably let her do it as it would solve so many of my current gripes about life.

Steve's death would make my life a lot easier, yes, but what if she swallowed the jewel? Then I'd have to wait around and dig through her shit to get it. That possibility was not cool; I had no interest in digging through a literal giant pile of shit and body parts for a jewel the size of my fist.

The queen shook him from side to side, her tits jiggling with the movement. "You wanna wanna your mate back? You gimme gimme my jewel." She smiled— though I use that term loosely with the size of her teeth and the twist of her face and mouth. Blood trickled over her lower lip and she slid an overly thick tongue out to lap at it. I grimaced. Disgusting creatures. How the hell they'd found a jewel and understood it gave them power was beyond me. Perhaps it was the emperor's way of making a joke. He'd stolen all the jewels from my mentor, Ish a hundred years before and handed them out to others to make her weak. Giving a jewel to creatures like the giants in front of me was a slap in the face.

"He's not my mate. And no, I'd rather not have him back." I grinned up at her, knowing I was playing a dangerous, reckless game. But what was new about that?

Nothing. Reckless was my middle name. No, really it was. Zamira Reckless Wilson. That's what you get when your ex-marine dad gave you your name. My mother chose my first name, and that had been good enough for her.

The giant queen frowned and I reached slowly to the left side where I'd stashed one of the other things I'd taken from the giants' hoard.

Steve had grabbed the jewel, and I'd taken two other items. A black jewel that was flashy as hell, and the flail with my family's crest etched into the wooden handle. The face of a lion in mid-roar, its mane a mass of hair, and eyes studded with tiny green emeralds. Coincidence that I should find it there, only a few hundred miles from my homeland? I think not. Anything with my family crest was rightfully mine, so I didn't consider it stealing, just taking back my birthright. The black jewel I'd taken, well, that was prep work for the next hunting trip for Ish. I was, if nothing else, prepared.

At least, that's what I liked to tell myself.

I let the flail slide through my hand until I was holding just the end of it, and the eyes of every giant followed the movement. A tingle started in my palm and rose along my arm, which I noticed, but ignored. So far so good. Lighter than any other weapon I had on me, I had no illusions about it. This weapon was not made for fighting; this show was to draw the giants to me—they were almost as bad as dragons when it came to guarding their treasures and what they believed was theirs. I swung it once, the two spiked balls hanging at the end of three-foot-long chains clicking, the chains holding them to the wood creating a nice patterned staccato of a rhythm. The tingle on my skin intensified.

"I have the jewel," I said. "So . . . what are you gonna gonna do about it?"

Steve groaned as the giant queen tightened her hold on him, lifting him as if to put him in her mouth. "I kill kill him. Eat eat him."

"He likes to be eaten. Don't you, Steve?" I laughed and he glared at me.

"Ish is going to hear about this," he yelled.

"Not if you're dead." I shrugged and turned Balder around with my legs, giving my horse silent cues. "No loss to me. He's a right bastard, that one. Nobody likes him back at home."

"Zam, don't leave me!" he howled. I lifted a hand, waving at him while I stared forward, my heart clambering up my throat. I didn't really want him to die. I just . . . didn't care like I had once if he lived. Bad spot for him to be, really. I'd trusted him at one time. I'd trusted so many people and they'd all shown me that trust was stupidity.

Trust would break your heart and get you killed all in one fell swoop.

I gave Balder a gentle nudge, urging him into a slow gallop. Fast enough that the giants would think I was running, not so fast that we used up everything Balder had left in his reserves. The sweat on his gray hide was still slick and he glistened in the light of the dying sun even in the cold of the northern desert. While he had amazing stamina, I knew we were pushing it if we had to go hard for very long.

This was a gamble and if I was wrong, I'd sentenced Steve to death and lost the jewel we'd come so far to find. His death would be bad, the loss of the jewel . . . worse. The closest thing I had left to family was depending on us to get that jewel. I took a quick look under my arm like a jockey on the race-track. Steve was falling to the ground, dropped like the useless piece of shit he was. Perfect. One problem down, one more to deal with.

My jaw tightened with each stride of the horse beneath me. The rumble of heavy feet reached my ears as the giants once more gave chase. I leaned over Balder's neck. "Time to go, my friend."

He plunged forward and once more we streaked down the gorge, drawing the heaving mass of giants after us. They were slow to get going, like a boulder rolling downhill. But once they were moving they were fucking hard to stop just like that same big-ass boulder.

I dared a look back to see them gaining on us once more, but the giants were not what I was looking for. No, I was checking to see if Steve was still alive after his fall.

I squinted, finally picking him out in the distance beyond the tree-trunk legs that hammered their way toward us. His golden hair and eyes seemed to catch the dying light as he turned his face toward me. He stood next to his horse and lifted a hand in a salute, then flipped me off.

That was about right for our current working relationship.

Saving him, keeping him alive was part of my job—and I hadn't failed yet, nor did I plan to. I might have screwed up everything else in my life, but keeping Steve alive was not on that list. My pride alone would never let me just give up. The taste of failure was not something I needed to have coating my mouth.

I put my boot heels against Balder's ribs, giving him the ignition spark he needed to finally unleash the remaining portion of his speed. He gave a grunt and then leapt forward as if I'd cracked him with a riding crop, when in reality . . . he just loved to run. I held my breath as he picked up speed, taking off as if we'd been standing still.

The giants behind us roared, the fury coming through clear along with a waft of horrible rotting teeth and soured stomach acid. I scrunched my nose, wishing not for the first time that I didn't have such a strong sense of smell.

The gorge widened in front of us, branching off to the left which would take us home, and to the right which would take us to a dead end. I urged Balder to the right. The only way Steve was going to make it by them now and get the jewel back to Ish was if I kept the giants busy long enough for him to make a clean getaway.

"Good thing I did my homework," I muttered. I'd scouted the gorge the night before, knowing we would likely need a quick escape and knowing there was a chance we'd be forced to the dead end.

I blew out a slow breath and once more dropped the reins so I had my hands free. This was going to be tight, there was no other way to look at it other than as a Hail Mary. I grabbed the shotgun from its holster under my leg once more. I only had two grenades left in the launcher, and they would have to be enough if we were making it out of this alive. The thing was, death didn't scare me anymore. It hadn't for years, which made me perfect for hunting the jewels in some ways. But it also meant that whoever I was working with was constantly put in situations far more dangerous than they needed to be. I couldn't seem to help it. But maybe if I could trust the partner I worked with, that would be different. As it was, Steve proved again and again that trusting others was not a good idea. End of story.

I didn't turn all the way around in my saddle but instead held the gun out to the side and pulled the trigger, shooting straight at the wall to my right. Before the recoil had even completed, I twisted to the left and repeated the shot.

Balder's speed got us out of the explosions' ranges, but just barely. The blowback from the rock wall sent shards of stone slicing through the air. One cut across my cheek, opening the flesh like a razor blade, and Balder stumbled, hit somewhere on his back end by the feel of the change in his stride.

He began to slow, his smooth gallop turning into a lurching leap.

Shit, this was not good. I looked back.

The rock wall had come down on either side, blocking the giants. For the moment.

But already they pulled at the boulders, throwing them out of the way, screaming at me.

"Pulling pulling her head off."

"Eating eating her horse."

"Take take our jewel back."

"Spray spray her face."

That last one made me shudder. Far worse than the others, spray was a term used for a giant's mating so I didn't want to think too much about it. Not when I was in the middle of seeing if we were even going to survive this race to the end of a dead-end gorge.

I let Balder slow, feeling the limp start to really set in on his right hind leg. I hopped off and ran beside him. There was a gash over the thickest part of his rump, deep enough that it was bad, but not so bad that it wouldn't heal. Assuming we got out of here, that was.

"Just keep moving," I said. "Keep moving, Balder. That wall over there? It doesn't look like much, but there's a goat trail winding up. If we can get on it, we can get out of here. No problem, right? We've been in tighter spots. You remember the jewel we took from the murder of griffins? That was rougher. And the coven of witches in India, that was no small thing either."

He snorted as if he didn't believe me any more than I believed me. I hurried our pace and then suddenly we stood at the bottom of the "goat trail." I'm not sure I'd even call it that. When I'd seen it the night before it had looked bigger, wider somehow. The narrow twisting path was barely a foot wide, and in many spaces crumbled into nothing. A true switchback trail, it wove its way to the top of the fifty-foot cliff. The giants were fifty feet tall at least. Which meant we had to be all the way to the top before they got through the barrier I'd made.

Staring down at us from the top were several goats, brown and white with tiny nubs for horns. And then one of them grinned at me.

Not goats, or not only goats.

A satyr waved at me from the top.

Fucking hell, the last thing I needed was a bunch of randy goat men leaping around us. They liked to cause trouble just because they could. I grabbed at the necklace with the thick man's ring on it, the only true talisman I carried. We could do this, we had to.

I put one foot on the bottom of the path and from behind us there was a massive crack and a boom as if a rock had been split and tossed out of the way. I didn't look, I didn't need to. I could feel the rumble of the giants' feet as they pounded toward us.

This was going to be tight.

CHAPTER TWO

Merlin leaned back and steepled his hands under his chin as he stared into the crystal ball. They'd been watching Steve and Zamira steal from the giants, watched now as Zamira fought for her life. He itched to help, but they had to see if the young woman would be able to save herself.

"Flora, what do you think?" He touched a finger to the glass of the ball and the image tightened on Zamira's face, the green eyes and swath of dark hair tipped in auburn as it swept around her.

His companion, a young voluptuous woman with stunning raven-black hair and bright green eyes, snorted at him in a most unladylike fashion. "You can't be serious about her? That . . . girl is barely a shapeshifter. She's a runt, Merlin. She has no power, so to speak; how exactly do you think she's going to bring down the western wall exactly? Not to mention that curse she's carrying. If *that* gets loose, there will be no helping her then."

He ran a hand over the spinning ball in front of them again. The girl was trying to push her horse up a trail that had very little footing. From the angle he looked, he could see the flash of fire in her eyes. "Reckless, determined. I like her."

"You would. We need someone who actually has a chance at the task at hand. Someone who could face the challenges and has the potential to survive. That other one, the one who has the jewel in hand would be better to help, I think." Flora leaned forward and tapped a finger on the sphere, changing the image to show the blond man and his horse, racing down the left branch of the gorge. "He has a strong sense of survival."

Merlin's eyebrows shot up. "You can't be serious? He's out for himself, he just left his partner there to deal with the giants on her own after she saved him." This turn of decisions was a surprise. Flora had been a champion of any underdog she could be in the past; now, though . . . it seemed that gaining back her youthful visage had made her a bit more ruthless.

"I know. But if we give him a reason to go after Maggi and her three guardians, then I think he could be persuaded." Flora leaned back, her green eyes thoughtful. "Why don't we each help our champion of choice?"

He sighed. This was the side of Flora he'd hoped was gone, but as it was, he would deal with it. She loved to win, at any cost. "A challenge then?" he asked.

She smiled, and there wasn't an ounce of malice in it, nothing but excitement which made it easier to accept that this was fun for her.

"Exactly. We need to see this through. You can't directly be involved, and I will hold myself back too. We can be like fairy godmothers to our chosen champions."

His lips turned up in a slow smile. That did sound like a bit of fun. After all, as serious as this was, he wouldn't turn down a challenge like that, especially if it got him something he'd wanted for a good period of time now—well, the last week if he was truly counting.

The bigger issue that Flora was unaware of concerned the emperor. The emperor was still alive and well and was one of the few people Merlin couldn't outright stop, which were two rather problematic points. The emperor was the reason he couldn't take care of the Ice Witch himself. The reason Merlin was trying to figure out this mess. He sighed.

If Flora knew about that side note, she'd be gone

faster than a snowflake disappearing in the desert. He had to make her think this was nothing more than a silly game with only a hint of danger. Not enough to scare her, just enough to intrigue her.

"And if I win?" He leaned forward and caught the edge of one loose raven-colored lock off her shoulder and wound it around a finger. "What will you give me, Flora?"

She smacked his hand away. "Get over yourself, Merlin. I'm too old for that shit."

He laughed. "Please, you're Greek, and you've been returned to your youth. You've probably got so much pent-up sexual energy you're ready to take on a satyr just to release some of it."

Her jaw dropped. "I may be a priestess of Zeus but that does not mean I'm *like* him!"

Merlin winked. "Too bad. I always liked you, Flora."

Color swept over her high, pale cheeks, and her green eyes glittered. Perhaps he was not so far off the mark after all. This would work in his favor if he could keep her eyes on him, and not on what was out there behind the wall.

She looked away from him and to the sphere. "Fine. We will each choose a champion. You want the little girl?"

He nodded, trying not to breathe a sigh of relief. "Yes. We can help them, but not directly influence. If we do that, we'll draw the attention of the Desert Guardians, and we do not want that." Worse, they'd draw the attention of the emperor. They did not need him showing up, not until they were ready for him.

She snorted. "No, we don't want that."

"We could have them work together," he paused, "like we are doing. Burying their differences and learning to love perhaps?"

"She'll never go for it. She hates him." Flora's eyes softened. "Worse, she doesn't trust him—or anyone for that matter. That much I understand."

In that he *did* agree, but it had to be offered on the off chance they could make the two desert shifters work together. They would be stronger together, and the oracle had pointed out that it would take two from the desert to tackle Maggi and her guardians.

Flora frowned. "Perhaps in their journey, they will learn to work together."

"I'm with you on your initial assessment. I doubt it." He leaned back, but his eyes were not on the sphere. "I mean, look at us. Together, but not working together."

She rolled her eyes. "That's because you're a donkey."

"But a handsome donkey, with much power and a great need to feel your lips on mine." He grinned as she blushed once more. Yes, there was something between them. He just needed the time to make her see it too. Apparently, he was losing his touch; normally a week was plenty of time to bring the ladies to him.

Of course, taking down the Western European Wall would elevate him in her eyes. He wasn't entirely sure she realized he'd been the one who built it. At the time, it had seemed prudent to keep the emperor contained. To put the supernaturals inside a very, very large cage, and keep the humans out. Only it hadn't worked that way. The supernaturals were already too far spread to be contained properly. Which had only meant more walls.

More divisiveness.

Now, the emperor was building his power again. And Merlin was the only one who seemed to realize the danger they were all in. Which meant he had to move fast, and with great discretion to get someone else to do the work for the job he should have done if not for problems he was dealing with. He rubbed the back of his neck. If there was so much as a hint of his magic on the wind, the emperor would sniff it out. He'd have to be damn crafty to help Zamira without using magic. Zamira's life would be on the line and he wasn't sure he could so much as light a fire for her without drawing unwanted attention.

Flora would have no such constraints in helping Steve.

Maybe we should switch was his last thought.

Green eyes flicked to him as Flora arched a delicate swoosh of an eyebrow, as if she knew something of what he was thinking. "Then we are agreed? I help Steve, and you help Zamira?"

Merlin held his hand out to her and she set her tiny, warm hand in his palm. He tightened his fingers over her hand before he brought it to his lips. He spoke against her skin as he raised his eyes to hers, seeing the flush of desire spread up her neck. "Agreed. Let the games begin, Flora."

CHAPTER THREE

The winding goat path beckoned and I didn't hesitate another second. Couldn't hesitate, to be honest, not if I wanted to live a second longer. With a rush of giants behind me, and safety at the top of the path, there was no reason to hold back. I mean, other than the chance that Balder or I could be snatched off the wall like some sort of fast-moving food if we dawdled.

I pulled Balder forward but he refused to take a step up the slope. I spun around and stared at him. "Not the time to act like a jackass, Balder!"

He grunted and I yanked on the reins, something I never did, but panic made me harder on him than I liked. The rumble of the earth increased as the giants once more picked up speed, seeing us standing there as if we were waiting on them. I ran around behind

Balder and pulled my leather belt off from around my waist.

"Sorry," I said as I raised it and brought it down hard on the left side of his ass, the crack resounding in the air. He dove forward and I kept at him, driving him up the hill. This was not the time for being careful despite the shitty footing. This was the time for running for our lives and praying to the desert goddess that we survived.

"Fucking Steve. Fucking idiot. Flipping me the fuck off instead of helping me get us out of here like the fucking douchecake camel's dick that he is. Shit and smegma for brains, only ever thinking with his tiny, useless cock, goddess damn him and his stupid, frigging lying face . . ." Somewhere in my tirade, about halfway up the path, I realized the giants had reached us and were not doing anything.

I didn't dare look at them. And in a flash, I knew why they'd stopped. Steve had said the reason, last night as we solidified our plans.

"You know, if you get stuck, just start swearing." He leaned back against his saddle across the fire from me.

I curled up by my own saddle and ignored him. That was best. If I said anything, we'd be fighting in a matter of seconds and be loud enough that no amount of stealth would help us.

"Kiara told me she read about giants. They love new curse words and people losing their shit in a rant. Or the

potential of learning new words. It's nice to have someone who's smart and *beautiful."*

I hunched further against my saddle, wanting nothing more than to strangle him.

Okay, so they liked learning new curse words. They loved to hear someone get cussed out, and especially if it was a tirade. We were halfway up the path and now Balder didn't need me to push him. He fought to get to the top, his back leg working hard not to give out under his weight.

Anger spurred through me, anger at myself along with a tentative hope that we would make it. My bestie Darcy would be howling with laughter at me, seeing me here now while I cussed out Steve to the entertainment of a rush of giants who'd only moments before been bent on pulling my head from my shoulders.

"I should never have trusted that cockwomble, cheating camel's stinking rotten asshole who thought no one would notice he was playing around, no one would notice because he thought he was smarter, but in truth, he was as always dumb as a sack of hammers that have their handles on backward. Useless, no good for anything—not even *sex*. Fucker couldn't even seem to figure out that the woman should *enjoy* it, too, but what does he care? He'll just damn well go onto the next one and then the next, not bothering with anything other than what he wants . . ." I let the words pour through me and out my mouth, the pent-up anger and hurt that stemmed from my relationship with Steve and having to work with him after said relationship had broken into a thousand pieces.

And people wondered why I had trust issues.

We were ten feet from the top and I didn't slow my feet or my mouth. The giants obviously liked foul language, and a good sordid story, but I had no idea that it could be so effective. Or mesmerizing. There was no way I was telling Steve *he'd* actually helped me.

"I hope the rest of his life he spends with a woman covered in warts and yeast infections, that even a whore wouldn't sleep with his infected tiny, smaller than a worm, limper than an overcooked noodle for a manhood . . ."

Balder reached the top and bolted away from the edge, away from the giants. I stumbled forward, and the words stopped as I took a deep breath.

From behind me came a screech that ended in a bellow. I felt the air swoop around me as a giant hand swept my way. I spun and fell backward as I pulled a blade from my side. The curved kukri knife was sharper than any razor, and I gave everything I had in that swing as I fell. The three fingers that came for me were curved, grasping, and I saw the queen's eyes at the edge of the cliff.

The knife cut through her palm, opening it like a ripe peach in a perfect line. Dark blue blood poured from the wound, spilling on the ground, leaching toward me like a floodgate opened. She yanked her hand back and I pushed my way farther from the cliff's edge as fast as I could, scrabbling while keeping my eyes on the tops of the giants' heads. The sway of their scraggly strands of hair was like some weird floating forest of dying trees.

A pair of hands caught me under the arms and I jerked away from them, fear making me clumsy. I spun with my knife up, still dripping with the giant-ess's blood.

Above me stood a young satyr, the same one I'd seen grinning at me from the top of the hill. His legs curved backward and were covered in hair, and on his head peeking between dark brown curls were two nubby horns, which meant he was young, mid-twenties at best. He grinned at me. "That was amazing. Really, I don't think I've ever seen anything quite like it. Or heard anything quite like it." He laughed. "I wish I had something to record it with."

"Thanks?" I pulled a little farther from him.

"I meant the story mostly; fighting I've seen before. Were you really cheated on by some guy with a tiny dick? I mean, wouldn't you be glad that he cheated, because I thought women didn't like small . . . packages?"

I snorted and pushed to my feet, wanting more space between me and the cliff edge. For all I knew, the giants would start lifting each other up and over to get to me and the treasures I'd stolen.

The satyr settled into a tight trot beside me as I strode away, following Balder's hoof prints. Scrub brush grew here and there, and smaller stunted trees, but I couldn't see my horse anywhere. No doubt he was pissed that I'd smacked him.

I grimaced. He wasn't like a normal horse—but to be fair, most animals on this side of the wall were not normal. They'd been around the supernatural creatures here for generations, locked in with us, and with that, had learned some tricks of their own, making them smarter than their domesticated cousins, and better survivors all the way around. At least, that's what my father had always said. I sighed. I would be paying for this for weeks if I didn't treat Balder right, if I didn't apologize. Oats, carrots, a nice warm mash at the very least would be the start of my apologizing.

"You can slow down. They won't climb up here," the satyr said. I glanced at him.

"Thanks . . ."

"Name is Marcel." He smiled and I felt the flush in my belly spread upward. Satyrs had sex magic and that could make it very hard to keep your clothes on. I gritted my teeth and closed myself to his magic.

"Knock that shit off," I growled as the shiver ran through me right to my middle and then lower, curling across parts of me that hadn't been touched in a long time.

"Oh, come on. From that story, if even half of it is true, you could use a good flouncing." He got in front of me and jogged backward, showing off, contracting his pecs and even going so far as to flex his arms.

Flouncing . . . that was a new one to me. "Yeah, no flouncing for me. That shit gets old fast."

"Not if it's done right. In fact, I bet if you had a *really good* flouncing, you'd enjoy it for weeks on end. At least." He winked at me. "I didn't catch your name, pretty lady."

"Zam." I looked past him, seeing Balder under a couple of trees, his head low and his back leg cocked, favoring it.

"Well, Zam, you escaped the queen of the giants, which in and of itself is impressive. But I have to ask, did you know they would stop and listen to your story?" Marcel did a little half-step, a hop and kick as if a bug had landed on him. I raised an eyebrow.

"No. I'd forgotten that part of the information pack I read until the last minute."

"Information pack?" He let out a noise that I suppose was a laugh, but to be honest, it sounded like a goat being strangled. Which made my lips twitch upward.

"Dude, you cannot laugh like that." I shook my head.

"Can't help it." He did that same braying, strangling goat scream and I had to stop walking.

"Sweet baby goddess, stop it!" I took a half-hearted swing at him. "Every predator within a ten-mile radius will hear that and think you're being tortured and then come looking for what's left of you!"

He slowed his horrifying laugh to a low-end chuckle that was at least not so friggin' loud. I shook my head. "Go on, get out of here."

"You don't want my help?" His face fell as if we were best friends and I'd just told him I hated his goaty little guts.

I tried to push past him but he moved with me. "What are you going to help me with exactly? I already turned down the flouncing."

"I could help your horse over there, stitch him up, make him good as new."

I sighed and tried again to go around him to get to Balder, but Marcel kept himself between us. I flicked an ascending eyebrow and held up the kukri blade I'd not yet put away. "Seriously, get the fuck out of my way."

He held up both hands as if surrendering. "I also saw your buddy, the big blond dude on the black horse. I can tell you what direction he went." Marcel waggled his eyebrows and fingers at me at the same time. "And for all that, just a quick flouncing. Twenty minutes, tops."

I stared hard at him, his words slowly sinking in. "You saw Steve? When?"

"Oh, right about as your horse crested the hill. He took one look at you coming over the top and the queen's hand coming for you, and took off fast as he could go. Not real brave, is he?"

Any gratefulness for keeping Steve alive, saving his ass—again—fled in a flurry of anger so hot, I thought my clothes would burst into flames. Not that I had that kind of magic, but in that moment, I could almost feel it under my skin, like a phoenix rising with a fury as scorching as any blaze.

Marcel's eyes widened. "You okay?"

I put a hand out to him, palm against his chest, and shoved him out of my way. I didn't think I could handle speaking right then for fear of what would come flooding out of my mouth. As it was, my mind raced, dancing forward with just what Steve was up to.

He'd take the jewel back to Ish, show her that he'd gotten it all on his own, hoping I was killed by the giants. Thinking I was dead, he could take all the glory. Again.

"Satyr-flouncing face-sprayer, I'm going to kick his ass all the way to the desert and back."

Marcel laughed behind me. "I'm going to steal that one. If you don't mind."

I reached Balder and he gave me a dirty look, his ears pinned to his head. I held up both hands. "I'm sorry, my friend. But you had to get up that hill or end up inside a giant's belly."

He snorted and one ear flicked forward. I reached out and touched his uninjured hip and he leaned into my hand. I had to let my anger with Steve go while I worked on Balder. The horse was far too sensitive to my emotions to give him that anger when he didn't deserve it. I stroked a hand over his side and pulled my medic bag from the back of the saddle. In a matter of minutes, I stitched the wound closed, making tight, neat wraps of the thread so the sutures would hold and heal while he walked.

"Half a flouncing to make him whole? Ten minutes. I can't go less than ten minutes if we're both going to enjoy it," Marcel said behind me, so close that if I so much as took a big breath, I'd have pushed my back into his front and I could only imagine what was there. He blew a soft breath against my ear and I swatted backward at him like I would a fly.

"Nope." I pulled out a jar of red sparkling paste and Marcel grunted. "That's right, I have my own magic."

"That's not really yours," he pointed out. "There is no way you made that hacka paste."

I shrugged. "Does it matter? It'll work, and Balder here and I will be leaving in a matter of minutes."

"Where did you get it?" Marcel came around to my side to peer at me while I smeared the healing paste onto Balder's stitched-up wound.

"A friend." I capped the jar and tucked it into the bag. I wasn't about to tell him that Ish made it for me. Ish didn't like other supernaturals knowing she was capable of certain things. Like healing paste.

"You aren't going to light it on fire?" Marcel leaned on Balder and the horse stepped away so Marcel stumbled. I wiped my hands on my cloak.

"Nope. It'll work, just slower without the flame." I walked up to Balder's head and took his reins.

"Wait, just like that you're leaving?" Marcel called after me. "Seriously, you're like the first *flounceable* woman I've seen in ages—"

"You'd flounce a piece of rotten twenty-day-old cheese if given the chance," I shot back.

"Ahh, you wound me. I would never flounce cheese without consent." He laughed. "Come on, just ten minutes. Pretty please?"

With my back to him, I let the smile slide over my lips. Satyrs were, if nothing else, funny as hell. As long as there was no flouncing involved, they could be good, light company. Totally untrustworthy, but fun.

Balder bumped me with his nose and gave a low snort.

"Yeah, he's a fool. But he's not a bad guy. Just a guy like all the other ones out there."

Maybe I was bitter. Shit, scratch that, I knew I was. But I was trying not to let it rule my life. Hard when the one person you thought you could trust with everything turned out to be the person you should have trusted the least.

My family hadn't helped in that department, and even my best friend . . . I shook my head. No, I wasn't going there. Not today.

From behind us came that awful goat-strangling laughter. "I heard that! And I take offense. I'm worth twice any of the other men you know! I've got the manhood to prove it. Twice as big!"

I turned as I walked, a laugh trickling through me, the lightness of the moment a balm to the anger, stealing me away from the dark place my head was going before it got too bad. "Good luck flouncing whatever woman comes through next. Or consenting cheese, as the case may be." I gave him a floppy salute and he returned the gesture.

"I'll see you again, Zam! I know it! Just you wait. We will have a great time together!" he shouted after me.

I had a feeling he was right and I'd meet him again, which was strange. I hadn't gotten that sensation in years. Not since I met Ish, I suppose, and she'd taken us from the Oasis, broken, injured, and without anyone to look after what was left of our family.

I walked beside Balder, heading northwest toward home. I tried not to think about what Ish would say when Steve got there alone. Would she care that I was dead? He'd spin his story in such a way that would make him look a hero who tried to save me, and then be overjoyed to see me survive, as though he couldn't believe that I'd made it out alive without him.

I couldn't help the anger that built with each step that took me closer to home.

And what would it do to my brother? He was there waiting to see if I survived too . . . Would he care? Something like heartbreak, an emotion I didn't want again, twisted through me and tried to set my eyes to flooding.

"No, no crying behind the wall," I whispered to myself. I refused to think that perhaps my brother would be relieved if I was dead, that he would no longer have to bear the shame of a sister who'd strayed so far from the way we were raised. I had to fight not to hunch my shoulders under the weight of those thoughts. Under the guilt of what I should have been but wasn't.

The only person who'd be happy to see me was

Darcy, but that was a given. She'd been my best friend since we'd been rescued from the Oasis. My mind tried to take me back to the moment I realized she was not quite the friend I'd thought.

"You'll be glad to see Darcy and Pig, won't you?" I ran a hand over Balder and he snorted. Pig was his horse girlfriend and he adored the scruffy little bay mare Darcy rode.

I spoke to Balder to fill the space between us. "Darcy will have gotten the jewel from the Ice Witch, and then we'll only have two left to get. Ish will be okay because she'll have more of her magic back and maybe she can help Bryce then." I frowned, thinking about how long it had been since we'd started this journey. I'd made Ish swear she wouldn't tell my brother why I was so willing to be a thief. That every jewel I brought her gave us both hope she'd be able to help Bryce.

"Bryce really hates me, I think," I said softly. "He believes Father was right about everything, and he wasn't. I know he wasn't. The world is not as black and white as either of them believe." *Believed*, I should have said, in the past tense for Father. I blew out a breath.

Balder snorted and I sighed. "I know. I know. We've had this conversation a thousand times at least. But maybe this time, I'll find a way to tell him Dad was wrong. That there is no black and white, that being a thief doesn't make me a heretic or a stain on our family."

Balder flapped his lips, and I slipped him a mint I had in the front pocket of my cloak.

Around us, the world had gone quiet. Most likely, it was our presence, and not anything else more sinister, but still I kept my ears perked. Surviving was something I was very good at, and I wasn't about to let my guard down now.

I checked Balder's wound. Already it looked days old, maybe even a week. The hacka paste was good shit, as my brother would say.

"How you feeling, my friend?" I tugged on Balder's tail once and he swished it.

I turned, the sensation of being watched heavy on me, but there was no one behind us. Just in case, though . . . I held up both hands and flipped up my middle finger. "Whoever you are, I don't have time for whatever shit you want to throw at me."

Balder bobbed his head a couple times in agreement, then dropped to one knee on his front leg, inviting me to mount. I didn't argue. If he was ready, I wasn't going to question him. I leapt straight up and landed in the saddle as lightly as any cat, then picked up the reins and Balder stepped into a ground-covering trot. There was only the slightest hesitation in his stride, a mere whisper that he'd been injured.

"We might not be able to beat Steve home, but we can show up right on his ass," I murmured.

I touched the ring hanging from the chain around my neck. The bump of it under my shirt was a comfort. Without it, my life would be a mess of epic proportions. With it, I could make my own choices without a curse dragging me down. With it, I had a chance at catching up to Steve—like a burr he didn't notice stuck to him until it dug into his skin and drew blood. I grinned to myself.

Home was the northernmost tip of the Caspian Sea in a town once known as Atyrau. Not that there were many people left in the town, humans or supes. Balder picked his way around the bubbling pits of waste that smelled of sulfur, cinnamon, and death. Weird combination, but I'd learned not to question why they smelled that way, just to avoid them. They burned, though not like the toxic waste that had been in the giants' home. That shit would eat you whole, an acid that cut through bone and tissue like it was nothing. No, this waste was hot, cooked from somewhere under the ground and then pushed to the surface—it would burn, but you could wash it off and survive.

Balder and I had ridden through the night, not

pushing hard but keeping up the steady pace because I knew Steve. He'd push his poor horse so hard, he'd be forced to walk the last ten miles before home. At the least, if not more. At the two-mile mark, we found his horse limping his way home, head hung low.

"Batman . . ." I called to him and he lifted his dark head, his eyes fogged with pain and fatigue. I slowed Balder, slid from his back. Batman took a few stumbling steps toward me and I struggled once more to contain the anger.

Save it for the bastard. Save it for Steve. Narcissistic camel's-dung-covered asshole that he is.

The need to help Batman allowed me to put the growing anger aside and focus on the horse in front of me. I grabbed my medic pack and pulled out my oat balls I'd made for the trip. Camel fat rolled up with oats and honey, then stuffed inside a leather pouch for storage. The horses didn't take to them right away, but when they were at the end of the journey, they gulped them down like they were manna from heaven.

"Eat up, boys." I held one out to Batman and he took it with soft lips. Balder pushed on me from the other side. I gave him one ball, but saved the last two for Batman. He was not as fit for these runs as Balder; Steve didn't put the time into him he needed. I put it on my mental to-do list that I would condition Batman with me and Balder from here on out. The horse didn't deserve to suffer because of Steve's asshole-ness.

"You know that's a stupid name he gave you. That's what you get when you start hanging out with humans. Batman, who names a horse Batman? Ridiculous," I muttered as I stroked the dark horse on the neck, then slid my hands over his body checking for wounds. His legs were swollen and a bit warm, but that would be expected with the headlong gallop through rough territory. I'd have to watch him for a fallout from this bullshit.

I held up my water bottle and tipped it so Batman could drink. Once he was as fueled up as I could get him, I loosened his cinch so he could breathe deeper, and took his bridle off. He would follow us home; I wasn't concerned about that. Balder leaned over and nipped at Batman's cheek.

The dark horse flinched, which wasn't like him, and showed just how exhausted he was that he didn't try to bite the gray back. Batman was a bit on the bossy side, so Balder taking the lead was unusual. I shook my head, mounted back up, and me and the two horses walked the last two miles home.

The stables came into view first and we went straight there. What had been a stockade was now a dual-purpose sprawling living area with a stable we'd added on. I got the two boys settled into their stalls with water and food. I'd have to walk them later so they wouldn't stiffen up, but for now, they deserved to just rest and eat. I checked the other stall for Pig, Darcy's mare.

While there were a few horses, none were the scruffy little mare. Which meant Darcy wasn't back yet. My belly rolled with a sharp tang of fear. Darcy and her crew had headed out weeks before Steve and me. They were supposed to have been back by now. We'd planned it that way so we could celebrate with two jewels at once. Ish had planned it that way, really.

"Where are you, Darcy?" I whispered. Balder pushed his nose against me, shoving me out of his stall. "Yeah, yeah, I'm going." I stripped off my cloak and hung it over the stall door, which left me in nothing but dark pants, tall black riding boots, and a plain white tank top. And my weapons—I was never without those. The twin kukri blades were strapped to my upper thighs, and the flail I kept in my right hand with the two spiked balls dangling just above the ground. If I was going to carry it as an actual weapon, I'd have to look at getting a strap for it. Maybe across my back.

At the moment, though, I had only one thought outside of my concern for Darcy.

"You are about to get your ass handed to you, Steve," I muttered under my breath as I strode out of the stable toward the main hall. Darcy would love this. I only wished she was back already so she could see me finally put Steve in his place—I wasn't the only one he'd hurt. That made me grin. Perhaps it would be more than a little fun to finally give him his comeuppance. And it would take my mind off Darcy not being there. She'd be back soon. I was sure of it. That's what I told myself while my instincts screamed that something was wrong, off.

My home was huge, far bigger than it needed to be for the small number of us that served Ish, but she liked us all to have room to ourselves. Especially considering how poorly we got along.

Or at least, how poorly Steve and I got along. No, that wasn't fair. There was also Maks, the lone human in the group. Nobody liked him, but that was because he was human. He served Ish faithfully, I supposed, so that was enough for me to leave him alone.

I'd give the human one thing, he was nice to look at. If he'd been a supe, he'd have had all the women fighting over who would have been in his bed with his electric blue eyes and messy sand-colored hair, big arms, and bigger . . . well, you get the picture.

Steve picked on him, but Steve picked on anyone he thought was lesser than him. Including me. Including Bryce. Including Batman. My jaw ticked with the anger that grew and burned out other thoughts.

The main door that led into the hall was open a

crack and Steve's voice flowed out to me even though I was thirty feet away.

"Ish, I'm so, *so* sorry. I couldn't save her. I tried. I fought through the giant's legs, and I reached out to her but she wouldn't take my hand. Her hatred of me for something I didn't do . . . it killed her in the end. As I always said it would."

I pushed the door open slowly, knowing it wouldn't creak and give me away—I'd oiled the hinges myself. Steve knelt in front of Ish, his blond head bowed in submission. Ish stared down at him, her face twisted with what could only be called anger.

She was an older woman, but still beautiful, tall, slim and with thick dark hair streaked with silver strands. But in that moment, I saw only a woman who didn't know how to react to the lies—goddess of the desert help me, she *had* to know Steve was lying again. This was not the first time he'd tried to lose me on a run, or the first time he'd tried to let an accident take my life. But the thing was, Ish always gave him the benefit of the doubt, something I just didn't understand. How could she not see what a fucking tool he was? Out for his own best interests.

Which made me wary of Ish, no matter that I wanted to trust her. That she held him above me made me doubt her ability to understand fully who and what he was.

"Maks," she called out, and her human servant

stepped from the shadows. Even though I didn't like Maks, it wasn't the same way I didn't like Steve. There was nothing really wrong with the servant except he was weak in a place where weakness equaled death. I should know. I was about as weak a supe as there was out there, much as it galled me. But that was why I worked so hard to fight on two legs, to improve my chances.

That was why I did all I could to be strong enough to come home every time, not in a body bag.

Ish put her hand out to him, as if to set it on Maks's broad shoulder, but he moved so her hand missed him. He didn't like being touched much more than I did. She didn't break her words, as though there was no slight toward her in his movement.

"Take a horse and ride out. Follow Steve's path backward and bring her home. Alive or dead, she does not deserve to be left behind. She has been a faithful ward of mine, and I promised her I would never leave her in the cold. *Ever.*" That last word came out as sharp as the crack of a whip and Steve flinched as a ripple of power swelled out around her. As well he should.

Ish was a strong mage, and with each jewel we brought her, her strength grew, and her ability to help others and keep us safe increased. A swell of love grew in me. Ish was looking out for me when she could have turned her back. She was going to send

Maks to find me. I felt bad for doubting her in that moment, wanting nothing more than to give her the belief that she deserved.

"I swear to you, there was *no* saving her. Perhaps her horse escaped, but there is no way that Zamira made it out alive. I saw her go under the giant queen's hand. I saw the fingers close around her."

Ish leaned over him. "Did you see her body, though?"

He drew a slow breath. "I . . . could not watch her die. For all that she hates me, I still have feelings for her, Ish. I could not bear to see her beauty crushed, snuffed out like a candle in the wind."

Another time not so long ago, I would have melted with his words, but now . . . not so much.

It was about time to make my entrance into this theatrical play he had going on. Oh, I wished I could see his face when he realized I was very much alive, and about to kick him right in those cheating, shriveled balls of his.

CHAPTER FOUR

S teve stayed where he was, on his knees, but his head was raised now as he looked Ish in the face. "I do not mean to distress you, my lady, but there will be nothing left of her. Do not waste Maks on a trip that will end with bits and pieces of her body, nothing to even call a body really. You can trust me, I swear to you she did not survive. The giant queen crushed her body."

What a fucking dumb-ass. Then again, he was trying to make sure I didn't survive. So, if I was injured out there, but still alive, the last thing he would want was me being brought home to convalesce. With me out of the picture, he would have no challenge for leadership of the rest of the supes here. As it was, I was the only person with enough attitude to face him down. He might be stronger than me, but leading a group of supes was about more than just strength. They had to believe you were there to look after them, that you would fight for them. Everyone —except Ish—had seen how fickle Steve was, which made him at best, a dangerous choice to lead our group.

I might not trust anyone else, but I made damn sure the people around here could depend on me.

I shook my head. Where I stood in the shadows of the room kept me from being seen unless someone was looking. Someone who knew me better than Steve did.

Behind and to the right of Ish, my brother sat at his work table, his hands unmoving on the flare gun he'd been tinkering with before we'd left three weeks ago. His eyes found me in the shadows of the doorway. Those golden orbs narrowed, flashing with anger.

"You sure that's the story you want to stick with, Steve? I mean, now is the time to change it if you're going to, if perhaps you were confused about what really happened," my brother said, his voice carrying through the room like the alpha he should have been.

"It's not a story, Bryce. *Cripple*." Steve's head snapped up, and he followed his words with a low snarl that my brother met with a snarl of his own— two alpha males was not a good idea in a small space when neither was truly stable. Bryce gripped the edge of the table but stayed where he was, chest heaving with the snarls and the desire, yet inability, to shift.

Foolish, foolish brother. He might not want the shame I brought to our family, but he'd still try to stand with me against everyone else. Figuratively speaking anyway. But there was no way he could stand against Steve in a challenge, not with the way his body was broken.

I took a step, bringing me into the light and drawing Ish's eyes to me. They lit up and she put a hand to her chest as her shoulders sagged a little. Relief, she was relieved I was okay. "Zamira, you are home."

She swept around Steve and came to me, put her hands on my face, and then gave me a hug. I leaned into the embrace, closing my eyes and breathing in the only smell of home I truly knew anymore. She was the closest thing I had to a mother and her relief that I was alive was a balm to my battered soul. Too many people had walked away from me in my life, too many people had broken my trust. I wasn't sure what I would do if Ish joined their ranks. If suddenly she wished I were not here. Like Bryce and Steve.

"I am," I said. "Did he give you the jewel?"

She smiled and touched a pouch tied to her waist over her long gray dress. "He did. It is beauty and full of power that I can use to help us all."

My eyes shot to hers and she shook her head at

my unspoken question. She was stronger, but not strong enough to help Bryce.

"Zam, you . . . how did you escape?" Steve was on his feet and headed our way, his disbelief plain, but under that, his anger bubbling upward. He was pissed that I was still alive and struggled not to show it. Ish stepped back. She rarely put herself between those she took care of, leaving us to figure out our own battles.

"Do not kill one another," was all she said.

I flicked the flail once, spinning the dual spiked balls and slowing Steve's approach, that same strange tingle moving its way up from my hand to my shoulder. His eyes followed the weapon's trajectory and he moved so he stood outside its range. "I fought for my life, Steve. *That's* how I escaped. You aren't going to get rid of me that easily, you know. You'll have to cut my throat yourself if you want to take over here." There was no point in trying to explain that I'd saved him, drawn the giants away and then watched as he'd fucked off and left me to die. No, that was not how things were done here. We all had to pretend that we really cared for one another when the truth was, that wasn't the case at all.

"Don't you dare challenge me," he growled. "Because I'll choose four legs and I'll snap you in half with one bite."

I smiled at him even though a heavy dose of fear

and shame slid through me. I chose to answer as if none of that curdled my blood. "I'd still kick your ass on four legs. You're too fucking slow and stupid to realize when you're outmatched. It takes more than size to run things in a pride." I kept the flail spinning, wanting nothing more than to crush his skull with a few well-placed blows. He deserved that and more to be honest.

His eyes slid to the weapon again and his throat bobbed. The tension between us crackled and grew as I picked up speed with the flail, feeling it as if it were an extension of my own body. A humming began to ripple through the air and I realized it was the flail. Confidence flooded me and I opened my mouth to do exactly what he'd told me not to—nothing new there. A challenge would bring this all to a head and perhaps I'd finally be able to drive him out. We didn't need him. And I could be done with this one way or another.

I was stopped short by a soft cry from the side of the room. A young girl ran forward. She was as blond as Steve, and at first glance, everyone thought she was his daughter because of the age difference. She was built nearly polar opposite to me in our body types, with her big bust, wide hips and tiny waist—a perfect hourglass if ever there was one. I had none of that going for me, as I was slim from top to bottom like my mother, from what I knew of her.

Her arms swept around his middle and she raised herself on her toes to kiss him, forcing him to face her. But his eyes kept on me, anger simmering in them.

My stomach rolled and I wasn't sure I wouldn't throw up on them both. Her hands cupped his face, trying to draw his eyes to her. Finally, he looked at her and she smiled up at him. "You're alive, Steve! I saw the horses in the stable but I wasn't sure you'd make it back to me."

I grimaced and turned away from the vile sight. "Just because I'm his ex-wife doesn't mean I'd let him die, Kiara." I wanted him gone, not his death. Notwithstanding today.

"I never said that," she whispered, her eyes wide with horror. I almost felt bad, almost. She was a nice kid, and I liked her, but the reality was he'd used her, groomed her to fall for him as her mentor, and in the end, he'd fooled us both. I'd been the one to get away from him, and she'd chosen to stay, even after she found out he'd been . . . flouncing us both along with a few others, as my new friend Marcel the satyr would have said.

"What, no challenge?" Steve threw at my back, snapping something inside me. There was no thought as I spun, drawing a kukri blade and throwing it in a single motion that didn't leave me any time to consider if it was a good idea or not. To be fair, I aimed to his right, to miss him and drive the blade into the wall behind him. A good scare was what I'd been going for.

The idiot dodged the wrong way. The kukri blade buried deep into his shoulder, driving through with both the force of the throw and the wicked edge of the blade that was designed to cause as much damage as possible.

He threw his head back and roared, the sound echoing through the big room as he grabbed the knife's handle and tossed the blade to the floor. Kiara cried out—again—and put her hands over the wound as she stared back at me with horrified wide amber eyes. "Why would you do that? Why would you do that when you just said you didn't want to kill him?"

Fuck, I'd made a mess of this. I touched the ring around my neck to make sure it was still there before I answered. "Because he's a fucking set of saggy camel balls who's lucky I don't kill him for leaving me to die! Any other alpha would challenge and kill him, Kiara. Remember that." I took a few steps forward and picked up the blade. Hard to believe I used to love him, that he was my world, and I thought we would see each other through anything. But there was that old saying in the desert that I knew now was a truth.

The surest way to hate someone to the core of

your soul is to love and trust them with all your heart first.

I'd given him everything I was, and he'd thrown me away like I was worthless, like my life and heart were nothing to him.

I wiped the blade off and put it back in its sheath on my thigh. Behind me, Steve snarled curses at me, Kiara sobbed and Ish did her best to calm them both. I looked for my brother but he was gone, leaving the scene of the crime yet again.

Leaving me to face the music alone. Classic.

I sighed and lifted my nose, catching the smell of grease, desert, and lion that was uniquely Bryce. I followed my nose away from the bellows of Steve as Kiara tried to soothe him, and deeper into the Stockyards. I knew where Bryce would be without my nose, but still, he'd surprised me here and there. Older than me by almost ten years, he'd been my protector my whole childhood, teaching me alongside Father how to fight, how to hunt and protect others, and now that the roles were reversed . . . well, let's just say he didn't handle it in a very polite fashion.

I knocked on the door to his room and workshop on the south side of the complex. "Bryce?"

"Yeah." He sounded none too pleased that I'd followed him.

I drew a breath and pushed the door open even as my worries over how he'd receive the news that I'd died and then showed up alive made me want to hesitate.

"Hesitation will get you killed," I said as I stepped into the room. His head snapped up and his deep amber eyes narrowed.

"Why would you say that?"

It had been something our father had taught us when we were training to fight. Hesitation killed. Someone would die if you hesitated. Leap in and fight for what you need to fight for, don't hold back, don't let uncertainty rule your thoughts. It was something I still struggled with, the uncertainty of who I was holding me back from making the snap decisions that were needed. Sure, throwing the knife had been a snap decision but even as I'd thrown it, I'd known it wasn't the best decision, and therein lay the rub.

I smiled but the smile fled as I walked closer to him and the table he sat at. "I wasn't sure you'd want me to come back alive, so coming in here to talk was . . . hard."

"Harder than sticking the pig?" He lifted an eyebrow and leaned back in his chair. He folded his arms over his chest, and I was struck as I was so often at the near-perfect reflection he was of our father.

"Nah, that's easy. No hesitation there. Talking is harder." I ran a hand over the edge of the work bench that hid his legs.

"Then don't talk. Go rest." He leaned forward and picked up his tools, his eyes avoiding mine.

"Is Darcy back yet?" I asked, hopeful that perhaps I'd just missed her somehow. Now that Steve wasn't in front of me, that feeling of fear for my best friend grew once more. No matter that we'd left on perhaps not the best of terms, she was still my friend. One of few.

And Bryce had a soft spot for Darcy, though he would never tell her. He would never want her saddled to someone like him. In our world, weakness was death, remember? Bryce was about as low as you could go—weaker than me, weaker even than the human Maks. Because it hadn't always been that way, he was . . . unpleasant most days.

He shook his head. "No." There was more, I knew there was and I didn't like it when he got like this. Moody, to say the least. That was what happened with a trapped lion forced into a cage there was no escaping. It made them mean and dangerous in their words.

My shoulders tightened, bracing for what was coming. "Say what you want to say, Bryce. I can take it."

"You came in here, you say what you want to say first," he snapped and tossed the tools on the bench. I opened my mouth but he beat me to it.

"I don't like you going on these hunts for the

jewels with Steve. We both know he doesn't give even a single shit about your life. We both know he'll leave you behind and one day you aren't going to come back. We both know he wants full leadership here and only your life is stopping him. You need to stay here and take on more of that role, you need to lead."

I swallowed the emotions that rioted inside my body. "Would it matter to you if I came back?"

He frowned. "You're my sister. What the hell kind of question is that?"

This had been coming a long time, and I'd held back because of his situation, but I didn't have it in me to pretend right then. I was tired, and my mouth had no one to hold it back.

"You hate that I don't follow what Father taught us. You think I'm breaking some kind of code of honor by being a thief, for killing for more than just survival or protection, and I wonder if maybe sometimes you might wish I'd just not come back. I wonder if you wish you could just bury me, too, and be done with our family."

Bryce stared at me, his eyes sparking with fury, and I stared back with no emotion because he didn't deny the words that I'd said, and I wasn't sure how to respond to that.

"Okay, I got it." I turned my back on him, leaving him there to rot in his workshop for all I cared. I tried not to think about being cast aside by one of the last people I'd thought I could always turn to. Stupid, so stupid of me to think my brother would actually stand with me when he couldn't fucking stand at all.

I found my way to my quarters which were closest to the stable. I flipped open the window above my bed and Balder stuck his head in, a mouthful of hay sticking out on either side of his face. I ran a hand over his nose but I couldn't find any words in my too-tight throat. I flopped myself down on my bed and closed my eyes. Maybe a few tears leaked out, I can't be certain because I fell asleep, exhaustion finally taking me, my hand wrapped around the ring that hung from my neck. You'd think I'd taken it off for all the problems happening. You'd think my curse was in full effect and not held back at all, not even by the talisman Ish had given me to keep myself clear of the Jinn's curse.

There were no dreams, and I woke hours later with a start. Not because I'd woken naturally but because something had broken the rest. The room was pitch dark and only a faint bit of light came through the window around Balder's head.

A creak from the doorway and I caught the scent of grease. "What do you want, Bryce?"

"Ish wants to see you."

I frowned. "You aren't a messenger boy."

"I . . . something's happened." He trailed off and I froze.

"Are we being attacked?" It hadn't happened often, but there was some lash-back from stealing the jewels from other supes. Occasionally they tracked us down and we had to beat them back.

"No, something with Darcy." There was enough worry in his voice that my heart kicked up more than a few notches. I stood and headed toward the door.

Where he was fair, I was dark, my hair a tangle of curls black as the night, fading to a ruddy brown at the ends. My eyes were green, bright like the jewels we searched for, and even my skin was darker from being out in the sun so much. Bound as he was to his crappy old wheelchair, Bryce didn't venture out much so his skin was paler than anyone else's here.

I brushed past him and he sucked in a breath like he wanted to say something, but there was nothing for him to say, at least I didn't think there was. I knew the truth between us and so did he. We were done. I could treat him like one of the other supes, no different. Not my brother anymore.

I was on my own, again. But maybe I'd always been on my own and just hadn't known it. That thought slowed me, but it was not the time to be reflective on my life.

Without another word between us, I hurried away, down the hall to Ish's quarters. The door was open and inside a fire burned hot, driving the cool air of the winter night away. Ish sat in a big chair in front of the fireplace. "Come, sit with me, Zamira. Something has happened that you need to be aware of." She beckoned me forward with one hand, holding a thick pottery chalice in the other, bubbling with something I couldn't place. I took a deep breath, holding the scent against the back of my tongue, finally pinpointing the spices. Aniseed was the strongest spice with a touch of nutmeg in the backdrop and beyond that, straight up vodka. A calming drink then, which did not bode well if Ish needed it.

I made my way to the fire, the animal in me almost groaning in pleasure with the heat that spilled from behind the grill if not for the worry gnawing at my insides. I sat with my back to the fire and crossed my legs. "Bryce said you needed to speak with me about Darcy. Is she back?" Hope, it was something I could hang onto for only a little longer.

"No, she is not." She shook her head. "Her horse came back with a note attached to the saddle."

She held a scroll out to me and I took it, fear making my mouth dry.

I unwound the paper and read the bold black ink out loud.

"Your golden cat is a lovely prize, Ish. Marsum will thank me for her. Do not bother to come for the jewel. It is mine and I will not give it up. To be crystal clear, I will slaughter all your pets if I must."

I read the words over and over. They were not signed, but they didn't need to be. "The Ice Witch has Darcy?"

"Yes." Ish's eyes were clouded.

"What about Richard and Leo?" I turned the paper over.

"Dead," Ish said. "They slipped by the White Wolf, the White Bear, and reached the White Raven. The Raven killed them and took Darcy as a prize. A threat to make sure . . . I do not try again to regain what is mine." There was an edge to her voice, grief and anger mixing through her words.

The world around me seemed to sway. Richard and Leo were not close to me, but they had worked with Darcy for years and she trusted them implicitly. The two men had a relationship she and I had both wished we could have with the mate of our choice. And just like that, they were gone, dead. Wiped out.

It had been years since we'd lost anyone on a hunt for a jewel. Years, and the shock was making me slow. I knew the importance of the jewels. I was the only one who truly understood why we were doing this and why the cost in lives was worth it, even if it hurt.

But Darcy, she could still be saved before she was sent to Marsum.

"Then we have to get her back." I handed the scroll back to Ish. "That's all there is to it."

Ish's eyes were hard to read as she spoke. "You wounded Steve badly, and while I do not blame you for your anger, it will make regaining the jewel difficult. I would send him to the Ice Witch to gain the jewel with his mate. I need you here to guard us on the off chance the witch sends any repercussions."

The words were like a gong inside my head, a big, angry fucking gong that resonated to the center of my bones. His mate? He'd claimed Kiara as his *mate*? They'd been together less than a year, and claiming a mate took longer than that. Not to mention the women I knew he'd been with while he was with Kiara.

Ish continued. "When he comes back with the jewel, I've told him he will have leadership here. He is the last alpha male capable, and it is time he took that responsibility."

I struggled to pin down the anger, hurt, and confusion, to not let it all come roaring out my mouth. No such luck. I shot to my feet, vibrating. "He cannot lead here. He'll fucking enslave the rest of the supes. He'll do exactly as he always has, lie and manipulate and break what little peace we have in this place!"

Ish frowned. "You think I would allow him to do that?"

"I think he would try and spin it so you believed him, just like he tried to make you believe I was dead." I began to pace. "He's a manipulator, he always has been."

"That is your broken heart talking," Ish said softly. "He was not always—"

"He was!" I yelled at her, ignoring the way her eyes narrowed. "I was just too young and stupid to see it. He likes his women young for that reason, because he can control them easier. It wasn't until I started questioning him that he wanted her. Only when I no longer let him make me his doormat, his yes woman, that things changed between us."

Her eyebrows rose slowly. "You think he controlled you?"

"He tried to." I shrugged, not wanting to say the truth. I'd let my love for him blind me to what he really was. "Look, enough of that, it's the past. I'm going after Darcy. And when I get back, I'll damn well fight him for leadership if I have to."

"No." That one word stopped me mid-stride. Did she mean no to the fight, or to me going? "When Steve is healed, he will go for the jewel with Kiara. You will go to Dragon's Ground to see if you can find a way in prepping us for the next jewel."

I closed my eyes, my heart breaking on what was left of my belief in Ish. I thought she would understand. I thought she of all people would grasp the importance of not leaving anyone behind. "You would leave Darcy to the Ice Witch? You would leave her to be sent to Marsum?"

"Steve will save her, Zamira." Ish's words were soft, but not particularly soothing. "You are not strong enough to see the final three jewels back to me on your own, or even *with* Steve. The final three jewels are held by guardians of the wall and they are . . . they are not a rush of giants or a coven of witches. They need a true lion of power to take them down. I'm sorry. But it is the truth."

Her words could not have cut any deeper than if she'd used a knife on me. I forced myself to stand still and straight, to not slump under the shame that had just been heaped onto me. "Not strong enough." I repeated the words.

"It is the truth, Zamira." Ish reached for me and I pulled back. "You know it is the truth and the sooner you accept it, the sooner you can move on with your life. You are living as though you can truly stand next to those in your pride, shoulder to shoulder, and you cannot. You are not that cat. You will never be."

I swallowed hard, turned and strode away from her. Away from a truth that while it might be my reality, was fucking hard to hear from the mouth of my surrogate mother. To hear that she thought so little of me, thought me incapable of . . . anything.

My whole life I'd fought one thing: being weaker

than the others. All I could do to counteract that weakness was by training, learning weaponry, gaining skills that helped me be the fighter and thief I was. But there was something else I struggled with almost as much as being weak. I'd screwed up who to trust enough times now that I didn't see the point in trusting anyone. Even Ish—the woman who was my mother in everything but blood. She didn't trust me to complete what I set out to do. She didn't trust me, and obviously, I couldn't trust her to know me well enough that she would allow me a measure of understanding.

The halls seemed to close in around me and I struggled to walk straight. I finally stopped and leaned against the rough brick and mortar to catch my breath that came in gulps, as if I'd been running flat out for miles and miles. But I couldn't slow the pounding of my heart or the racing of my thoughts as my world imploded. My ears twitched with the squeak of a wheel and I turned my head. "What do you want, Bryce?" The words were hollow, dead of emotion. It was time I felt nothing, it was time to shut this shit down. If I didn't feel anything, then I couldn't be hurt anymore. If I expected nothing from those around me, there would be no disappointment.

"Tell me you're going after her," he said with more pain in his voice than I'd heard in years. "I may never be able to love her the way she deserves, but I don't think I can go on without her being in my life. Steve won't save her; we both know it. No matter what was between them—"

"Don't." I cut him off. "Don't go there."

My throat tightened, making it tough to speak. At least Bryce loved Darcy. It took me a moment to pull my shit together, to push the past down so I didn't vomit it right out my mouth. "I'm not leaving her out there on her own."

He closed his eyes and then took a big breath, expanding his broad chest. "Then you're going to need help and I know who can go with you and not be missed, at least not right away. Darcy was flirting with the human before she left."

"Maks?" I stared hard at him and shook my head. "No, she didn't like Maks. She would have told me something like that." It was bad enough who she *did* like, and it wasn't my brother. Maks, while pleasing to the eye, was human. I was sure Darcy wouldn't take him into her bed. My gut twisted. Then again, Darcy had taken someone to her bed that I would've never thought she would.

Bryce nodded. "She did. I'm sure of it. I saw them talking several times out my window. And the feeling was mutual. You were too busy hating Steve to see she was falling for him."

I wasn't sure if he meant Darcy was falling for Maks or Steve. No, that wasn't true. I knew he meant

Maks, but I'd never told him the other secret Darcy had. It was her secret to tell, or not tell after all, not mine.

"He's human; what can he possibly do to help?" I lowered my voice, not because Maks might hear me slag him, but *Ish* might hear us talking and she'd try to stop me. Because I'd already decided I was going after Darcy. No matter what happened, she was my friend and I wasn't leaving her in the icy cold north.

I wasn't sure anymore if she would do the same for me, not after our fight. But I wouldn't let that stop me. She'd saved my life years ago, and this was my chance to return the favor, to show her I could forgive her.

"Maks is cannon fodder." Bryce shook his head. "Shitty as that sounds. And he does have some skills, and you can boss him around easier than Steve. He can help, I think. He's survived on this side of the wall where other humans haven't lasted a week. You could use that kind of luck on your side."

I pushed off the wall and made a motion with my hand, an offer to push his wheelchair. He shook his head. The fight we'd had earlier was gone under the bonds of our broken family. That's the way it went some days. Screaming and yelling and hating, then banding together to save one of our own, burying the feelings so they didn't get in the way of what needed to be done.

I walked beside him, heading to my room. "I don't want his help. I'll be faster on my own."

Humans were so many things and none of them good in my opinion. Useless, prideful, stupid. I mean, I got what Bryce was thinking. It would be no big loss for Maks to die. Not really. And if he managed to help me a little along the way, I could understand what my brother was thinking. The problem was I knew I could move faster on my own. Never mind the whole issue of whether or not I could trust Maks —the short answer was I couldn't. No human could be trusted. No matter how pretty his blue eyes were.

"I've already told him he's going with you," Bryce said. "You aren't the big cat you were meant to be, Zam. You're quick, and smart, and mean as they come when you really put up a fight, but you need some muscle behind you in case things get tough. Maks can be that muscle. And you need someone to help push you into decisions you'd rather not make. You won't do that on your own."

His words stopped me. Complimentary and not, all at once. "Bryce—"

"No. For once let me lead our family as I was meant to. I'm giving you a direct command." Something in his voice deepened and I felt his power as an alpha all the way to my bones. My leader was speaking and the cat in me bowed under his demand, making me inwardly snarl at the submissiveness in me. "Get Darcy, bring her home. Take Maks and try not to get killed."

I nodded, bending to his will. And even though it was what I wanted to do—get Darcy home—I hated that my inner self was still the doormat cat I loathed. "What about the jewel?"

"Ish wants it, so Steve and Kiara can get it," Bryce said. "Two teams, two goals." I noted that he used the word *want*. He was wrong about that—Ish needed the jewel. Her secrets burned in me, and for a brief second, I thought about telling him the truth. About telling him what I knew. But I couldn't trust him with it. I knew that.

I put a hand on his shoulder and tightened my fingers as I struggled to let him direct me. It was his rightful place in our family, but things hadn't quite worked out that way. My cat wanted to bow to him, and at the same time, swat his cheek for trying to boss me. I finally lowered my chin to my chest, submitting fully. A sigh slid past my lips.

"Tell Maks to meet me at the stable. I leave tonight, in an hour."

Bryce nodded. "Take that flail with you. Father told me about it, said it was a powerful weapon."

"What do you mean?" I touched the handle of the flail hanging on my side. Not a good place if I were going into battle, but that hadn't been the plan when

I wore it into Ish's anteroom. It had been for show alone.

"There are legends around it, if it's the flail I think it is." Bryce reached out and grabbed one of the spikes, pulling the whole weapon up so he could see the designs on the haft. "But it isn't good. If that really is the weapon Marsum created, then it's powerful, yes. But the stories Father told me say it's dangerous to the user too."

For a moment, I stared at him, sure that I'd heard him wrong. I had to have heard him wrong. "Marsum. Did you say *Marsum's flail?*"

Marsum was the Jinn who'd destroyed our family, killed our father and maimed Bryce. No small thing in my world, and to have a weapon he created . . . I wasn't sure how I felt about that.

Bryce nodded. "I did. Our great-grandfather stole the weapon from the Jinn, and then it went missing on his next raid. Take it with you, but be careful. I don't know what it can do, but . . ."

I didn't know if I should snatch my hand away from the wooden handle or hang on tighter. "There were enough 'buts' in that little story to make a gay man giddy. You aren't leaving me with a lot of confidence in taking it at all."

He shrugged. "I only mention anything because of the seal of the lion on it." He ran his finger over the lion's head on the handle. "This is Grandfather's crest. The rest is just what I remember Father telling me and he wasn't sure on anything either. Bring her home, Zam." He raised his eyes to mine and again I found myself backing down, bowing my head to him. He turned his wheelchair and left me standing there. No goodbye, no come home, not even a be careful. Just bring Darcy home.

My heart ticked with discomfort, that once again, I was passed over for someone else. Despite our strained relationship, he was my brother. He should have cared for me a little. Then again, if he knew the truth of his injury, I wouldn't blame him for hating me.

I watched him roll down the hall, then opened my door and stepped over the threshold. His words worried me and I considered doing the opposite of his advice and leaving the flail behind. I knew my two kukri blades, the shotgun, and the other weapons I carried well. What did I need with some magic shit that could end up doing something weird to me?

I rubbed the heels of my hands over my eyes, indecision wracking me. Damn it. I needed to choose and choose quickly if I was going to get ahead of Maks. I paced the room for a good five minutes as I fought to figure out what would be best. Take it, don't take it.

It finally came down to one thing. Bryce was still my alpha and he said I needed the weapon, so for now, I'd take it. If things got ugly, I'd just drop it where I stood.

Right.

"I'm coming for you, Darcy." I grabbed my bedroll and saddlebags that would hold most of my gear behind my saddle. I stuffed them with what I would need for the colder country I was headed toward. Fur-lined clothing, gloves, a fire starter, dried food, more of the oat and fat balls for Balder, thicker blankets for me, collapsible buckets for melting snow into water. The bedroll was twice the size it normally was and my saddlebags bulged.

I grabbed the flail from my bed, rolling it over once so the lion's eyes glinted up at me. At least it was light and wouldn't add much to the weight Balder had to carry. That was the only thing I figured it had going for it. "I think you're just ornamental, but if you really are special . . . let's see what you can do." I rigged up a leather sheath that strapped the flail diagonally against my back, the handle sticking up over my right shoulder. I barely felt the weight. I looked over my shoulder to see the twin spiked balls also tight against my back, but I'd not tied them there. They didn't bump against me as I tested out walking around with it. "You really are magic, aren't you?" I muttered. Of course, the weapon didn't talk back. I mean, talking weapons, even I wasn't that far gone.

But still, the line of the handle against my back

seemed to heat in response to my query. Yeah, that was what I thought and that made me nervous, because if Marsum had made the flail, it would be bad news.

I had no more time to waver on the choice. I was packed and ready to go. I didn't go around to the outside to get to the stable, but crawled through the window right into Balder's stall. I still had half an hour before Maks was supposed to meet me at the stable. Half an hour and I'd be long gone.

Balder gave a grunt and a snort as I woke him.

"Sorry, friend. Let's get you saddled up before that human shows up." Much as I wanted Bryce to feel he was in charge, he was out of his mind. I wasn't taking no stinking human with me. We'd sneak out now, because there was no way the human would be ready to go before I was off and running.

I brushed Balder down, currying his coat and loosening the sweat stains from the ride in. His wound was completely healed and I knocked the last of the dried hacka paste from his hip.

A scent curled around my face that was not hay, horse, or anything else that belonged in the stable. Musk, the scent of musk that didn't belong on any supe, which meant only one thing.

"Damn it," I grumbled.

Maks was here.

CHAPTER FIVE

Maks was a big guy, especially for a human. If he'd been a supernatural, I could see why Darcy would have been interested in him—physically, at least, seeing as he was the most passive guy I'd met. He didn't fight, just let people roll right over him like a doormat.

His shoulders were almost as wide as Bryce's, and he was fit, athletic, and moved with an easy grace that came with being comfortable in one's own skin despite the submissive behavior. He had dark blond hair streaked with lighter strands from working in the sun all summer. Blue eyes and a scar along the edge of the left side of his jaw gave him an interesting face. In the six months he'd been at the Stockyards, I'd not spoken more than a few words to him.

That was about to change on an epic scale.

"Thought you'd leave without me?" he asked.

I tightened Balder's girth and then looked over my shoulder at him. "Yes. And I still am."

"No, you're not," Maks said, his voice confident in a way no human had a right to be, not here, not on this side of the wall they'd had Merlin create to keep the rest of us in.

The telltale squeak of Bryce's wheelchair made me grind my teeth for only a moment. Without words, Bryce's presence meant that his previous command came home to roost on my shoulders. "Maks, get Batman and saddle him up," I said.

Maks laughed. "I don't take orders from you."

Now that was unexpected. "Fine, you stay behind and play with Steve, entertain him while his wound heals and I'll get Darcy myself."

Maks disappeared and Bryce grabbed the edge of the door and hauled himself up with an ease that showed how much he worked his upper body. "Work with him. Please."

It was the *please* that slowed me. Bryce never asked nicely, not for anything or anyone.

"I love her too, Bryce," I said softly. "She's family." No matter what history had passed between her and Steve while I'd been married to him.

"I love her best," he said.

I laughed and turned to see his face. He was smiling, but it was pained. "Okay, you love her best. I'll bring her back. I swear it."

"And . . ." he grimaced, "I love you too, little sister. I'm sorry I'm such an asshole."

I bit my lower lip and gave him a quick nod, not sure I could trust my voice. How long had it been since he'd told me he loved me? Was it a way to make sure I went after Darcy? Was it a form of manipulation? Possibly. Which made the sting in my eyes that much worse—that I doubted him.

He nodded at me as if he understood, then lowered himself into his chair so I could no longer see him. I dashed a hand against my pooling eyes. Crying, there was no crying on this side of the wall, that's what my father always said. Crying was for the humans, for the weak.

The door swung open; Bryce held it for me and Balder. I walked out, Balder followed. Maks and Batman were ready, and I noted his bedroll and saddlebags were at least as full as mine. That much was good, I supposed, at least he was prepared. Or what he thought was being prepared. He'd not left the Stockyards in all the time he'd been here. Maks had no idea what he was getting into.

There were no more words from Bryce, nothing but a salute. I gave him a wobbly one back, then flipped him off, which left him laughing in the court-yard of the stable. Sibling bonds were weird at the best of times. But more so when the roles reversed and the protector became the protected. I wanted to believe everything he said, the younger sibling in me wanted to trust him . . . but I just couldn't. Not again. Not after everything that happened.

Maks and I walked beside the horses, and with each step of their hooves on the old pavement road that led out, I expected Steve or Ish to come flying toward us, telling us we couldn't go. Then again, Ish *had* said she wanted me to go to Dragon's Ground to check things out, so I could always cover with that. But there was no one, and just like that, we were on the hard-packed dirt road that led north, away from the Stockyards and the Caspian Sea, toward the Witch's Reign and all that lay in wait for us.

"Are you familiar with where we're headed?" Maks switched sides to the left of Batman, closer to me.

I gave him the side eye. Part of my distrust in the human was simple. Maks didn't remember anything before he'd come stumbling out of the desert and all but fell into the horse's water trough, sucking back water like he'd not drunk in days. He knew only that when he'd been in the desert, he was being chased and running for his life. The other part of my distrust was simpler yet. He was human—cut from the same cloth as the people who thought it a good idea to pen all the supernaturals into one area and let them slaughter each other. Ish had told us the full story when our father had only given us bits and pieces.

My father had always said the wall was meant to protect both kinds of people, human and supernatural. Ish had shown me the truth—that it had been a powerful political move to contain the dangers of the supernatural world so the weaker humans could thrive and pretend none of us existed.

Penning us inside the walls, there was hope we would all slaughter each other eventually. Or maybe that the emperor would massacre us all. I shivered. That was one story I hoped I never had to face in real life.

Finally, I answered Maks's question. "I've not been into the northern clime, no. But I know of it." Over the years, Ish had drilled us on the areas we would go into one day to reclaim the different jewels.

"Tell me what you know so I can at least grasp what we're dealing with," he said. I waited for him to continue with a *please*, but none came. Humans—seriously, they had zero manners.

I drew in a breath of cool air and held it for a moment while I thought where to start. "Dragons hold the middle part of the wall and we have to get by them before we even touch down on the Witch's Reign. The dragons protect the wall from both the humans and the supernaturals who would work to tear it down. Far as I know, there are ten varieties of the lizard brains. Hopefully we don't run into any of them and can head straight on through to the Ice Witch's territory. She protects the northern portion of the wall for the same reason the dragons do." That and power. The guardians of the various points of the wall were all about power. The jewels they held helped them in that respect, too, boosting their strength and magic.

"Details, what kind of details have you got on the dragons we could face?" he asked, and I glanced at him. His face had gone thoughtful and I realized he truly wanted to know what I knew, and maybe it had to do with loving Darcy and wanting to be able to understand her world better. Not that loving her was hard. She was sweet and kind and treated everyone with care. She was our peacemaker, and I knew why Steve had gone to her. In theory. I sighed and stepped around a hole in the hard-packed earth. The moonlight lit our path. We had that going for us at least.

"There are ten kinds of dragons. The largest four hold a connection to the four elements. Fire, wind, water, and earth. But they aren't the ones we have to worry about. We'll be skirting the edge of the forest, so we have to watch for the sap suckers."

"Sap suckers?"

"Yeah, they eat the sap from the trees and then turn it into acid that can eat through anything—flesh, bone, metal . . . It's nasty shit. And while the bigger

dragons are bad, those sap suckers are friggin' deadly."
From the corner of my eye, I saw him pale.

"How do you deal with them?"

"You talk to them. And give them a gift they might like."

"Like what?"

I patted my bedroll. "Something I grabbed from the giants' stash. I was going to keep it, but I can use it here."

He was quiet a moment, thoughtful.

"Steve is going to be pissed that we took his horse," Maks said.

I shrugged and then smiled, flashing my canines at him. "Yup, he is. But you're big enough you need him to carry you. Steve can always shift and use his own damn legs to reach Witch's Reign." Because there were no other animals big enough to carry the two-hundred-plus pound shifter. I grinned again at Maks, and miracle of miracles, he grinned back.

"I like the way you think, Zamira. Steve is . . . not my favorite person." At least on that, we agreed. No doubt Steve had been a right bastard to Maks too.

"Just Zam," I corrected him. Zamira was what those who could boss me around used. The name my father had growled every time he caught me red-handed stealing from the cookie jar, as it were. The name Steve, Bryce, and Ish used to corral me into doing what *they* thought best.

I turned to see Maks talking softly to Batman, sliding his hands over the big horse, rubbing his neck then lifting the horse's head so he could breathe into his nostrils, giving the animal his scent as they walked.

"They're going to be on us fast," Maks said. "We should hurry."

I shook my head. "First off, Ish wanted me to scout the Dragon's Ground so we're covered. We'll go slowly on foot the first few days. Both horses need the rest after that last run in. Steve will take at least two days to heal, possibly three." It wasn't much of a rest for Batman or Balder, but the movement would help them keep from stiffening.

"Even with the hacka paste?" he asked.

"Yes, even with the hacka paste. My knives are designed to cut deep and do serious damage to supes." I didn't feel like elaborating more, like how Ish had dipped the blades in a vat of something that made them deadlier than any other blade.

Maks and I walked through the last of the night, heading due north. The terrain was not particularly hard, and we were able to use the old roads the humans had built years before.

"You ever wonder what it would be like if the wall came down?" Maks asked me sometime around noon on that first full day.

"No." I didn't elaborate, but apparently, Maks was

feeling chatty. Yippy skippy, a chatty human, just what I wanted on a six-week round-trip journey.

"You mean you never wondered what it would be like to live side by side with humans?"

I looked at him across Balder's back. Batman had cozied right up to him, bonding with him so quickly, I would have sworn he was a true horse whisperer. Then again, it could be the treats he kept slipping the horse too. Mints, if the flash of white, sound of crunching, and whiff of peppermint I caught now and again was on point.

Exasperated by his foolish question, I sighed. "Seeing as we're going to be riding together for a long damn time, I'll explain. My father thought the wall should come down. I was raised on the idea that the wall was a blight on the world and should have never been built. Ultimately it cost him his life, and Bryce his body, and me most of my family. So, no, the wall can stay up until the fucking end of time for all I care."

"You're not like the other supes," he said. "They all want to be free of this place. To be free of the threat of the emperor."

He had a point. I decided to turn the tables on him. "Don't you want to go back to your home, wherever that is?"

"America," he said. "I'm from the West Coast near a little town called Seattle. I remember it in bits and pieces. Not my family or what I was doing out here, mind you. But old memories, like when I was a kid. I think my family traveled a lot or something." He frowned and rubbed at the scar on his face with one hand.

My heart twanged. "My father was from America. New York."

"Nice town that, biggish, full of people and action."

I looked at him again. "You've been?"

"Few times. I think. I mean, I'm guessing because again my memories are full of holes and gaping chunks of time." He nodded, frowning again. "But you're avoiding my question. You're different from the other supes, why? Why wouldn't you want the wall to come down?"

"I'm cursed, doesn't matter where I go. Might as well stay here." I touched the ring around my neck, the cool of the metal a comfort. As long as I wore it, I was safe. The people around me were safe.

He laughed but I didn't join in, and he slowly let the laughter die. "Shit, are you serious?"

I shrugged. "I was cursed by the Jinn when they killed my family." His eyes popped wide and his mouth hung open as he stared at me. Gobsmacked. The definition in the dictionary would have that face he was making next to it. Why the hell was I telling him all this?

Because he was being nice to Batman . . . that was why, as stupid as it sounded. He had a soft touch with the horse and that meant something to me. Cruelty to animals—especially those who needed us to care for them—was not a quality I tolerated in other people. I'd seen too many people haul off and beat an animal because they'd had a shit day. People like Steve.

So, for that I cut Maks some slack, and maybe a little because he was easy on the eyes. That, and he was human so he truly didn't understand this world, or what resided in it. I supposed some answers were in order if he were truly going to live here.

"What kind of curse? If I can ask?" he said softly, carefully, as if he knew it was a tender spot.

I shook my head. "Doesn't matter. I have this." I pulled the necklace out and showed him the ring that hung from it. Made of solid silver, it was crafted in the likeness of a roaring lion. When I was younger, I'd wanted to believe it was a perfect image of my dad, so I had something to remember him by. But now . . . I knew it was just a lion. Just like all the other lions out there. "Ish found me and Bryce after the attack. She took my father's ring and blessed it to offset the curse the Jinn laid on me. Long as I have this, I'm good."

He was quiet after that, his eyes thoughtful. Thank the goddess he was, because just those few words had stirred up memories. Memories that Ish had helped me lock away so I could go on with my life. She'd always said the past was the past and that you needed to move forward with your eyes on the goals you made. She was right about that. Memories could cut you down and eat you alive if you let them.

I knew that better than anyone.

For a week, we headed north without running into anything bigger than a few tiny supes that scattered as soon as we approached. Which was good, but also made me wonder what was going on. I knew the time of year was bad for dragon attacks, so it could've been as simple as that. But still, I wondered if it was something more. Our path just seemed to be miraculously clear and that made me nervous, especially as we rode through the steppes.

The steppes were known for having good horses. The tribesmen who bred them were always on the lookout for more horseflesh and often would come to bargain, beg, or steal your horse if they thought they were worth it. I'd come this far north a few times. This was where I'd found Balder and had to give up a fair amount of gold to take him home.

I patted his neck. While he was bred for speed, he was also bred from the hardy steppes ponies infused with blood of the desert breeds. Endurance, stamina, heart, speed, brains.

That made him the best horse who'd ever carried me.

Then there was Maks. He helped me make camp each night without being asked, hiking out to find water, carrying buckets back to our fire. He cooked most of the meals and made sure the horses were hobbled. All things that I'd done on my own before. I'd admit it only to myself, but it was nice to have someone around who didn't make me do everything on my own. Not that I told *him* that.

Maks was making it difficult for me not to like him.

Especially when he bent at the waist to pick up wood for the fire. I grinned, thinking about that image as we began to turn northwest. The temperatures began to drop incrementally. I pulled out my thicker fur-lined cloak and pulled it on. Maks did the same, though his coat was shorter—but still lined with fur.

"You said something back there that stuck with me," Maks said. We rode side by side now and I looked across at him. Batman had fully recovered and was bouncing along, happy to have a rider who looked after him.

"And what was that?" I asked. We'd barely spoken two words over as many days, the work to keep our camps going not needing much speaking. Pretty much "back there" could mean any number of things.

I hated to admit it, but we worked well together, taking up the tasks needed to set up and take down camp. I didn't have to tell him what to do, or even ask. He just did what needed doing. Bryce had been right about him. Maks was submissive, which meant there was no fighting, no arguing. He just did as he was told for the most part.

I might have to change my opinion of him and say he made a better traveling companion than I expected. Better than Steve, that was for damn sure.

"You said Steve didn't need the horse, that he could catch up on his own feet. What is he exactly? And why do you need a horse then, because . . . aren't you the same as him? Isn't that the deal, no inter-species relations? Right?"

My eyes widened, surprise cutting through me that he didn't know the basics about the supes he lived with, but the surprise gave way to irritation. My jaw ticked as I debated telling him all the truth and settled for just some of it. Which . . . was not really lying, right? Omitting some of the details he didn't need to know would hurry the story along.

"First off," I shook my head, "you're telling me you never figured what we all are in the last six months living with all of us? Why didn't you ask someone? Like Darcy?"

"Ish kept me separated, in case you hadn't noticed. She was worried I might run into an . . . accident." He rolled his shoulders and stretched his lower back. "I didn't push it because I didn't want to upset her. And Darcy's and my conversations were circling other things, not what she was."

I wasn't surprised. Ish had a soft spot for the underdogs. Or under cats as the case was with me.

"Steve is a lion shifter," I said. "And yes, my family is—check that, was—all lion shifters."

"Bryce?"

I gave a quick shake of my head. "He can't shift, not with the injuries he sustained at the Oasis." Again, a memory bit at me and I shoved it back, the pain of it catching me off guard.

Blood all around us, the smell of my family's blood filling my senses, blinding me.

"Shouldn't that have healed, though? Like isn't that the perk of being a supe, fast healing and all?" Maks kept at it, and while I understood the curiosity, I didn't like the direction the conversation was taking. The past and the things from that time of my life I worked hard to make sure would never be recalled were not something I wanted to discuss with anyone, especially not a human.

I ran my tongue over the inside of my mouth and the tips of my canines before I answered. "Some injuries can't be healed. Like with my kukri blades, they're, well, I call them blessed, but they cut deepest on a supe, and the wound won't heal like it should, disabling them. Which is why Steve will need time to heal, buying us time to get ahead of him and stay off his radar."

"You mean it wouldn't cut me?"

"That's exactly what I mean. They'd be like butter knives on you. I'd have to use blunt force to make them work at all," I said.

"And Bryce? Did he get a knife like that in the back?"

His words were a little too close to home and the memory I'd just banished. Hesitation made me stumble as I debated how much more to divulge. The minutes ticked by as I struggled and finally decided to give him some of the story. I could do this. I could give him info and not go back to that dark place.

I drew a breath and let it out slowly before I answered. "Some supernaturals, when they injure others, can cause a deep kind of damage. Ish thought he might heal over time, and then she thought she might be able to help him, but that . . . that's not been the case. Maybe if she gets all the jewels she needs and gains all her strength back, something could be done." I had not planned on saying that much to him, but really what did it matter at this point? The chances were good he wouldn't make it back with me.

"You said she *needs* the jewels. Everyone else has only said she *wants* them. Which is it?"

I stared at him, the blue of his eyes unwavering as they stared right back at me. "Needs. She needs them. And so does Bryce." There. Let him make of that what he would.

I gave Balder a slight tap to move him a little faster. "Enough girl talk. We're coming up on the southern edge of the forest and we need to be on guard."

Maks and Batman caught up and I pointed ahead. The start of Dragon's Ground was marked by a massive petrified tree that stood nearly a hundred feet in the air. Ish had told me about it, but hearing about it and seeing it were two different things. Etched into the entire trunk were markings I couldn't read, and didn't need to. Ish had explained they were warnings about all the horrible things that would happen to you if you dared to cross into the dragons' lands. All the ways you could, would, and should die.

"That's . . . impressive," Maks said.

"That's not the word I'd use, but sure, go with impressive." I shrugged. "We're going to stay to the outside edge of the forest and make our way north as fast as we can. The sooner we're into the Witch's Reign, the sooner we get Darcy back."

"This is why we held the horses back the last few days, isn't it?" he asked.

"Yes. There's a good chance we'll end up running

for our lives and we need them to be at full speed." I pulled Balder down from the trot and settled him into a fast walk. "Check your gear and make sure it's all strapped tightly. Do not pull any weapons on them. Let me do the talking if any of them show up. If they find out you're human, they'll eat you without hesitation." I wasn't entirely sure of that last bit but I needed to make sure he didn't say something and get us both eaten.

"Shit." He breathed out the word. "Wait, so why aren't we going farther east to avoid this whole party with the lizards?" Maks spoke as he worked at his straps.

"Because Darcy doesn't have much time. This is the fastest route, as the crow flies." I swept the area around us with my eyes, looking for anything that would tip me off that we were being watched. So far so good.

"Why does she only have so much time? I mean, I know she's a captive, but the note didn't say anything about her being killed, only kept as a prize."

Ish had shown him the note? Again, I wondered at his relationship with my mentor. I wrestled with giving information, but again, the reality was he likely wouldn't be around very long, so whatever secrets I touched on, he'd not be alive to share. "The Ice Witch has a connection to the Jinn in the south. The Jinn hate the lion shifters because we stood between them and the other supes in the area, doing our best to protect the weaker. The Ice Witch will send Darcy to the Jinn and Marsum as a gift—she is like me, a daughter of an alpha. It would keep the Jinn happy to have a princess in their grasp." I knew because I'd been hunted before by the Jinn and only Ish's strength and Darcy's quick thinking had saved me. The Jinn hated the women of the lion prides more than the men. Why? I didn't know the answer. But they did, and it was why Kiara had been kept at the stronghold and not sent after the jewels. I was . . . disposable, seeing as I wasn't really a lion. And Darcy had demanded to take her place in hunting the jewels Ish so desperately needed.

He adjusted his seat, his eyes thoughtful. "Wait, I thought the Ice Witch is some crazy bad-ass everyone is afraid of?"

I snorted. "She is. I don't know if the Jinn are stronger but it wouldn't surprise me. They're horrible, Maks. The worst of the wall's guardians by far. They kill without reservation for nothing more than power. At least the dragons eat their kills. At least the Ice Witch doesn't bother anyone who doesn't bother her. The Jinn hunt down those who they hate, they hunt them until they have their hides." A shiver ran down my spine as if speaking their name had drawn their attention to me once more.

"You're sure about all that?" he asked softly.

"Yes. I . . . I've lived through their dominion, Maks. I know the darkest side of their nature."

He drew a breath and slowly nodded. "Okay, so back to the present. We're on a time crunch because Darcy's going to get shipped off to the Jinn. We move fast, don't engage, and get Darcy out of there. Sound about right?"

I turned and looked at him. He was frowning slightly, his eyes serious, and I realized he meant every word. Strange, when I'd been raised to believe humans were nothing but self-serving assholes, afraid of everything around them, to see this kind of behavior. "I don't want to like you, Maks."

He grinned and a laugh slid from him. "Well, I'm sure I'll piss you off at some point, slothful human that I am."

"True enough, and you do have balls, and that's the surest way to end up in my bad book right now." I nodded and an answering smile on my own lips caught me off guard.

There was silence for the space of about three heartbeats.

"Any idea where Darcy will be exactly?" Maks asked.

I frowned. "I assume in the castle the Witch holds court in. Pojhola. Northern part of what used to be Finland. She's got guardians that help her, three of them. But they won't bother us, I don't think.

We'll slip through the borders and be in and out of her castle in no time. We aren't going for the jewel. They will have their eyes on Steve and Kiara, not looking for two very quiet, very stealthy travelers."

He grunted. "Are you deliberately trying to make this sound easy?"

"Yes." I flashed him a smile. "Because the truth would make you pee yourself."

"Well, we can't have that. I'd end up frozen to my saddle," he grumbled and I laughed.

Damn, I really didn't want to like him. Humans died here, and I'd already lost enough people I cared about. Adding a weak man who had a thing for my best friend to the list was not something I would consider a smart idea. I sighed, the laughter dying out.

A few moments later, I held up a hand, cutting off anything else he might say.

We drew close to the petrified tree and the first official marker of the Dragon's Ground. Like a doomsday sentinel, it rose far above us and the engravings in it shone in the winter sunlight, glinting like cut gemstones in the blackened and aged wood spire.

A sense of foreboding scampered up my spine. We weren't being watched exactly, but it was like the forest itself knew we were there, and we didn't belong. Or maybe like we'd set off some alarm system like Bryce had been trying to set up for the Stockyards.

I shook my head and urged Balder into a faster walk. We wouldn't bolt unless we absolutely had to— as in if a dragon popped out and decided to have us for lunch. I eased Balder closer to Batman and Maks.

"The dragons are whelping right now. That makes them especially vigilant, and testy, which is the last thing we need while we are trying to sneak by quietly. Keep your voice low and your eyes open."

"You mean they're having babies?"

"Yes." Goddess, he wasn't really that dumb, was he? What else did he think I meant when I said whelping?

A crack in the trees to the left of us sent my heart rate up a few notches. I put a hand out and grabbed Maks's arm, slowing him. Damn, those were some fine muscles under my hand.

Focus, Zam. Focus. The nice muscles are attached to a dumb human likely to get killed in the next short bit. Cannon fodder, remember?

I blew out a breath and let go of Maks. I put a hand to my hood and pulled it back so I could uncover my ears. I tipped my head sideways, working the way the wind blew across me so I could pick up on the noise I'd heard, and there in the distance was another crack and . . . a cry of someone being hurt.

Or scared. And it was small enough that it likely wasn't a dragon.

Likely, but not for sure.

Hesitation slowed me, and we probably sat there too long. Long enough that Maks started shooting me looks with his eyebrows so high, they almost hit his hairline. I closed my eyes and let myself listen to the cat inside me. She was curious, pushing me to go look. My instincts when I'd listened to them had rarely been good in the past, but something told me I had to check out the noise.

I flexed my jaw, decision made. "Stay here. I'm going to see what's going on."

"Shouldn't we let them be distracted and keep moving? This could work to our advantage, Zam. Whatever is going on is keeping them away from us." Maks's voice was barely above a whisper. "You just said we didn't need to draw attention to us. You snooping around could do just that!"

He was right, but there was something about the sound that drew me forward. The cry of pain struck a chord in me I couldn't deny. I slid off Balder's back and handed his reins to Maks. "Keep north along the borderline of the trees. If a dragon comes out before I get back to you, the black jewel for our passage is in my bedroll."

"Wait. And what happens if you get killed?" He made a grab for me but I dodged his hand with ease.

I grinned widely, flashing my pointed canines I rarely showed off. "Trust me, I won't be."

His eyebrows shot up again and I turned my back on him, hurrying through the skiff of snow. I had my kukri twins on my thighs, and the flail was strapped to my back. Lucky for me when I shifted to my feline form my weapons and clothes shifted with me, becoming a chain around my neck woven with whatever color cloth my clothes were. A perk the bigger shifters didn't have. They all went naked when they shifted and often lost their weapons. My weapons became a part of the chain as far as I knew.

I glanced back as I stepped under the cover of the trees. Maks had done as I asked and continued onward. Which was good. Because I didn't like anyone seeing my shifted form and realizing just how small and weak I truly was.

Shame curled around me and I batted it away as best I could. Being from a lion pride should have meant I had power and strength to spare, that I should have been a literal force to be reckoned with. But I'd gotten the shit end of the barrel when it came to my other form. Much as I wanted to believe it was the Jinn's fault, there was the chance I was just born broken.

How long had it been since I'd shifted into my animal form? Over a year, at least. I didn't like to use it much, the embarrassment it brought was heavier than any weight on my shoulders.

I crouched to the ground and put my hands into the snow, flexed my fingers and let the change come. For me, it was like opening a door and stepping through. One side was my human form, and the other my feline.

My bones adjusted quickly, losing mass and density; my skin rippled and was quickly covered in a thick black fur that insulated me from the cold better than any coat. I blinked and was looking at the world from about two feet high. The first of my two curses in all its glory. That I would never shift into anything but a measly black house cat. I thought when I was younger I'd grow out of it. But that hadn't been the case. This was who I was, through and through.

There would be no lion form for me, no fearsome predator that would be able to take on the most fearsome enemies with a roar and the swipe of a paw.

Whether my small form was the Jinn's fault or not, it didn't change my opinion of them.

The Jinn were assholes of the greatest kind to add a second curse to the one I'd been born with.

CHAPTER SIX

I tried to tell myself that my shifted form was not all bad. I tried to think of the ways it could have perks over being a true lion. Keeping my clothes and weapons was good. The bigger shifters didn't have that ability; buck naked in the snow was no way to swing things if you didn't have to.

The one other half-decent thing about being a house cat was the sneak factor. Ten points for me there. To the outside world, I made out like I had the better end of the deal, that being a house cat shifter was brilliant, a fucking glorious reality that everyone should've been jealous of.

The truth was a lot different, of course. I'd have given up those perks in an instant if offered the chance to be a lion in truth, to be able to stand with those of my pride, without shame and weakness.

I crept through the snowy forest with no sound, my small paws making indents in the top crust of snow but no true noise. I hurried toward the cries that grew louder with each step.

Someone was being hurt, for sure . . . but there were other bigger voices now.

"Aww, look at the runt. Are you *crying*, Lila the Gnat?" That voice was thick, male, rumbling and sounded like it needed to choke up a foot-long snot log.

I slowed my pace, creeping up behind a big pine tree where the sap had exploded from the cold and ran down the bark. There were several marks where oversized teeth had dug into the trunk to get at the sap. The heavy scent of the tree should help me stay off the radar of whoever was in the clearing. I peered around the thick trunk to see what was going on.

Curiosity killed the cat was not a saying for nothing.

In front of me were three dragons about the size of Balder. Two of them were shades of green and brown with traces of gold scales scattered along their spines and on the front of their legs. Eyes of deepest brown, they were predatory in a way I'd only ever seen in hawks and eagles. Like they could see right through you if they chose. Their wings were not very big, which told me they were land-bound.

This close to the edge of their territory along

with their coloring made me think the two were Grasslanders. Dragons that lived amongst the trees, using branches and leaves as camouflage to hunt for their food. No fire, and no acid in their mouths, as far as I knew, but they did have a serious venom if they got their teeth on you. Venom that paralyzed but didn't kill. The third one was black and blue and had big wings that laid over his back. He was a flier. Probably a good chance he was one of the elemental dragons. I curled back my lips into a low hiss, not liking the odds for whatever it was they were bullying.

The three large dragons stood in a circle around something my size. I frowned and squinted.

What I was seeing couldn't be right. Not possible.

There were no dragons that small, yet that was exactly what was in the middle of their circle. A dragon with blue, gray, and silver markings, no bigger than the average house cat, trembling in the snow at the feet of the bigger dragons as she fought to keep away from them. She bared her teeth, crouching and lunging, as she tried to keep her eyes on all three at once.

"Go flounce yourself," the little dragon—Lila, I assumed—snapped. She spun in a circle, her minuscule teeth flashing. One of the other dragons tipped his head back and laughed.

"You ain't even got a good amount of poison,

runt, barely enough to kill a bug. What are you going to do, nip at my toes?"

She was a sap sucker? She was all the wrong colors. But I didn't doubt them. They would know what she was capable of, not me. I did not need any of that venom on my skin. I crinkled up my nose and took a step back, my eyes still on them as I put distance between us.

Meddling in the affairs of dragons was not smart. Not if you liked the placement of your head on your shoulders as it was. The little dragon would have to fight her way out to show her worth. I knew the feeling, trying to prove yourself when you were the smallest kid on the block. But it would make her stronger and I wouldn't take that from her. Being the smallest meant you had to fight harder, meaner, and smarter.

"Just kill her already," the biggest of the three dragons said, the one with the wings.

"Ahh, but I want to have some fun first. They didn't say we couldn't play with her. I want to pull her wings off and see if she looks like a snake with legs."

My feet stopped moving and a ripple of chills slid down my spine. Lila spun and launched into the air, but was batted down before she rose more than a few feet. I felt the snarl rolling up my throat and I couldn't stop it. The desire to protect those who needed defending was as ingrained in me as my ability to shift. I might only be a house cat in form, but the lion in me didn't like odds stacked like this.

Damn it.

Part of my brain tried to stop me, told me I was an idiot, that there was no way I could save her. But I had to try.

That much of my father's teachings had stayed with me.

Protect the innocent, save the children, you are the last line of defense.

The dragon with wings was closest and had his back to me. Funny enough, there was no hesitation for me this time. I went for him first. If I could distract them, maybe she could get away. I'd slip into the forest and that would be that. Over and done before anyone even knew I was there.

I raced across the snow, belly low and eyes locked on my target. At the last second, I jumped up and landed between his shoulder blades where I was fairly certain he wouldn't be able to reach me. I dug in my claws, cutting through the thick armored hide with an ease that shocked me. I'd never actually tried to fight anything bigger than me in this form. What would be the point? But here I was actually doing damage!

There was a moment of silence and then he roared and tried to whip his head around, his tooth-filled mouth snapping. But I was too far up and he wasn't flexible enough. Score one for the kitty cat.

"What the fuck is that on your back?" One of the Grasslander dragons laughed at him. "You've got a fuzzy black growth! A snarling tumor!"

They came toward us, laughing, while I clung to his back and he bucked and fought to dislodge me.

"You shouldn't pick on those smaller than you," I snarled. "Some of us have claws and teeth."

"You . . . pussy cat, I'm going to peel your hide from your bones!" He flicked his wings out wide and the muscles under him bunched. There was no way I was going to fly with him.

I might have been stupid to think I could take him on, but I was not so stupid as to let him get me in the air.

Right before he launched skyward, I twisted and let go, leaping for one of his buddies. I caught him on the side of his neck and once more dug my claws in. I was lower this time, closer to his chest, and he flung himself backward as my claws cut deeply into his hide. This was insane. How was this even happening? A strange sense of glee filled me and I bit him, tearing away a tiny chunk of dragon meat with a wrench of my head. Heat flowed through me, and in a flash of understanding, it hit me.

This had something to do with the flail. Magic,

Marsum's magic. It made my claws and teeth stronger and sharper than they had ever been.

Giddy the fuck up!

In the tumble between me and the dragons, Lila shot into the sky. Her crystalline blue eyes met mine in a flash, and I thought she was going to leave, escape, as was my plan. In fact, I expected no less of her.

Apparently though, I wasn't the only one with claws and teeth and an attitude to back them up once royally pissed.

She dropped like a stone, landing on top of the third dragon's head. He screeched and then I couldn't see them because I was tumbling with the dragon I was attached to.

"Get it off, get it off! Ahhh, the claws burn! Let me go!"

I grinned and decided to add to the pain, forgetting in the melee that I was supposed to be flying under the radar as it were. For the first time, I felt like a lion, tackling something I should never have tried as a tiny cat. And it was glorious.

I dropped my mouth and bit into his hide, shaking my head and growling as I tore at the armored scales, peeling them off like peeling an orange, hunks of hide ripping and falling to the snow.

If I thought the screeching was bad before, it was

nothing to what erupted out of him now. You'd think I'd poured acid into the wounds.

"Let me go, let me go, let me go!" The words squealed into high octaves and I realized he was nothing more than a teenage dragon. Young and easy to scare once he realized he was outmatched. Part of my brain could not comprehend what was happening. The other part was practically crowing.

I was besting a dragon. All. By. Myself.

"Only if you promise to let her live, and let me go too!" I shouted back at him.

"Done, done! Lila lives!" He screeched the words, and from where I hung on, I could see his jeweled eyes rolled back in his head and his body slumped.

Did the pussy of a dragon just pass out? He fell to the snow and I leapt free of him before he could tumble and crush me. Damn it, he had!

The other two dragons were gone, leaving just me and Lila. She flew about five feet in the air.

"Why did you help me?" She shook her head. "You shouldn't have helped me."

"How about we get out of here first before we have a discussion about who should have helped who?" I countered. She bobbed her head and I raced away from the clearing and the dragon we left behind. "Will others come?" I asked.

"Maybe," she said.

Maybe was the chance we had to take. Without

the blood lust driving me, my common sense showed back up. Lila was right. I should have walked away because now we'd caused a ruckus and were at least three days from the border of the Witch's Reign. Three days of dodging dragons in subzero temperatures did not sound like a good idea at all.

There wasn't enough breath for talking anyway. We raced through the trees, heading north. We had to get to Maks before the dragons did. They'd be looking for a cat and a tiny dragon. Not a woman with a big hood on. Already I knew Lila would fit in the hood; she was just small enough if she stayed still.

We burst out of the trees along the edge of the forest and there was a snort and a whinny behind me. I spun around to see Maks sighting a crossbow at me. Shit, I did not want him to see me like this. But what did it matter? He wasn't going to make it out of this trip, of that much I was sure. I tried not to feel bad about that. But I couldn't help the shame. It had been with me so long, it was a companion all in itself.

I opened the door inside my mind to my two-legged form and my bones and body shifted fast so I was upright in a matter of two blinks of the eyes. Maks's eyes went wide and he lowered the crossbow. Behind us came a boom of trees being shattered and then a roar of a much, much bigger dragon. The teenage dragons had bigger friends, apparently.

"I have to hide!" Lila cried.

"In my hood, now. Don't move. Don't say a word." I held the edge of the hood open and she hesitated a moment. "I won't let you down, Lila. You can trust me."

She shook her head once, indecision flickering across her face. But she had no choice. She had to trust me and we both knew it. She flew down to my shoulder. She couldn't have been more than six or seven pounds. Almost identical in size to my house cat form. With a liquid ease, she slid into my hood, settling herself across my shoulders.

Maks handed me Balder's reins and I mounted. "Trot. Not fast. Just moving away from here," he said. "We need to make sure they don't put two and two together."

He was right, exactly what I was thinking. Dragons were smart, and if they saw the exit of my paw prints from the trees intersecting with the horses, we were screwed.

The horses happily broke into matched trots that put distance between us and my prints.

Lila shivered inside my hood. "They'll kill us all. You should never have helped me. You don't know what you've brought on yourself."

"No, they won't." I reached back to my bedroll and fumbled with it until I found the black jewel. I held it in one gloved hand. Warmth rolled from it, and I clung to the stone, terrified I'd drop it in the snow. That would . . . not be good, to say the least.

"You sure about this?" Maks was beside me and I glanced at him.

"Of course, I am."

"You're a terrible liar, you know that, right?"

I grinned, a wild sensation rolling through me, covering the hesitation that crawled through my veins. That recklessness Bryce and so many others had accused me of, what my father had named me after, and it made me want to believe. With the attack on the dragons, something in me had shifted. "Of course, I am."

He shook his head. "We need to survive this to get to Darcy, Zam. Not play dodge the dragon."

That sobered me and I clung to the new strength I'd seen in myself. I didn't want to hesitate anymore. I wanted to take life by the balls and run with it. "We will, but we have to be bold to see this to the end. There can be no other way."

"This isn't bold. It's stupid," Maks said.

"Maybe. Maybe not. Shit happens for a reason, Maks. You should know that by now, living on this side of the wall."

Lila tightened her hold on the back of my neck and pressed her head against me. "You should have just let them kill me."

"Not going to happen," I said. No way was I letting someone die just because they were smaller.

Funny how that struck a chord with me.

The snap of wings and a snarl wet with fluid— acid most likely—told me our time was up. I slowed Balder to a walk and Maks did the same with Batman. The horses shivered as though they were covered in flies. They knew we were being hunted by a predator large enough to snap them in half. I knew the feeling. Just walking along while a massive dragon flew toward us was not a natural inclination. I wanted to bolt as much as they did.

"Steady." I breathed the word and let myself sink into the saddle, a sense of calm flowing over me. Whatever happened would happen and we would either survive or we wouldn't. Darcy would understand . . . it was a cat thing. Or maybe a woman thing. Maybe both.

There was no point in worrying about having to face the dragons now. We were facing them whether we wanted to or not.

"Stop!" The word reverberated around us and the two horses reared up as the world seemed to shake with the thunder. My hood trembled as if it would fall off and I grabbed the edge with one hand. I couldn't let Lila be exposed. But that meant I dropped my reins, because I still held the black jewel in my other hand.

Mistake number one.

Dropping my reins was to Balder a sign to run flat out. Which was not really the plan I had in mind.

He leapt forward and Maks cursed me as Batman followed his lead.

The dragon behind us roared again and I knew it wouldn't matter if we slowed now. The chase was on. We'd either outrun him or we wouldn't.

"Lean into it, Maks!" I shouted.

"You said we were going to negotiate!" he shouted.

"My mistake!" I glanced at him racing beside me. His brows were knitted but he didn't look behind us. I did.

The dragon was coming fast, far faster than the giants, which meant outrunning him was no good. His wing span would swallow us both and liquid that sparkled in the sun dripped from his chin. I assumed it was acid. His neck rippled, the muscles contracting.

Like a camel right before he spit . . .

"He's going to spit at us!" I yelled. Maks twisted around then and shook his head.

"Damn it, this is not how things are supposed to happen!" he said, and lifted a hand. Like he was going to do what, shake a fist at the dragon and make him run away?

"Throw the jewel in the air!" Lila yelled. "It will distract him!"

I didn't hesitate. I threw the black stone up with all my strength, the light catching it as it tumbled over and over, glittering in the weak winter light.

I couldn't help myself. I watched as the dragon's eyes shot to the jewel, mesmerized. Treasure, he wanted the treasure for himself and he was willing to let us go if it meant he got it.

He went for it, his front clawed hands outstretched, reaching for the tumbling jewel. It slid through his fingers and fell to the ground behind us. He dropped, scrambled around like a cat diving after a mouse, the skiff of snow bursting into the air.

"Faster!" I said. I leaned into Balder and Maks did the same with Batman. What surprised me was that for the first time Batman kept up, matching Balder stride for stride. I guess the long, slow trek we'd made had built up good muscle and stamina in him.

We raced along the tree-lined ground that should have taken us all day in the biting cold and snow, in a matter of a little over an hour. The horses began to show signs of initial fatigue after the adrenaline burst, but I didn't dare suggest slowing. Not yet. Near the end of their energy, they gave a surge like they'd gotten a second wind somehow, turning on the speed again, surprising me. I wasn't questioning it, not with a dragon on our asses.

I put a hand to my hood. "Lila, can you look and tell us if we're clear?"

Her head edged out and she looked at the forest to my right as it whipped by. "I think you can slow, we're into new dragon territory. For now, at least." She tucked into my hood once more as though she'd been doing it for years. As if she belonged there.

I give Balder a gentle pull on the reins and he broke his gallop into a trot and then a side-heaving walk. I slid from his back and walked beside him. Maks once more followed my lead, dismounting and giving Batman a break.

"What the hell was that shit back there?" He strode around the front of the horses to face me. "Seriously, is that how you always do things?"

I shrugged, doing my best not to get defensive because to be fair, it was not what I'd planned at all. I wasn't going to show him weakness, though. "Depends on the situation, to be honest."

"So, all the stories Steve told us about you fucking up, of making bad choices because you couldn't make a decision, those were true then?"

Anger snapped through me, anger and shame and horror that Steve had been talking smack about me. "You don't understand anything, *human*. So, why don't you shut your mouth before I shut it for you." So much for getting warm and fuzzy with him. For almost liking him, or enjoying his company.

"*Human*, what, wait? Are you serious?" Lila stuck her head all the way out, her tail and tiny claws hanging onto me for balance as I walked. "I've never seen a real human. He's not as ugly as I thought he'd be. I thought they all looked like giants, just in miniature. I mean . . . well, you know what I mean." She tipped her head and I caught a flash of her blue eyes again, assessing Maks.

Maks glanced at her and his lips tightened. "What are you going to do with a dragon, Zam?"

I shrugged. "Saved her."

"You . . . aren't serious, are you?" He stared at me. "Dragons can't be trusted, you know that. Hell, even I know that."

I fought the grimace that wanted to take over my face because there was some truth to that. Dragons were actors to the nth degree, able to make you believe anything they wanted. Then again. "Humans can't be trusted, either, according to Ish and my father. Which means I can't trust you. Which is fine by me." I looked past him, my ears straining for any sign of pursuit.

"Who is Ish? Is that your mother?" Lila came out a little farther so her front half was visible, her tail and butt still inside my hood.

"We can't take a dragon with us," Maks said. "It's going to be hard enough getting through the cold, never mind with a lizard that can't stand the frigid temperatures. It's cold here, but it's going to get far colder, and in case you've forgotten, we're here to save Darcy, not a runt of a dragon."

I whipped around and slammed a hand into his chest, shoving him back a few steps, I think shocking us both. "I have *not* forgotten. If anything, we're farther ahead now than we would have been otherwise. The horses covered a day's worth of ground in an hour."

"Yeah, but the dragons will come looking for us because we've pissed them off and given them something to chase along with taking someone that I assume they wanted to kill?" He shoved my hand away and glanced at Lila at the edge of my hood.

He wanted to throw her away because she was small and weak like me. She was trouble, like me.

"Then that means we have to go faster. Which means we get to Darcy sooner. Which means we go home sooner. All good things, Maks." I gave him a tight smile, fighting not to growl at him.

He shook his head. "I can see why Steve doesn't like to work with you. Not only are you impetuous, you're a damn house cat. I thought I was going with something truly bad-ass, not . . . that." His words were hard and disbelief filled them. Disbelief and condescension.

I flinched as if he'd slapped me. I turned to Balder and mounted up. "Fuck you, Maks." I gave Balder my heels and he broke into a trot that had us ahead of Maks and Batman. Batman whinnied after us as if he could hold us back.

Balder kept moving. He was used to leaving Batman behind.

"That was very unkind of him," Lila said. "I get picked on for being a runt. I thought you were very brave back there with my cousins." She tipped her head against my cheek. I swallowed hard.

"Those were your cousins?" I shook my head, reminding myself not to complain about Bryce ever again.

"Yes, all dragons are considered cousins. My kind believe any weakness should be wiped out, and I am too small. The Gnat, as they called me." Her big eyes blinked once, the lashes fluttering. She changed the direction of her words. "If you'll let me, I can try to help you. Maybe if I do that, your friend Ish will let me stay with you. I have no home now. I can't go back to Dragon's Ground."

There was a connection between this little dragon and myself, I wouldn't deny it. That was the world of the supernatural: when a friend came along, you held on tightly. Because there was no telling when you might need each other. Or like Darcy, lose each other. I was afraid to trust Lila, though. Maks wasn't wrong when he'd said dragons couldn't be trusted.

How the hell he knew that was beyond me, but he

had a point. Which meant I had to be careful and not let myself get too deep into caring for her.

I lifted a hand and ran my fingers along the top of her head. "I think that's a great idea, Lila. I feel like I've known you for years."

"Me too," she whispered. "I like you, Zam. Not just because you saved me either. You're what I want to be. Brave and fierce even if you aren't the biggest supe."

I smiled, my heart swelling a little, but it was strained as I stared into the distance, thinking about all we were going to face. This was the beginning of the journey, far from home and going deep into enemy territory. "Though she be but little, she is fierce," I whispered softly.

"Shakespeare." Lila bobbed her head. "I always loved that line."

I laughed. A dragon who recognized Shakespeare? "How about this one. 'Hell is empty and all the devils are here.' What play?"

"Oh, please. That's easy. *The Tempest*. How about, 'It is not in the stars to hold our destiny but in ourselves.'" She scrambled off my shoulder and up Balder's neck where she perched and faced me with a wide grin on her toothy face.

I pointed a finger at her. "*Romeo and Juliet*."

Back and forth we went, throwing lines, trying to stump one another. I let Balder slow again and Maks eventually caught up but I ignored him. Because he was a human, a stupid, stupid human man who had no idea what this world was really like. I remembered something my father had told me, and it made more sense to me now than ever before.

Zamira, there are times you must take a chance. You. Because maybe tomorrow, you might not be alive. Live for the moment. In order to get up each day and face the darkness—you need to embrace the moments of joy in life. One day, the inevitable will come for you and you will have no more todays.

Death was always waiting, and I knew it better than most.

Lila's eyes narrowed and she flashed a wink at me before she turned her head to Maks. She waved one tip of her wing at him. "Out of my sight! Thou dost infect my eyes."

"Oh, burn!" I turned my head to the side and raised an eyebrow at him. "Thou art a boil, a plague sore, an embossed carbuncle in my corrupted blood." Take that, human. Use all the F-bombs you like, you won't beat Will when it came to put-downs.

"Are you tossing Shakespearean insults at me? You two are out of your minds," Maks said. "We have acid-spitting dragons looking for us, we're racing to save Darcy, and have a killing winter ahead of us if the rumors of the Ice Witch are even half true, not to mention slipping past her three guardians. Do you recall these small yet rather important details? As in, we need to get the hell out of here? Not spend our time trotting out how many plays of yore you've read." He continued to mutter under his breath and I chose not to listen. There might have been more than a few damned house cat mutterings and those burned my pride and hurt something deep inside of me more than anything else could have. He was right. I was just a house cat.

Lila stuck her tongue out at him. "More of your conversation would infect my brain."

His face tightened and Lila howled with laughter, her whole tiny body shaking. I smiled. I might be stuck with Maks for now. But I had been right in saving Lila. She was a bright ray of light on what was otherwise a shitty fucking day.

I nodded to myself. "Though she be but little, she is fierce. And she's my friend."

CHAPTER SEVEN

L ila continued to throw insults at Maks even as the darkness began to fall around us on the edge of Dragon's Ground. I was concerned for two reasons. One, we literally weren't out of the woods yet, and two, the temperature was slowly dipping. That wasn't good for any of us.

"Thou art a boil." She flew between us doing barrel rolls and then shooting up into the sky to scout for any incoming dragons.

"You used that one already. Several times, in fact," Maks drawled.

"It's a good one. You look like a boil. Ready to pop." She flicked her tail at him, catching the edge of his ear in a hard snap.

He clapped a hand over it with a grunt. "God save

me from angry women, and even angrier lady dragons."

Lila landed on my right shoulder, preening. "There is a place up ahead we could camp, if you want to stop for the night? The dragons don't like it, so they won't come close. And yes," she looked at Maks, "you should talk to your deity about saving you from angry female dragons. We all bite." She stuck her tongue out at him again, flipping it back and forth. I bit back a grin.

"If you have a place, then yes, lead the way, Lila." I motioned with my hand for her to do just that. I was hoping for a trapper shack. According to Ish's information, the old structures were still here and there, dotted on the landscape, left behind by the humans before they scattered as the wall went up. A trapper shack would be perfect, small and meant to blend in with the forest so the animals being hunted would never see it. An extra level of camouflage would not hurt my feelings at all.

She pushed off from my shoulder and flew ahead of us, the glitter of her scales catching the last of the dying light. As soon as she was well out of earshot, Maks reached across the space between the horses and tapped my arm.

"You really think we can trust her?" He kept his voice low. "It could be a trap. She could be working for the dragons, drawing us in. Looking for a way to get back into their good graces by bringing home dinner."

I snorted, the desire to rub my face with both hands high. "Really? We aren't any special prizes here, Maks. You're a human, and I'm a freaking house cat. Even Lila is no big thing to them. They sent *juveniles* to dispatch her, that is how little they thought of her. If she'd had any value they would have executed her publicly. And we aren't here to steal anything from the dragons, we're just passing through. Dragons can pick up on the intentions of those they're around." That last bit was a fib, but I needed him to trust Lila, because I wanted badly to believe she was one of the good ones.

I rolled my shoulders and stretched my back with a big breath. Part of it was true, though, about the feelings. Lila had said she knew I truly meant to protect her, and because of that . . . well, I wanted to believe I had her loyalty. That I could trust her. I shook my head at myself. There was that *T* word again. Maybe this time, I'd be giving it to the right person. "I bet we aren't even on their radar anymore."

Again, that last bit was more hope than truth. I didn't need him freaking out about me being impetuous, or foolish, or indecisive. I was a grown woman and I'd survived in this world when a lot of people would have given up, lain down, and died where their spirits had been broken. But that was a cat for you, nine lives and all that shit. I'd keep going even when I wasn't entirely sure I should be still alive. I wasn't sure how many lives I had left after the last ten years hunting jewels for Ish.

Lila ducked into the trees, flicking her tail at us to follow her. She disappeared into the thick evergreens and I grimaced. I did not want to *go* into the Dragon's Ground until we absolutely had to, but it looked like the place Lila had in mind for us to stay was exactly there, into the den of the beast.

"See, yeah, that face you're making right there, that makes me nervous," Maks said. "This is a bad idea, isn't it, following her?"

"Not bad. But dangerous? Yes, I can say it would be that at least. To be fair, everything we do outside of Ish's home is dangerous. And Lila obviously knows what she's doing and she knows this place far better than either you or I," I pointed out. "So, we trust her and keep going."

"You're trusting a dragon you've known for hours. Hours. That's freaking ridiculous. Stupid, reckless . . . just . . . I can't even begin to understand how you can't see just how bad of an idea this is."

My jaw ticked because what he was saying was true and I knew it. But he was a human and that meant there were things he just didn't grasp in his little pea brain. I whipped around to face him. "*You* don't understand this world, human. Saving someone's life here is no small thing. You don't turn on them, no matter what, until at the very least that debt is repaid. No matter if it costs you your life or the life of someone you love, if it costs you your marriage, or your brother's respect, your values or anything else you might hold dear. You do *not* turn on them. You just don't. You repay the debt, and that's all there is to that, Maks."

His eyes widened. I pulled back, and yanked my hood over my face. I had not meant to say that much to him, but once the words started they didn't want to stop.

He was silent after that which was a blessing in and of itself. Minutes later, we crossed the tree line and walked into Dragon's Ground. Yes, we were farther north, but we were still at least fifty miles from the boundary line we needed to cross before we would be on the Witch's Reign. And that's when things would get interesting. That's when we needed to be especially careful.

As if facing the dragons we'd seen already wasn't interesting enough.

I sighed, feeling the weight of this journey on my shoulders like a living creature, one that wanted to strangle me if I let it have its way.

We had a long way to go, and a long way back, and a time crunch on top of all that, and a lot of lives at stake. I sighed again as I let Balder pick his path through the trees, but it wasn't long before we were forced to stop.

In front of us was a high fence made of . . . spears, it looked like, if I was seeing things right. They were old and rusted, shattered in places, and pieced back together in others as if they'd been there a very long time. I frowned and slid off Balder's back. Lila lighted on the top of one of the spears, balancing carefully on her two clawed back feet. "Here, we can camp in here, against that building back there I think is best."

I looked past her at the stones in the ground, the markings on them, the stone building she pointed at with the tip of one wing. "Lila, is this a . . . graveyard?"

"Yeah, but not for dragons; for the supes that used to live in this forest before the dragons. It's way older than the wall and hasn't been used in hundreds of years." She flicked her wings behind her and hopped off the spear and to the ground. She trotted forward on her four limbs like a tiny dragon horse. "Come on, there's a shelter not far from here, that building, like I said, I think is best."

I looked at Maks who just shook his head. "It's a good thing I . . . care for . . . her. I wouldn't do this for anyone else."

"You mean Darcy?" I tipped my head to one side. It was almost like he'd forgotten her name.

"Of course, I mean Darcy," he snapped, his eyes unable to meet mine.

Funny, but his words seemed stilted, like he knew he should say something about her. Like he hadn't really been thinking about her at all.

Easy on the suspicious aloysius, Zam, I told myself.

"Me either. Hanging out in graveyards isn't my idea of a nice night out," I muttered and stepped Balder through the opening that led into the graveyard. Fingers crossed it was a dead graveyard. Like really, really dead.

A chill flickered over me as I crossed an invisible barrier that had nothing to do with the cold weather around us. Like I'd inadvertently set off an unseen alarm for the spirits of the dead. The hair on my arms rose the farther in we went. Safe from dragons, but what else was here that wasn't so safe for us?

Ghouls were known to haunt graveyards, spirits of the dead, of course, and then there were worse creatures. Vamps for one, and even werewolves were known to stick close to the dead. I grimaced and reminded myself that, at least, a vamp would go for Maks first. The wolf would come for me, smelling what I was. Cats versus dogs and all that.

My lips twitched and Maks must have caught the edge of my smile because he frowned at me which made the twitch bigger. Of course, the smile was more nerves than anything else. Within seconds, I could feel my sixth sense dropping into overdrive, picking up on every noise, every smell, every creak that was anything but natural. The dead were restless, and they knew I could sense them.

Double damn.

Lila ducked behind a couple of bigger tombstones and then stopped in front of the old blocky house she'd pointed at from the fence. Twelve feet in height and about the same distance across, the carved stones were huge and would have been a monumental task to move. The front of it was peaked and drawn forward a solid six feet into an overhang that was covered in tiny figures. The more I looked, the more the figures looked as though they were writhing in pain, skeletal, and in some state of decomposition across the board.

Awesome.

"A crypt? Are you serious?" Maks snorted. "You can't be serious. Tell me you're joking, little dragon. That this is just a very bad sense of humor."

"The dragons don't like it here. I never knew why. They won't even talk about it. Certainly, not to anyone who isn't an elder, so it's really the best place. Unless you want to make camp somewhere they could easily find us?" Lila sat on her haunches like a well-trained dog, her wing tips trembling. The cold must be getting to her. We needed a fire for all of us.

He glared at her. "This is a bad, bad idea. If

dragons don't like this place, then we are fucking stupid to be here," Maks muttered even as he dismounted and loosened Batman's cinch, giving the horse a scratch on his neck and slipping him another mint.

I wanted to disagree with him, but the sensation of being watched, of not being welcome on this land, grew inside me with each passing second. I didn't dismount.

Balder stomped his front foot and there was a resounding crack. I looked over his shoulder to the ground at his feet. He'd snapped a bone that lay on the ground, as if it had been placed there. Not a speck of dirt marred the creamy white bone. My lips curled into a silent snarl and my body tensed. I forced myself to breathe through the sensation. "Maks, do you feel anything . . . out of the ordinary?"

"Cold and hungry and fucking irritated that no one listens to me because I'm just a *human*. You wouldn't treat me like this if I were a supe. I've had no say in all of this, and my life is on the line too," he grumbled. I ignored him and his complaint when another time his grumbling would have made me laugh.

"Lila, you feel anything?" I looked at the little dragon.

She shook her head. "I hate to agree with him but cold and hungry are about all I've got going on."

Except that her wings still shook even though the wind had subsided and, while I wanted to believe it was just the cold, I wasn't so sure. Her jeweled eyes locked with mine and she shook her head ever so slightly. She *did* feel something but didn't want Maks to know. And if I was right, she was as frozen in place as me. Why was she hiding it from Maks? An ego thing? Possibly, dragons didn't like to be known as weak, and that would be a struggle for one so small as Lila who was already fighting an uphill battle. Or maybe like me, she knew he'd make good cannon fodder if the situation demanded it.

If the spirits turned out to be more than just restless.

The two horses shifted their feet in tandem. I forced myself off Balder's back and slid to the ground, still holding onto him in case I needed to leap back into the saddle. As soon as my feet touched the earth, the sensation of being watched intensified. As if someone stood right behind me, breathing down the side of my neck, which was impossible, seeing as I still had my hood up. Sweat broke out along my hairline and trickled down my back. I stood there and did my best to breathe through it, knowing it for what it was.

Finally, Maks noticed. "What's wrong?"

"Felines are sensitive to the dead." I was trying to talk normal but it came out as a whisper. "And the dead know it. They tend to . . . want my attention. I was hoping this place was old enough that the spirits would have moved on by now."

Maks came around Balder to my side. "Then we have to go if it's not safe."

"This *is* safe, at least from the dragons, if Lila is right," I said, and my stomach rolled with the thought of staying more than another few minutes. "I just . . . I won't sleep is all." Or eat. Or relax. As it was right then, the need to whip around and tell the spirits to back the fuck off was strong enough that I had to work to hold in the words and fear. Because saying those things would do me no good.

I was no medium trained to handle spirits. Certainly, not pissed off spirits of dead supes crawling around the graveyard looking for attention and trying to draw me out to them. Some spirits could steal your energy and take you into a coma, and that's if they were playing nice. That was shit I did not need when Darcy was depending on me. I touched the ring that rested against my chest, taking strength from it.

I drew a breath and let it out slowly, still fighting the sensations that wormed around me. "Get a fire going. It's safer here than out there." I repeated those words, needing to believe them.

Maks watched my face. "You sure?"

"Yes."

No.

But that word didn't flow past my lips.

I wasn't sure at all, but I would give him a point or two for asking, at least, and trying to make sure I was okay. Maybe I could see a little of what Darcy saw in him. Maks was solid, and more dependable than any of the other partners I'd had on a trip. He turned away and something touched my elbow, a hand and fingers that tightened for a moment and then were gone. Letting me know *they* knew I was aware of them.

Again, just awesome.

I froze where I was once more. Balder turned his head and bumped me.

"Right, let's loosen your cinch," I said. I made my cold fingers work, easing his tack and then Batman's. Most nights, we took all their gear off, but not here, not inside enemy territory. We'd all rest with one eye open. Two eyes, in my case.

Lila swept into my range of sight and landed on Balder's saddle, her tiny claws clutching at the edges of the leather. "I've been here before, but I've never felt anything like this."

I drew a breath and caught a scent of salt in the air, like the ocean. It was there and gone. "How close are we to water?"

"Water?" She frowned, wrinkling her skin around her eyes. "You mean a river?"

"No, like an ocean."

"We aren't," she said. "Why?"

I drew a big breath and let the air rest on the back of my tongue, tasting it. "I can smell the ocean." Which made absolutely no sense whatsoever.

I didn't like it. This world was not one for coincidences. Not in the least. And smelling the ocean this far was a sign of some sort. I just had to figure out what it was trying to tell me.

"No dragons are connected to the ocean, right?" I crossed my arms and tucked my hands into my armpits for extra warmth.

Lila shook her head and Maks crouched in front of the crypt to set up the fire. He said nothing, but I had no doubt he was listening.

"No, we can't go near the ocean. That is the Ice Witch's territory, though the dragons would like to take it from her," Lila said. She shivered and I opened the edge of my hood. I didn't have to say a word, she leapt up and burrowed into my thick mane of hair. Her scales were cool against my skin, but I didn't mind. Better than having something undead touching me.

Lila shifted around inside my hood so her head hung out. "The Ice Witch rules from the edge of the water and we avoid it. She's a right bitch, that one. She used to take the youngling dragons as prizes. She skinned them and used their armor for her army of ice goblins. There was a battle and from what I know, a truce was called. She couldn't beat us, and we couldn't beat her. The Jinn stepped in and smacked them all soundly."

I didn't like the sounds of that. Like the Jinn were somehow running the show, even all the way up here.

I noted Maks listening intently, though he was trying to look like he wasn't. Subtle, I thought to myself, he was not.

I took a step away from Balder, then another, and another until I was across the pile of sticks from Maks under the overhang. His hands swept over the wood as he produced a flint. He struck it a few times, the sparks flying and then the wood catching with a rush of light and warmth.

My mind raced with thoughts of what might be out there watching us, and it didn't help that the sensation of being peered at rolled over me again and again, in waves. Ocean waves. I swallowed hard. "Maks, did anyone else know we'd left the Stockyards?"

"What do you mean? Your brother knew. Ish was sending you out to check on—" he glanced at Lila then back to me, "things." The firelight danced over his face giving him a ghoulish look.

"The servants, or other supes, anyone at the Stockyards besides Ish and my brother?" I crouched, pulled my gloves off, and held my hands to the fire, soaking in the heat. Because there was no way they would try to sabotage us. Was there?

Maks put a couple pieces of wood on the fire and the heat seemed to push back some of the weight of the eyes on me. "Not that I know of. Why? What are you getting at?" Maks shifted and then sat, putting his back against the stone door so he stared into the dark graveyard, his blue eyes flitting from one headstone to another. Searching for things he couldn't see.

"I think someone warned the Ice Witch we were coming for Darcy." I rolled my hand and the smell of ocean water and ice curled up my nose, making me sneeze. "Yeah, I think she's onto us." I thought for a moment, coming up with only a single answer. "It had to be Steve, but why?" And why would the Ice Witch care if we came for Darcy? Wouldn't she be more worried if we were coming for the jewel?

Maks snorted. "You hate Steve, and I get that, I do. But that doesn't mean he'd jeopardize Darcy's life. Didn't they have something going on at one point?"

I glanced at him and then away so I looked out into the graveyard too, his words creating a bitter gall in my belly. "He's too stupid to realize that he'd be risking her life. He only sees what's in front of him, not long-term repercussions. Hence the cheating. Hence the atrocious lying. If he thinks he can get rid of both me and Darcy in one fell swoop, he'd do it."

"You just said he's stupid. How would he have done this? And so quickly?" Maks asked.

I rubbed my slowly warming fingers over my face. He had a point. Either Steve was too stupid to see the consequences of hampering us, or he was smart enough to figure this out.

"Shit, I don't know," I whispered.

Laughter spilled out of the graveyard followed by a low whistle.

"Tell me you whistled," I whispered.

"Not me," Maks whispered back.

The three of us froze in tandem as a mist began to crawl between the gravestones. Mist that should not have been with the snow falling unless . . . I made myself move so I was on the edge of the crypt's step. I reached down and pulled a glove off so I could touch the ground with my bare hand.

Warm . . . the ground was warm and getting hotter. I watched the snow melt in front of us and the mist rose thicker, like a fog. A fog that turned into three distinct figures.

Maks reached for the gun he carried. "What were you saying about this being a good idea?"

CHAPTER EIGHT

Maks's question, about just how much of a good idea this was, was not unwarranted. But in that moment as fog turned into figures, and we stood at the doorway to a crypt of long-dead supernaturals, I wasn't about to go into just why coming here was still a good idea. Dragons looking for us being at the top of the list. Ghosts couldn't kill you if you were smart about it; dragons could no matter how smart you were.

I made myself stand and took a step forward so the fire was behind me, putting my face into shadow.

"We are not here to cause problems for you. Or . . . um . . . disturb you," I said.

The figures slowed their approach, stopping about ten feet from me. Laughter flowed through them—not nice laughter, but dark and throaty. Wet with blood.

The middle one lifted his hand, rolling it so his palm faced upward. "You trespass on our land, cat."

"Well, to be fair, we're hiding from the dragons that would like to eat us." Sweat trickled down my spine. Funny, I was less afraid now that I could see the wayward spirits. "Did the Ice Witch send you?"

The middle one swiveled his wrist all the way around so the palm faced up once more. "She did not."

I wasn't buying it. "Then why did I smell the ocean?"

Laughter again followed my question.

"Who are you talking to?" Maks growled at me.

Right, unless he was a sensitive, he wouldn't be able to see or hear them. He might pick up on a few things, but not enough to truly grasp what was happening. To be fair, not many supes could see ghosts, either. Most likely he just saw the fog and felt the presence of the spirits. "Keep quiet and let me work here."

Lila peered out from my hood. "Vamps, all three were vamps when they were alive."

The figures shimmered and then became clearer, as if her naming them had given them substance.

"This ground is cursed." The middle one took a step closer. "But so are you, aren't you, cat?"

"Yeah, that shit sucks," I said.

He solidified further so there was no seeing through him. If I hadn't seen it happen, I wouldn't have known he was dead. Maks said nothing behind me—even now he saw nothing.

"We are here to warn you, cursed one." He smiled and his fangs flashed through the mist that curled between us. "The Ice Witch did not send us, but she sent her spirits to watch you. They cannot enter here. We have no love of her, so we will warn you. This one time." He held up a single finger. "This is our haunt and we protect what's in it."

"Ah, you don't like sharing?" I almost smiled. Almost. But thought better of it at the last second. First rule in chatting up a ghost. Don't piss them off, don't make them think you're making fun of them.

He took a step closer and I could see the color of his hair, a white blond, and his eyes a sharp blue. "Don't push me, kitty cat."

I swallowed hard. "Got it. Sorry, it's hard not to be a sass mouth."

"I can see that." The dead vamp drew a breath and then shook his head. "The witch wants your hide, cat. And not everyone around you is as they seem. Betrayal. Death. Battle wounds. They are coming for you. Nothing is as it seems. The emperor is rising, and he will bathe our world in blood."

"Fun," Lila whispered.

"And you're warning me because?" I asked.

"Because the Ice Witch tried to take our souls. She tried to use us to attack you and that is not acceptable. We are not pets to be controlled," he said. "But she cannot control a vampire, not even when they are dead. That is not within her ability. Other spirits she'll manipulate and use to track you. I think a dark shadow will find you when you leave this graveyard."

The more he talked, the clearer his features became until I could see even the individual lashes on his eyelids. I had to swallow again; he was gorgeous. Too bad he was dead. And a vamp.

They bit. A shiver ran through me, maybe that wouldn't be so bad.

"Basically, this is just a big fuck you to her?" I arched an eyebrow, I couldn't help it. The vamp grinned.

"Something like that. And I'll admit, I have a weakness for strong women." He lifted a hand and ran it through a single lock of my hair. "Though I prefer redheads."

I didn't bat his hand away because he wasn't really touching me. "I'm not that strong." Ahh, I needed to keep my mouth shut.

The dead vamp smiled. "Strength has little to do with the powers you are given, cat. The strongest person I knew was weak by way of her abilities. Her strength came from her heart and the determination in her very soul." He took a step back, the smile lingering on his lips. "We will keep the other spirits at bay so you may rest. But when you leave this ground, you will no longer be safe from them. And they will follow you; they have your scent."

My mouth tightened. "Thanks. For the warning and everything."

That bit about the emperor was more than a little disturbing. Seeing as he was supposed to be just a story, not a real creature at all.

He bowed his head. "We are protectors of our world. You and I, no matter what others may tell you. I think you're going to find out the hard way where your strength lies, cat." He took a step back, and then another and another until his body blended with the mist and then he and his two friends were gone. The sensation of being watched eased off until it was nothing more than a tickle along the back of my neck.

I blew out a breath of air I didn't realize I'd been hanging onto. I turned and bumped into Maks.

"Seriously, what just happened?" He barked the question, snapping me out of the fog I'd been literally standing in. I held up both hands and made a shooing motion with them.

"Dude, back the hell off. We're safe for tonight."

Lila put her mouth to my ear. "You going to tell him about the spirits following you?"

I shook my head.

"Who were you talking to out there?" Maks had a sheen of sweat across his brow. "I mean, I could hear you talking but it was like you were far away."

"I was chatting with the dead that live here. The guardians of this place are going to look out for us tonight. After that, we're on our own." I slumped by the fire, exhaustion hitting me hard. Escaping near death did that to you.

Lila moved so she was on one shoulder and I could lean against the stone wall. It was cold but solid and that gave me a little comfort. With my front to the fire and my back to the stone, I let the fatigue take me. "Sleep while you can, Maks. We've got a long ride ahead of us."

"We aren't taking shifts?" The disbelief in his voice was straight up shock.

"No, I trust the one I spoke with, and I have a feeling this could be the last time we both get a full night's sleep." I closed my eyes and behind the lids saw the vamp with the blue eyes smile and wink at me. Yeah, he'd have been a ladies' man for sure. I sighed and sleep rolled over me.

But not before I heard Maks mutter, "This is fucking nuts."

❋

I woke to the smell of cooking meat and my mouth instantly filled with saliva even as my nose twitched with the rancid scent of burning hair. I leaned forward, eyes blinking to clear away the last of the sleep. To my left, Maks was still out cold, and Lila hovered above the fire, a whole rabbit cooking on the coals.

"Figured I'd get breakfast." She fanned her wings, which set the flames higher and a sizzle of charring hair flicked through the air, thicker this time.

I moved closer and pulled a blade from my thigh strap. "Here, it looks done." I stuck the point through the back leg and dragged it out of the fire. Using both knives, I sliced it open and cut off hunks of meat that was overcooked in some parts, and almost raw in others.

"You don't want the skin? That's the best part." Lila hopped on the stone beside me. I peeled the skin off where I could and handed it to her.

"Yeah, not so much. You can have it all."

She grabbed a hunk and threw her head back, dislocating her jaw like a snake to get it all in with a few good head tosses. I looked away in time to see Maks's face rapidly greening. I handed him a leg and thigh of the rabbit that was mostly done.

"Breakfast. Courtesy of Lila."

He shook his head and I gave him the best death eyes I could. *Do not offend the small, acid-spitting dragon, idiot man.*

With every muscle twitch screaming reluctance, he took the leg and I cut the second one off for myself. The meat was pink the further in I got, and the innards were still there, but that didn't bother me. I'd eaten my fair share of small rodents that were still squirming.

Maks, on the other hand . . . he got up and ran into the graveyard and heaved after just a few bites. I shook my head. He was not going to survive this journey. Not at this rate. It was only going to get harder from here on in, not easier.

"He didn't like it?" Lila's question was tinged with hurt.

"He's human. Which means he can't handle a lot of things." I took another bite, tearing the flesh off and mimicking her move of throwing my head back to get it down. "I like it. I could eat medium rare rabbit all day."

She grinned up at me, a piece of hide hanging from her mouth. She licked it in. Yeah, supes were not known for doing well in polite society. Good thing we weren't being invited to a tea party any time soon.

Maks cleaned up the campsite, scattering the hot coals, and fed the horses while I checked them over.

But from there on out, Maks was quiet and Lila chatty. She guided us through the forest, staying just inside the edge, using the trees for cover. "The dragons look for those traveling the outer edge. They know that no one wants to come onto their ground. Which makes this a perfect hiding spot."

"Your ground," Maks said.

She shook her head. "No, I meant their ground. It has never been my place, not really. I've always been an outcast." After that, she went quiet and Maks took her place in the chatty department.

"We aren't far from the edge of the Witch's Reign. We could reach it late tomorrow and we need a plan," he said.

"I know." I could feel the spirit or spirits she set to watch me, trailing behind us like a connection I didn't know how to cut. I twisted around in the saddle and saw a dark shadow duck behind a tree.

Yeah, that was what I thought. Damn it, the dead vamp was spot on.

"What about Steve? Should we wait for him and go into the Witch's Reign together?" Maks glanced at me. "Safer that way, maybe working with someone with a bit more . . . size?"

I snorted and gave him a pointed look. "Someone gave up the fact that we headed out early, that we're on our own, and now the Ice Witch knows we're coming." And if the vamp ghost was right, she wanted my hide for some reason in particular.

Just to add a little extra spice to the trip in case we were lacking any.

"So . . . why are we going into the Ice Realm again?" Lila said.

"My friend was taken by the witch. We have to get her back before she's handed over to the Jinn." I twisted around, catching a glimpse of the shadow stalking me. That was not going to bode well. I had to find a way to *un-attach* it.

"And the jewel that Steve is going after?" Maks asked. I looked at him. He shrugged. "I'm curious, what can I say?"

"The jewel is an ice sapphire, created when the witch took her seat in the north and agreed to hold her end of the wall. Far as I know, it's in her crown. At least, that's where Ish thought it would be." Which meant it was going to be a bitch to get, but that wasn't my problem. That was Steve's problem. The thought made me smile. I didn't want Ish to not get the jewel, I just wanted Steve to fail miserably.

Lila landed on Balder's neck, near his ears, using his bridle as a strap for balance. "How are you going to get it then?"

"We aren't." I grinned at her. "But if it were me, I'd go in as a cat, grab the jewel and be out before she even knew we were there. As it is, that's up to Steve and Kiara now. And they'd better not fail Ish."

To be fair, that was always the plan when I worked on a heist, but so often Steve fucked it up because he wanted to go in too and he was a hell of a lot harder to hide considering his size as a shifter. He didn't want to wait on me and lose out on any glory, as he saw it.

"That sounds easy enough," Maks said. "But it never goes that way. At least, not from what Ish has told me."

I spun to glare at him, my defenses going straight the fuck up. "What would she tell you about anyway? How could she trust you with anything, *human*?"

He shrugged and looked away, a faint pink on his cheeks. "I might be human, but I do have feelings, you know. Ish has been kinder than she needs to be to me, and I have done what I can to reciprocate by listening to her."

"She likes charity cases," I said.

"I'm not a charity case." There was more than a hint of anger in his words.

I rolled my eyes. "You're a man, which negates any feelings you might have as a moot point. And trust me, Ish showing you kindness has done you no favors. You're human, and you're going to die here weak and afraid."

Lila snorted softly. "I don't want to die like that."

I didn't either, but Maks had to get it through his head that his life was on a timer.

"You understand, Maks? You'll die here, because you are of zero use to anyone. Zero. You don't have the balls to be an alpha and take charge, even if you were a supe."

Then Maks did something I did not expect. He dropped his stirrups and pushed off his horse, strode over to me, and grabbed my leg, his fingers digging into my calves. I arched an eyebrow at him, not comprehending just what was going on until it was too late. He yanked me out of the saddle. I let go of the reins so I wouldn't pull Balder with me.

"Hey!" I yelped as he threw me to the ground and jumped on top of me. What the fuck was going on?

His hands were on my wrists faster than they had any right to be, and he pinned them to the ground with an ease I didn't like. I twisted my body out from under him—my flexibility was a bonus here—and drove a knee into his side as hard as I could. But he didn't let go and I didn't have the leverage to break any ribs.

Instead he pulled me harder toward him, using his size and weight to overpower me.

"Maks, get off me now!"

His face was flat, no emotion showing in his eyes —not even a flicker. What was he thinking? For a moment, fear sliced through me. Bryce had said it. I wasn't strong enough, and Maks was loaded with muscle. Even though I was a supe, he was stronger than me.

"You want help?" Lila flew above us.

"No." I growled the word and then the fight began in earnest. I managed to get a leg around his hip, and with a heave, rolled him off me. But he didn't let go. I tried head butting him, but he held me at arm's length—like it was easy to keep me held down, which did nothing but piss me off more. I tried getting my legs between us to kick him in the balls but he blocked me with his thighs, twisting with each blow I landed.

"Let me go!" I screeched finally, losing my temper and whatever sense of control I might have had.

"Apologize. You need to apologize for being a snot, Zamira," he said as calmly as if he weren't holding me down.

And then suddenly I was on my belly, my face shoved into a bank of snow. It was like I was wrestling with Bryce again, unable to move, unable to truly fight his strength and speed. When Steve and I had been a couple, he'd never out-wrestled me because he'd not had the speed. Strong, yes, but not like this. Never like this. So just what the hell was happening? It was like Maks was seeing past me, to my next move and blocking it before I had a chance to see it through and turn it on him.

He pushed my face harder into the snow so the ice crystals went up my nose and bit at my closed eyes.

"Apologize, Zamira. I get that you're bitter, but it's not a good look on you. Not all men are assholes, not all men are useless. Not even a human like me. And if you hadn't noticed, I just made you submit." His voice was right in my ear as I lay there, humiliation flowing through me like I'd never felt before. I'd just been thumped soundly . . . by a human.

"No." I gritted the word out, my pride not letting me buckle under his demand, as simple as it was. I would not admit I was wrong.

"Never thought I'd say this, but I think I feel bad for Steve. That he married you that is. That he had to put up with your shit day in and day out." He pushed off me and I scrambled away from him. Part of me wanted to lash out at him, to prove I was stronger.

But . . . he'd already shown he was tougher than me, and the cat in me buckled to that truth and submitted. Just like it buckled under Bryce's demands that I listen to him. Because there was a time when he'd been my alpha—my brother, yes, but my boss, too, and I respected that.

I didn't want to respect Maks.

I didn't want him to play an alpha to my submissive smaller form.

I turned my back on him and stumbled to where

Balder was, shaking with the need to go to my knees in front of him and bow my head. Did he know that would be my reaction? Did he know that if he bested me I would be fighting my own instincts once he made me submit? It didn't matter that I hadn't verbally given in, my body knew it had been beaten and every instinct tried to force me to give in to him, to do as he wished.

I pulled myself into the saddle and gave Balder his head, and he tore away from Maks and Batman. Shame, hurt, and uncertainty flowed through me. I'd been cruel to Maks, bitter as he'd said. But he was human. He didn't deserve anything else. Not with what they'd done to us. Locking us away like animals.

Caging us.

Making us fight each other to survive. I clung to the old truths as the last bit of armor to keep myself safe from this new twist between us.

I didn't know where I was when I stopped. I only knew it was hours later. I'd run from all the truths that a simple fight had shined a light on. I was weak, and as useless in some ways as a human, more so seeing as it was a human that had beaten me. I shook from head to foot even though I wasn't cold. Balder picked up on it, prancing on the spot. I put a hand to his neck. "I'm sorry."

A sigh from behind me turned me around. Lila sat on Balder's saddlebags, her eyes on me.

"Why did you run?"

My shoulders slumped. "I . . . I'm hard-wired to give in when someone proves they're stronger than me. The best I could do was run to give space between us. He cannot be my alpha, Lila."

"But he's your partner, and he's here to save your friend, isn't he?"

"He's human. They did this to us." That was my father coming out of my mouth, his beliefs, but they were mine too. Weren't they? Steve had believed it. Bryce believed it.

Did I?

"And I'm a runt of a dragon, who cares? We all have abilities even if they might seem small and insignificant. He needs you. He might be physically stronger, Zam, that much is true. But he can't navigate this world like you. And if your friend Darcy is truly in danger and he could help you save her, shouldn't you go back and get him? I mean . . . otherwise, aren't you doing to him what you're accusing all humans of doing to us. Judging him based on all the others?"

I closed my eyes. "Fuck, Lila. Why did you have to say that?"

"My father used to call me Blunt for a nickname. As in I said the truth regardless of what it did to others. I'm sorry if I hurt your feelings, but I think you're being a brat and meaner than you really are."

My eyes flew open. Blunt indeed. She stared back at me and I slowly nodded.

"Damn it. You're right."

I turned Balder back the way we'd come.

"I don't think he's all that bad," Lila said. "I mean, I like teasing him, but he's trying real hard to help. I shouldn't have egged you on. Obviously, he thinks his emotions are important and that he has value. So maybe tread carefully."

She was right, I knew she was. But my whole life had been nothing more than a litany of 'humans are assholes, the human men are the worst, the only thing worse than a human man is a Jinn.'

But maybe this was one human I could be friends with, could work with to help Darcy.

I nodded to myself, letting the truth fill me. I'd been the asshole this time. Maks had been trying to help. And maybe, just maybe, I'd been pushing him away for more reasons than being human.

More maybe because those blue eyes of his were haunting my sleep more than I wanted to admit.

"You like him, don't you?" Lila said and I sucked in a sharp breath. "Ha, I knew it! What's wrong with that? He does have big muscled arms, and those eyes are lovely. I knew a male dragon with blue eyes like that, they were lovely on him too." She swept around in front of me and I shook my head.

"I *don't* like him." The words were strangled,

though, and even I heard the lie in them. Damn it, when had this happened? Somewhere in the last week I'd seen him work, seen him help me without having to be told or prodded. When I'd been staring at his ass and thinking about those eyes and starting to wish he'd been a supe.

He'd been a partner rather than the dead weight I'd thought he'd be. I urged Balder into a faster trot, shame driving me.

Why did I have to be so thick in the head? Pride, it was a curse of a lion in more ways than one.

An hour later we'd not found Maks, or any trace of him or Batman. They shouldn't have been this far back. Sweat and nerves bit at me. What the hell had I done now? Cursed I might be, but I still wore my necklace, which meant the curse was not supposed to be in play.

Lila broke the silence. "Is that blood on the snow?" She shot into the air above my head.

I stood in my stirrups and looked where she pointed with a wing tip.

My nerves tightened as I stared at the bright red blood. "Yeah, yeah it is."

CHAPTER NINE

The marks in the snow, the perfect imprints, led southeast. I flicked my hood off, turned and leaned into Balder. Because while I could see the blood on the snow and the hoof prints, I could also hear the thunder of another set of hooves ahead of us. We'd be able to catch Batman, I was sure of it.

The snow flew up around us in a spray as if it were liquid water and not frozen. Through its mist, I could just make out Batman as he slid to a stop, reared up, and threw Maks from the saddle.

"Damn it," I growled.

A part of me that I didn't like tried to pull me back, to hold me away from helping. Not to be an asshole, but because I was a cat and he just finished whooping my ass so he should have been able to take care of himself. That was nature for you.

We raced toward him but I couldn't see what was attacking him. If it was a dragon, it wasn't a big one. "Lila, what is it?"

She swept up ahead of us then called back, "Pack of wolves. Normal as they can be." She swooped down and grabbed hold of my shoulder. "Five."

Five wolves were not insurmountable. We could do this.

I grabbed the flail from its holster across the back of my saddle and pulled it free, my palm tingling as I tightened my grip. I whistled for Batman and he spun, kicked out at a wolf and caught it in the jaw. We closed the distance, my body tensed for battle and then there was a blur of golden fur and a snarl of a lion.

Steve had caught up to us.

He burst out of the trees in full lion form, his body fucking glittering in the sunlight as if he'd indeed been touched with 24k gold. He slammed into the first two wolves, mowing them down with no effort, using his weight and size to his advantage like always. His big paws swiped the next one off its feet, downing it hard enough that it lay there, stunned. A second later the remaining wolves scattered like leaves before the storm, tails tucked between their legs. Just like that, it was done. Maks was safe.

And I was saddled with my ex-husband once more.

Kiara rode out from behind Steve on one of the smaller horses. She was bundled up against the cold. Her eyes went to me and then narrowed as she blew out a short puff of air.

"Holy shit," Lila breathed out. "That was fast. You mean, you should have been like that, but you got stuck with . . . wow."

Steve turned and let out a roar that echoed through the trees, rattling the branches and reverberating through my chest. "Shut up, you moron!" I slid from Balder's saddle. I put the flail on my back again, once more unused. Maybe that was a good thing. That tingle on my skin had to be some sort of warning.

I went to Maks first. He stared up at me as I held a hand out to him. "Why'd you come back?"

"Because I was being an asshole. I can admit it when I'm wrong."

And I kinda like those blue eyes of yours, human man.

He took my hand and I helped him up.

Steve trotted close to us and then shifted into his human form. "Give me my clothes."

I stared at him. "We didn't bring clothes for you."

"I meant Kiara," he growled. She and her horse cut between us, pushing me aside as she handed Steve a pile of clothes.

He yanked them on and I turned my back on him. Didn't need to see any of that. I'd had my fill of his naked body over the years in more ways than one. I bumped into Maks and he caught me by the arms, steadying me as if he understood. But he didn't, and that was okay too.

"Let's go," I said. He dropped his hands, confusion cutting across his face for just a flash.

"Yeah, listen to her, human. She'll get you killed faster than if you were here by yourself."

Maks's back stiffened. I turned and smiled at Steve. "Good luck getting the jewel, asshole. We're out of here before the wolves bring back any friends." Maks nodded, catching my drift. The White Wolf was the first guardian for the Witch. We did not want to tangle with him, and for all we knew, the wolves would report back to him and lead him straight to us. That was a distinct possibility.

Steve, though, was too dumb to see the connection. "I can handle wolves, hell, Kiara could have handled them. But not you, not you, Zam. You're too much of a fucking pussy to be able to save anyone. Darcy is going to get shipped off to Marsum, your human there is going to die, and I doubt even your shit luck will get you out of this one alive."

I kept moving, my mouth clamped shut, taking the lead much to the chagrin of my inner cat. She didn't want me to be bossy, she wanted to rub up against Maks and let him be the boss. Maks had slammed me into the ground, held me there, and proven he was stronger. I shook off the need to submit. I refused to be like the rest of my kind. Like Kiara, mincing and mewling at the men who could tackle them to the ground.

Nope, that was not me. Not me and I wasn't going to let that kind of stupidity rule my life, not even for those baby blues. I looked at Maks and he lifted an eyebrow.

"We're good," I said. "I just had to get over a case of the dumbs."

His lips twitched. "Even though I'm just a human?"

"You light a good fire, and cook a mean stew. I'll give that to you, though you need to work on keeping rare rabbit down." I was not going to admit within earshot of Steve that he'd caught me off guard. That because he was a human, I'd not thought him a threat, and in another context, it could have meant my life.

"You know, the next time we fight, I'm not going to go easy on you," he said.

I could have strangled him. "Next time wolves come to eat you, I won't come running back."

"Touché," he said softly. "Then are we agreed to work together? Properly?"

Lila bobbed her head, hanging out the side of my

hood, and I slowly followed. "Partners. Darcy needs us both."

"STOP." The voice was Steve's and I cringed, knowing already what he was going to say. "What the *fuck* are you doing with a dragon?"

"She's a guide. I've paid her to help us," I said. Yeah, this was not going to go well. Ish's rules were embedded in my mind.

Don't befriend the enemy. No matter what. They will use you.

Lila flew above me and she bobbed her head, her eyes wide. I knew Steve was out for himself and he finally showed his true colors to someone other than me. I had my back to him. "We need a guide to get through here, and maybe she'll help us with our next trip." I didn't want to say out loud that as soon as the dragons were done making babies, we'd be back here searching for their jewel too. But with my back to Steve, Kiara and Maks, I missed the first part of what happened next.

"Steve, what are you doing?" Maks said and then there was a thud. I spun in my seat to see Maks fall to the ground and Steve leap into Batman's saddle. My ex stared hard at me and lifted something into the air.

A flare gun. The same one my brother had been working on in his workshop.

"Don't you dare!" I reached for the flail. If he

didn't put the gun down, I'd take him out. Funny how I was afraid of Maks beating me, but with Steve . . . I'd fight him to the literal death if I had to in order to prove myself. I would *never* submit to him.

He smiled as he pulled the trigger, the flare shot into the sky and burst open in a shower of sparkles. "Leave the human," he said, "or die with him. I don't care which. You're about as useless as him anyway."

Kiara's horse danced under her and she smiled and blew me a kiss as she turned away. Oh, I'd like to smack that saucy grin right off her stupid face, give her some scars so she wouldn't be so fucking smug. Smart, she was the smart one.

It hit me then who had set us up, who had let the Ice Witch know we were coming.

Kiara.

Darcy and I were both ex-lovers of her new mate. What better way to rid him of any temptation but to have us killed?

Batman bucked once under Steve and I just stared at him. The words he'd spoken finally sunk in, those words that shouldn't have hurt after this long apart, after all he'd done to try and leave me behind, they cut into me like claws tearing at my flesh.

Shocked, I sat there.

I shook my head to throw the immobility away. Steve took off at full speed on Batman, Kiara and her horse tight beside him. I made myself speak, forcing myself past that hurt.

"Maks, come on, we've got to get the hell out of here. That flare is going to bring down the heavy on us." I moved my foot out of the stirrup so he could use it. I didn't have to prompt him more than that.

He was up and behind me in the saddle, his arms around my waist and then we were off. Balder might have been carrying far more weight than he was used to but he gave it his all, going as fast as he could, breathing hard as he worked to keep up the speed. Maks hung onto me, his body warm and solid, that musky scent of his curling around me. Another time I might have let myself enjoy it a little. The smell, that is.

"Lila, tell me we can hide somewhere," I called up to her.

Behind us came the snap of branches and trees, the roar of a dragon drawing close once more.

"I've not been this far north; your best chance is to run hard for the border. And hope the White Wolf does not wait for you there."

"We're too heavy," Maks said. "Either you leave me behind or you shift."

Shift, to my useless house cat form.

This was no time for arguing. I nodded and did the only thing I could to help as he'd suggested. I shifted down to my house cat form, grimacing as I went. On four legs, I turned and looked up at him. "Take my spot, Maks," I said. He seemed shocked that I could speak in my cat form, but he slid forward and took the reins without hesitation.

Balder redoubled his speed with the reduction in weight. I hopped up and sat on Maks's shoulder, digging into his thick coat with my tiny claws so I could watch behind us. The motion of Balder galloping rocked me back and forth, but that didn't change what I was seeing behind us.

The dragon that burst out of the trees was brown, like the earth, his scales a multitude of the same shades of color over and over, highlighted in the sparkling light of the still-dying flare. His head whipped around until he caught sight of us. And then he let out a roar, a call for his other buddies to come see what he found. There was an answering roar farther away and more tree crashing that set my heart pumping harder. The only upside I could see was that his wings were small, so he wasn't a flier.

I crawled over Maks' shoulder and down onto Balder's rump and dug my claws in. He burst forward in an attempt to get away from me. I backed up, pricking him with each step as I let out a long low hiss.

"What are you doing?" Maks yelled as Balder grunted under us.

"Hurrying him up," I said. I knew Balder's drives

and that a hiss was about as close as I could get to the oversized snake that had tried to eat him a few years ago. Fear drove him now, more than anything else.

"If you can get to cover, Prince can't smell. He hunts by sight alone," Lila called down to us. "Assuming you don't make it to the border, that is."

Maks urged Balder faster—though it really wasn't needed now that I'd done my part—and all I could do was hang on for my life. I hated it. Hated not being able to do anything while those around me had their lives on the line. Because I could always slip away, my size saving me. But I didn't want to do that, not again.

I climbed up to Maks's shoulder once more, watching the dragon draw closer despite Balder's speed. That big fucker—Prince, as Lila named him— was moving fast, and we were not going to make it. I could feel death hovering, laughing at me. Death had come more than once my way, and I'd always dodged him. Or her. Maybe it was a her; that would explain the grudge she held against me for escaping that first moment in life that should have ended me.

A memory tried to surge up through me and I pushed it away. Not now. The last thing I needed was a flashback to another time I'd been helpless to save those I cared about. I was not going there.

The brown dragon raced along the tree line, his body humping and undulating like a snake on legs.

His eyes were locked on us and his mouth hung open, flashing a rather alarming number of teeth in row upon row.

"Hurry." I breathed the word out and Maks put his boots to Balder. My horse leapt forward and bucked out and I cringed. "No boots, hiss at him."

"Hiss?"

"Just do it!" I let out a hiss, drawing the sound out as hard as I could. Balder surged, and I could feel the panic in him and I felt bad for his mental state. But it was our only hope.

"You aren't going to make it," Lila said from above and then she was gone, shooting back the way we'd come.

The bigger dragon behind us laughed as I watched Lila fly straight up and over him. "Runt, what are you doing?"

"You leave them alone!" she screeched. My eyes locked on her above the brown dragon. Her body heaved and then a stream of sparkling green glitter poured from her mouth and landed right on his face, splashing across his eyes.

The reaction to the sparkle stuff she dropped was instantaneous. He flailed his head side to side with a roar that bent into the upper octaves until it was nothing but a shriek of pain that went on and on. Balder reacted, driving forward, plunging through the snow. He stumbled and went down on one knee and then was back up and racing forward again.

"Slow, some. He won't be coming after us," I said, sure I was right. Lila had saved us, but at what cost? Her people would know it was her.

Maks reached up and cupped my small body, but in doing so basically grabbed my ass. I let out a growl and he let go. "How do you know?"

"Lila just dropped acid on him," I said.

As if my words had produced the little dragon, she appeared above us, and flew closer. The sparkling green clung to her lips. "You might want to roll in the snow or something, because I'll be honest, I have mad respect for what you've got going on but I want none of it on me," I said.

She nodded and dove into a snow bank and came out, sparkle free.

The thing was, I wasn't surprised this journey was turning into a shit show of epic proportions. That had always been the way, right from that first moment at the Oasis. If not for the ring I carried, though, it would have been a thousand times worse, that much I knew.

Moments later, we crossed the border into the Ice Witch's territory. How did I know? Because the trees went from being green with the occasional bit of snow, to nothing but a blanket of white with ice crystals hanging from the tips of the trees. Even the temperature dropped so rapidly, the hairs inside my nose crinkled with ice. I sneezed and pawed at my face. As long as we only had one horse, I would have to stay small. A shiver rippled through me.

"You need my second cloak." I looked up at Maks.

"I'm bigger than you."

"It will fit, put it on. Then Lila and I can curl inside the hood." I blinked up at him, daring him to challenge me. "You need our warmth and we need yours. That's the only way this is going to work as long as we're riding together."

Those blue eyes of his filled with uncertainty, but he did as I said and pulled out the thick black cloak lined with fur. He swung it over his shoulders and Lila swooped down and stuffed herself into the hood the second he had it up.

"And where are you going?" he asked and I heard the concern in his voice.

"In with Lila." I jumped up and tucked myself into his hood, my hood I should say, and set myself on his left shoulder. "This way we can discuss just what we're going to do, how we're getting in and out of the castle, get Darcy, and escape back to the Stockyards."

He grunted. "A devil on one shoulder, an angel on the other is the normal way of things. Here, I've got two devils, I think."

I didn't want to grin but it was kinda funny. Lila snickered. "Be nice, or I'll spit on you."

He laughed which caught me off guard. I didn't think he had it in him to take a joke that well, after how he'd reacted to me earlier. I almost wondered if he'd taken offense on purpose, so he could show off that he was stronger than me.

A shiver ran through me. He wasn't like that. Then again, I'd always been told that humans were smarter than they looked.

"What is the plan then?" Maks asked.

"We let Steve take the lead through the Witch's territory but stay close. He'll draw the big guns to him and nobody will even notice us." I tucked my legs so they dropped into the back of the hood and I hung over his shoulder, peering out at the world. If I concentrated, I could still feel that dark spirit tracking me. Which meant the Witch knew I was on her turf now. "If we stay close to him, the Witch will know he's coming. She'll send her guardians to him and he'll have to deal with them. We'll slip by then."

"Ish needs the jewel," Maks said slowly. "You have a plan for that I'm assuming?"

I smiled to myself as my plan began to form. "We're going to get Darcy back, and with her safe, I'll slip in and we'll get that jewel too. Steve won't know what hit him."

And neither would the Ice Witch.

CHAPTER TEN

Now as plans go, keeping up with Steve and Kiara was no real problem. We caught glimpses of movement ahead of us through the trees, the swish of a tail, the flash of Kiara's bright yellow cloak. The bigger problem would be making sure the Witch's guardians didn't end up coming at us first. But we were headed north, and the Wolf, in theory, should be coming south. At least, that was the hope.

"The White Wolf, you want to tell me about this mythical creature? Weaknesses, strengths, that sort of thing," Maks asked. I rocked on his shoulder, my claws digging into his thick coat for balance.

"He's not a real wolf as far as I know," Lila said from the right side of the hood. "His howl can freeze a person and he has some ability to sense when anyone comes into his territory."

Maks twisted his head toward Lila. "Are the dragons afraid of him?"

"They respect him, I suppose," she said. "They know he would be backed up by the Ice Witch and her other two guardians."

"What are the other two guardians?" Maks asked.

I grimaced. "If all goes well, we won't even see them. But . . . the White Bear and the White Raven are the others. Each worse than the previous, which is why we don't want to tangle with them at all. We want to use stealth to slip by and into the castle. We're thieves, Maks, not fighters. And Darcy needs us to be the best thieves of all so we can steal her away."

"Oh, good, for a minute there, I thought you were going to tell me we were going to have to face them one at a time," he grumbled.

I batted his nose with a paw. "Have you seen me? I wouldn't go in swinging even if I were a *real* lion shifter. That's about as close to suicidal as you could get, going after the guardians." What I didn't want to tell Maks was that when we'd started out after the jewels years ago, there had been three teams. The third team had started with the Ice Witch's realm and had never come home. We'd put off trying for her jewel as long as we could.

My heart twanged and I wondered if we would see some sign of them. Rushton, Lars, Petra . . . two lion shifters and a young mage. Petra was my cousin from a pride adjacent to our own. I shook my head. No, they were gone, long gone, and I knew there would be no coming back for them, not like there was for Darcy.

There was still a chance we could save her.

The light shifted as suddenly as if someone had blown out a candle, and darkness fell around us like a giant blanket had covered the sky. "Slow down, we'll catch up to them in the morning."

Balder slowed with my words before Maks gave him a signal. We continued while the temperature dropped, and the snow around us began to glow with the moon's light. I didn't want to call a stop, not when Balder still had energy, which meant we kept going—slowly—for another couple hours.

Somewhere in the second hour, my eyes caught movement through the trees ahead of us and I frowned. Had we caught up to Steve and Kiara? A shadow figure moved fast toward us, limping but trying not to. Too big to be Steve but . . . I scrambled out of the hood and dropped to the ground, shifting in mid-air before landing on two legs.

"What is it?" Maks leaned forward, going for his shotgun.

I didn't answer Maks but sprinted toward where

I'd seen the shadow coming through the trees. Behind me, Balder let out a whinny and from the trees ahead came an answering call. Batman limped toward me, blowing hard, his flanks heaving and scored with claw marks. Blood splattered his one side and I scented it on the air. Horse, but not his, a mare's. Kiara's mare.

"Easy, easy, man," I whispered as I caught the edge of a broken rein. His coat glistened with sweat and froth from a hard run in the cold. By the looks of him and how he was puffing, Kiara and Steve had taken off at top speed the second we slowed down. Idiots. But then they must have run into something to dismount Batman. That couldn't be good.

I grabbed an extra blanket from his pack and put it over him. In this cold, the sweat could literally freeze him to death.

Maks jumped off Balder and strode toward us. He handed me the reins for Balder and ran his hands over Batman. "Hello, friend. You had some fun out there, did you?"

Batman put his head against Maks's chest and leaned into him, a heavy sigh flapping between his big lips.

Lila left Maks and swept over to my shoulder. "Those marks on his hide, they aren't from a lion. They're far too big."

I nodded, the scent of dog whispering past my

nose. "Yeah, I agree. Those are wolf scores if I'm smelling right. And the blood is from the other horse."

Without another thought, I lifted my head and scented the air around us, trying to pick up a hint of how close the White Wolf was. But the air was still and gave me nothing I could use. That did not bode well.

"We need to keep moving so he doesn't freeze." I patted Batman as I walked past him in the direction he'd come from.

"You want to go that way right now? How about we wait until the Wolf wanders off maybe, huh? I heard what you and Lila said, that the Wolf did this." Maks caught up to me, Batman bumping along beside him.

"We have to. We'll veer to the east a bit, but we must go this direction. We can't go back into the Dragon's Ground," I said. "Batman is hurt. We need to take care of him if he's to carry you the rest of the way, and we need some warmth to keep both them and us from freezing till morning. Veering off track will cost us time we don't have. In the morning, we'll reassess."

I hated that we were going to slow down yet again, but we would do Darcy no favors by coming for her exhausted and half dead, ending up by her side in matching chains. Or straight up killed, that was always an option too.

Some sort of shelter would have been nice, but out here that wasn't likely to happen. The best I was hoping for was some big cliff or tree at our backs that would help shelter us if it started snowing.

A cold flake landed on my cheek, then another and another. I looked into the sky as the snowflakes dropped around us, picking up in speed and size even as I watched. As if that weren't enough, I could feel the temperature dropping *again* at a rate that would kill in very little time.

A killing winter was what Maks had said, and he was right.

"I'll scout ahead." Lila was gone in a flash without having to be asked.

Maks was quiet a moment. "You think she's going to find us another crypt?"

I smiled to myself in the darkness. "Sweet baby goddess, I hope not. But I'd take it at this point. Hell, we'd have to get into the crypt to survive this cold." I struggled to draw a deep breath, the cold so sharp, it hurt my lungs. This was bad, and getting worse by the second. A cliff or a tree wasn't going to be enough. Not at this rate with the temperature falling.

A few minutes later, the sound of Lila's wings tugged at my ears. "This way," she chattered out between her teeth.

She dropped to my shoulder and crawled in.

"Ahead and to the right. There's a stand of trees that will work."

My heart sunk. A stand of trees would not protect us from the cold, not this kind of cold. I looked at Maks and he shook his head. "We need something better than that." He knew as well as I did that we were in deep, freezing shit. We layered up with the clothes we had, blanketing the horses too with the extra ones, tying them down to hold out the blasts of arctic air.

This was not a natural winter—*that* we'd come prepared for. This winter of ice cold had magic on the wind driving it.

Ish had not warned us that this could happen.

I nodded and Lila shifted as if to launch out again. I put a hand up, stopping her. "You're too cold already. Stay in there and warm up."

Maks and I pushed through as the snow came down harder, blowing straight into our faces with the icy wind that suddenly picked up and shoved its way into us, stealing our warmth when it shouldn't have been. We were prepared.

But not for this.

I kept my nose up, though, scenting for something that would help us. Was this how Petra and the others had died? Not by the Wolf himself, but sheer exposure to the wicked winter cold that never left this land, the winter that the Ice Witch created? That would make an awful kind of sense seeing as there had been no note from the Ice Witch when they went missing.

As another temperature drop curled around us, the certainty that the cold had killed them grew to an almost absolute knowledge. Their deaths had been from exposure. And if Steve and Kiara weren't dead by the Wolf's jaws, they would be by the end of the night with no clothes, no horses, and no shelter.

Just like us.

I drew a big breath, coughing on the ice crystals that filled my nose and tried to form inside my lungs, but . . . there was something else along with the cold.

Wood smoke. To my right the scent came and I turned toward it with the hope of a warm fire pushing me even though my body hurt with each movement. Though it was faint, our only chance of surviving this onslaught of a killing winter temperature drop was finding the source of the fire. I just hoped it was not a hallucination preceding death.

Maks was huddled against the wind and snow but he kept up. The horses were slowing too now, winter's bite chewing on their limbs like a dog on a bone.

I squinted through the darkness and there it was, a flicker of light to match the smell of the wood smoke. I pulled on Balder harder and he did his best to hurry into a stumbling trot. The tiny shack came into view. Barely twelve feet across and a single door and window that were shuttered tightly. I stumbled up to it, realizing just how close we were to freezing as a sudden spurt of warmth trickled through me. False warmth, the kind that came right before you succumbed to the ice in your veins.

I banged on the door, unable to find my voice. There was no answer. I grabbed the handle and shoved the door open to find the place empty, a fire raging in a battle against the outside weather. I grabbed Lila from my hood and tossed her inside, then turned to find Maks gone.

"Around back," he yelled.

I followed the sound of his voice to a three-sided shelter against the back of the house. He had Batman's gear off and the wool blanket on him. I moved as fast as I could, doing the same for Balder. There was a thick bedding of straw underfoot and hay spilling out of the feeder. Like someone had been waiting for us.

"Here. We can block the wind for them with this." Maks's words shook with the cold as he pointed at a large old barn door propped against the shelter. Too good to be true, it was a straight up friggin' miracle. We lifted it together and positioned it in front of the horses, essentially locking them in and sealing in whatever heat they provided for each other.

Maks grabbed my arm and all but dragged me to

the front of the shack. We stumbled through the door and I kicked it shut behind me. The warmth in the room was instant and my face and hands began to hurt right away as they thawed too rapidly.

Lila was on the edge of the brick fireplace. "There's a stew cooking too."

"Is this a trap?" Maks shed the thick cloak and boots despite his words.

I did the same as I shook my head. "If it is, we're dead. Because we can't go back out there. Where, if you don't realize it, we'd also be dead. That cold. It is not natural."

We made our way to the fireplace and soaked up the heat, our limbs slowly gaining back the heat they'd lost.

"Fuck, that was close," Maks whispered. "I was starting to not feel the cold."

"I know, me too," I said.

The room was no more than twelve by twelve, a single small table and one chair, a single small bed laid out in the corner covered with a bunch of blankets and then the fireplace. There was wood stacked high and I fed some into the flames.

"Here," Maks grabbed a bowl off the table and handed it to me. "We should eat while we can."

Except there wasn't much more than a bowl's worth of food left. I scooped it all out, ate a third, gave a few bites of meat to Lila and then handed the rest to Maks. There was no room for talking.

Or so I thought.

"There's a bottle up there." Lila leapt into the air and flew to a shelf above the table. "It looks like . . . oh, it is!" Her little claws wrapped around the bottle and she brought it down to me, swaying with it in a looping circle before she handed it off to me. I turned the three-quarters-full bottle around. No label, but Lila was dancing around as if it were something amazing.

"Open it!" She squealed the words.

A chill swept through me and I put the bottle down. "You sure it's what you think it is, Lila?"

"It's țuică, a fermented plum drink from my home. It's amazing. Like *a-ma-zing*." She made grabby hands with her little claws. I grabbed the cork, and while the liquid sloshed in it, I wasn't fully certain it was liquor.

I looked at Maks who shrugged and smiled. "Unless there's a genie in there, I think we're good." Maks's words had almost stopped me right there.

The last thing I needed was a Jinn knowing I was still alive. While I was weak, I was also the daughter of the only lion shifter to truly stand against them, and there was value in my blood to them. As far as they knew, I'd died in the desert with Bryce and my father. I swallowed hard and the cork gave way with a pop. The smell of sweet plums flowed up my nose. I tipped it up and took a swig. Deep in flavor, the liquid slid down my throat and warmed me far better than the stew.

"Me too!" Lila grabbed at the bottle and I poured some into the bowl for her. She lapped it up like a dog, humming the whole time.

I offered it to Maks. He took it, and then I took it back and then suddenly we were finishing the bottle, laughing as Lila wobbled across the floor. How had we finished the bottle that fast? Maks stood and stumbled in front of me, I smacked him on the ass, laughing. Damn, even his ass was tight with muscle. "Out of the way, you're blocking the heat, human."

He grabbed a log and threw it onto the fire and then fell backward so he sat beside me. "I don't want to like you, Zamira. You're far too complicated for me. Too much baggage, too much sass, and too much of a mouth on you."

I turned to face him. "Well, I don't want to like you either, human man with the pretty blue eyes." Wait. Stop. Did I say that out loud? Lila snorted softly and then let out a long rumbling snore by the fire.

He grinned. "You think my eyes are pretty?"

I grinned back because I was fucking sauced with plum liquor that had gone straight to my brain and shut off any cohesive thoughts. I leaned into him. "Yes, but don't tell Maks."

He laughed and that rumbly sound did something really bad to me. How long had it been since I'd let a man just hold me? Over a year, closer to two if I were being honest. Since Steve and I split.

I leaned into him more and took a deep breath. He smelled like . . . the heat of the sun burning off the edges of the sand in the morning on the desert dunes, all of that under the musk I associated with him. I closed my eyes and let myself bask for a moment.

"I have to tell you that I do like your ass," he said softly, his voice right at my ear. "Like, a lot. Lots. Really lots." He was slurring his words as much as I was, which was funny and made me smile again.

Our faces were cheek to cheek and the heat in the room had nothing to what was going on between us.

Warning, warning! This is a bad fucking idea! That was the little, still-sober voice that I'd essentially drowned out in plum juice. I probably should have listened to it. The edge of his mouth grazed mine, the brush of his unshaven skin made me shiver and I turned into the movement so our lips skimmed across each other. Carefully, testing the waters.

He moved slowly, and I don't think it was inebriation so much as caution finally kicking in. I was a supe, he was a human. This did not bode well for either of us. But neither of us pulled back—thanks mostly to the alcohol flooding our brains.

What could I say? I obviously had a difficult time picking men if Steve was any indication, and now to move from him—to a human man? Jesus, my father would have had a heart attack. None of that registered though, not in that moment.

One of Maks's hands slid into my hair and pulled me closer yet to him, his tongue sliding into my mouth and mine reciprocating the move. I think I groaned and he murmured something unintelligible but it sounded nice. His other hand went to the small of my back and then lower, grabbing one side of my ass and dragging me into his lap with ease.

I wrapped one arm around his neck and the other around his shoulders as if I could hold him to me and hang onto that sense of home that he somehow, impossibly, had on his skin.

Bad, this is bad! STOP. STOP! I forced myself to pull my lips from his, though our foreheads still touched, our breath going in and out, over and over in a nice tandem movement that made my heart pound faster yet.

He bit my lower lip and I let out another groan as he pulled me into a second kiss that scattered what was left of my cohesive thought. Heat, fire, desert, home, the images and feelings scrambled what was left of my brain. My one hand found the back of his head, my fingers sliding into the silken strands of his sandy hair. I tipped my head back, inviting him to my neck, a truly submissive move, an invitation to my most vulnerable spot. His breath ghosted across my skin, and I arched toward him anticipating the warmth of his mouth. He rubbed his cheek across my collarbone as if marking me and I whimpered, writhing in his lap.

And then he let go of me and stood, sending me to the floor with a crash. Shocked, I sat there and tried to figure out just what had happened. What . . . where had he gone?

"I'm sorry, I can't. This was a bad idea." Maks stumbled away from me to the far corner of the room, his hands on his hips even as he swayed where he was, obviously still drunk but pulling his shit together. I watched as he struggled to breathe in and out, his back lifting with each deep breath. "You take the bed."

I sat there, stunned, doing what I could to pull *my* shit together. "You're right. Bad idea. Too much drink." And he liked Darcy . . . didn't he? Was that why I was drawn to him, because I wanted to hurt her the way she'd hurt me?

No, I wasn't like that. But a bed this close to a human I'd just been making out with would be too much. Too much temptation with my brain in the stupid state it was. Because even right then with him rebuffing me, I wanted to grab him and rip his clothes off and bite into him, and let him bite me. I sighed, a shudder running through me.

"You take the bed, I'll sleep next to Lila." I forced my body into a shift. My bones protested a second shift this close to the first, but they did it. I crept on four paws to where the dragon slept on the fire-heated tiles and curled up next to her, tucking my nose under my tail, hiding yet again.

I closed my eyes and tried not to be hurt by the fact that a human, a man that by rights should have been damn well overjoyed to have the interest of any supe woman, had just rejected me.

The morning came—or what passed for morning here in the northern clime. I woke with a shiver, and twisted to look at the fire dying. I shifted into my human form and stood far too fast. My head throbbed and my tongue was thick with the distant taste of plum liquor. I grabbed a few smaller pieces of wood and laid them on the glowing coals. I got the fire going hot again, building it up quickly. The least we could do for whoever this shack belonged to was leave it as we found it. Warm.

Maks lay on his belly, snoring lightly into the blankets of the bed. I stared at him, thinking hard. What happened last night? Had something gone on that I was not remembering?

The kiss came back to me in a flood of sensation that made me want to strip down and crawl into the bed with him and see if the sensations were real, or just a fantasy. I cringed and backed away, horrified at my own thoughts. I opened the door and went out to the horses, the cold air cooling my overheated skin. While it was still cold out, the temperature had risen to survivable instead of full-on killing.

Whatever magic had been driving it was gone. The horses were fine, toasty in their makeshift shed, their heads low as they slept soundly.

Which meant I had nothing to do but go back inside the shack. With Maks. Whose lap I'd sat in as I'd kissed him and he'd kissed back and I still wanted to kiss. A human who I'd pretty much invited to mark me as his. Shit, had I truly lost my mind? Just the day before, I'd been ready to run from him, leave him to the literal wolves. And now, here I was struggling with desires I had no reason to have. None at all. If my indecision had ever had a high point, this was it.

There was one upside, though, that I could see.

"We had a lot of liquor, maybe he won't remember," I whispered to myself, my hand on the door.

"He probably won't," a male voice said behind me.

I whipped around, drawing my kukri blades so fast, they sang against their sheaths.

The man behind me was dressed in proper winter gear, all lined with fur from the cloak and the edge of his pants to his boots and gloves. He held up his hands and swept the cloak back so I could see his face. He was younger than I'd have thought with a grin that spoke of trouble and magic. Brown hair, brown eyes, seemingly an average guy. Which set my alarm bells ringing.

"What are you?" I didn't lower my blades.

"That's rude. You're not supposed to ask people what they are." He tsked at me.

I let out a low growl. "Rude doesn't even begin to cover me, buddy. What the fuck are you?"

I didn't want him to get close enough that I would be able to tell myself. Something about him made my skin itch.

"Warlock." He smiled. "And that's my shack you-all shacked up in last night."

Horror flushed through me and my cheeks blazed with heat. "We did *not* shack up."

He winked. "It was close enough though to call it that, don't you think?"

"We're just leaving," I said. "Thanks for the use of your home." I would not call it a shack. I would not!

He smiled. "Wait, I wish to talk with you. I think perhaps we can help each other."

I didn't need to know what he wanted. I already had the answer to his request. He was a warlock and that meant only one reply. "No." I had my hand on the lever of the door and was pushing it open, letting the cold in. "Maks, Lila, time to go," I shouted but my eyes stayed on the warlock.

"Ah, of course, you distrust me. Being a warlock does not leave me in good standing with most super dupers—pardon me, supes as they are called here." His smile hadn't slipped. "But I can tell you two things. Darcy is alive, and the Jinn will arrive in two short days to take her. The Ice Witch, Maggi, also has Steve and his mate now too, and you need him. You will need him to tackle Dragon's Ground and the Dominion of the Jinn, to take the jewels back to Ish."

If I thought I was horrified before, it was nothing to what washed through me now. "How can you know that? I mean about . . . what we're hunting for? Darcy. Steve. All of it."

He swept a low bow from the waist. "Because I'm Merlin, creator of the wall that holds the supernaturals back from the humans."

CHAPTER ELEVEN

I stared hard at the warlock in front of me who'd just claimed to be *the* Merlin. Not that he was named after the fool who'd made the walls that held us in, but the actual Merlin who'd made them over two hundred years before when the humans began to realize they were not alone.

For a moment, I thought about laughing in his face. But then I could see he was dead serious. That or a lunatic. Neither one was good for me and my companions.

"Then perhaps I should do us all a favor and just kill you right here." I lifted the tip of a blade to point it at his face. I was bothered by the fact he didn't seem bothered at all. He batted the blade away as if it were a fly.

"Here's the thing. I've had an awakening, if you

will. I realize now it was wrong what I did building this wall and the others, and I need to rectify that wrong." He shrugged. "You do stupid things when you're young. Like kissing the wrong species." He winked at me and I wanted to punch him in the nose. He had to have been spying on us, the perv.

"What do you want from me?"

"A little of your time is all." His smile was as greasy as any snake charmer's.

Well, that was a damn lie if ever I heard one. I frowned at him and he held out his hand. "I wanted to show you this, a picture of your friend Darcy. As you know already, the Ice Witch has her the same as she has Steve. I thought perhaps this will help you continue on when things get tough, seeing the condition she is in."

He held out a thick piece of paper—a photograph, something I'd seen before but not often. I reached out and snatched it away from him. There was Darcy chained to a stone wall, most of her clothing gone, her blond hair tangled and matted, but I knew her as well as I knew my own reflection. Her body was rail-thin, emaciated from lack of food and the cold. Sores were scattered over her limbs, open wounds that even in the picture looked painful.

While I didn't give two flying fucks about Steve or Kiara, Darcy was another matter, and it was obvious she was in pain by the bend of her body. "Where is she?"

"I told you, the Ice Witch has her." He tipped his head.

"I mean *where* in the castle?" I snapped. He went on as if I'd not questioned him at all.

"You'll need to defeat her guardians first if you want a chance at actually saving your friend. Because if you get her out of the castle and they are still around, they will kill you all." He stared hard at me. "Taking them out is, well, it's going to be tough considering your . . . lack of size. But I have faith."

The door behind me opened and heat flowed out around me. Lila landed on my shoulder and I clutched the photograph in my hand before throwing it back at Merlin. "Go flounce yourself, warlock. I'm not going to believe your lies. We don't need to face anyone, certainly not her guardians. We're just going to slip in and out and be gone before the Witch even knows we were there."

Maks stepped out beside me and I watched Merlin's eyebrows shoot up. "Well, isn't that fascinating company you are keeping, little lion. I had no idea you would be willing to work with someone like him."

His words were not for me by the way he stared at Maks. The energy around us seemed to tighten and shift, and for a moment, I thought Maks was going to launch himself at Merlin, which was insane. I put a hand on his arm, feeling him tremble with energy. "Let's go. He's just looking for trouble. That's what warlocks do best."

Only I was pretty damn sure that wasn't all he was looking for.

Merlin wanted something from me, that was the only reason he would have shown up to speak exclusively to me and not Lila, or Maks.

We strode around to the back and tacked the horses up, silence between us. I pulled myself onto Balder's back and he twisted in the snow, dancing, his energy high after a solid night's rest, food, and warmth.

I blinked and stared at the shed and the three-sided stall. Still there, so no illusions. Smoke curled out of the chimney, faint, wisping away to nothing before it reached the top of the trees.

We rode around the front to see that Merlin was gone, most likely inside his house. Fine by me.

I urged Balder forward, away from whatever it was we were leaving behind. The thing was, I almost believed him, the warlock that is. The photograph could have been faked, but how could he have known about Darcy in the first place?

Or about me kissing Maks? I snuck a glance sideways at the human with pretty blue eyes riding beside me. A frown still sat on his lips as his eyes scanned the area in front of us. Maybe he had forgotten, maybe the alcohol had burned away his memory. That would be good, the best thing really in the scheme of things. I sighed and Lila tapped the side of my neck with a single claw.

"What's wrong?"

I shook my head. "Nothing really. I just . . . we need to get to Darcy and get her home as fast as we can." Because what if Merlin was not lying and we were going to face the three guardians? That was not going to go well. Darcy would have no one to rescue her then. What if we got her out and the guardians came after us? I could tell by the picture, she was not well, the cold and captivity eating at her, tearing her down and stealing her strength.

Never mind the fact that the Jinn were on their way here, or at least one of them was on his way to fetch the daughter of an alpha.

Maks looked at me. "What next?"

"Kiara was sent to help Steve, which means she would have had gear and maybe even maps in her saddlebags. Those maps could pinpoint where we are going to find Darcy."

"Not that those would have been good to grab before we left," he said with more than a hint of sarcasm biting through the words. "I mean really, let's dive into this completely blind, that'll improve our chances."

I gritted my teeth, the tips of my canines pressing against the inside of my lips. I took a breath before I answered. "Because we aren't supposed to be going to the Witch's Reign. We're *supposed* to be watching the dragons. Ish never would have handed over the maps." I frowned. "So, if we can find the maps, we might have a better idea of where inside the castle Darcy and the others are."

"Wait, what others?" Maks spluttered.

"Merlin said that Steve and Kiara were taken too," I said. "I don't like them, hell, I don't like them enough to put my life in danger for them, but if they are there, then we'll get them out too."

Lila frowned. "Merlin? As in THE Merlin?"

"So he says," I said softly. "I don't know if he's to be believed, but the reality is it makes sense."

Maks was quiet a moment before he blew out a heavy breath. "Well, if we're going to find where Batman and Steve parted ways, and where Kiara's horse was killed, we should split up to cover more ground. All that snow last night is going to make it hard to track them."

I nodded. "Lila, go with Maks. If he gets into trouble, come get me."

She bobbed her head, all the laughter from the drunken night before gone. Something had shifted with Merlin's visit. The reality of where we were and how dangerous it was had sunk in further as if the near-death experience in the snow hadn't done its job. The night would fall again, and we would need shelter or end up frozen on our path once more. And Darcy would be handed off to the Jinn if she didn't die of exposure in that dungeon.

Maks, Lila, and Batman peeled away at the first hint of a path branching in two directions. I followed the trail to the left, my mind occupied with what had happened. The kiss. The warlock. The picture of Darcy. The Jinn headed our way. I shook my head, trying to clear it of thoughts that were doing nothing but distracting me.

Balder trotted along slowly, eating up the path until it came an abrupt end. Or maybe more like it ended at the backside of a warlock.

Merlin turned around with his eyebrows high. "Wait, are you following me?"

I frowned. "No, of course not. I thought you went into your house." He had to have been moving fast to have gotten this far ahead of us. In fact, there was sweat sliding down the side of his face.

"You don't have magic at all, do you?" I laughed at him. "No warlock worth his grandfather's beard would allow himself to be caught on foot, sweating."

He grimaced. "I have a fair number of enemies here as you can imagine. If I use my magic, I'll draw their attention. Not only do I not want that, you do not want that."

"Enemies?" I arched an eyebrow at him, still laughing softly.

"The emperor for one," Merlin said. "I cannot beat him, and so I must stay rather quiet if I am to do anything here. Now, let us get to the important bits of this conversation."

I stared at him, feeling that same sense of power that I'd picked up on before. Every instinct in me was screaming that this really was the true Merlin.

"No, let's not." I steered Balder as if to go around him but he grabbed the reins.

"Zamira Reckless Wilson. I knew your father. I know that flail you carry and the power in it and in you. You need to stop thinking of yourself as too small, as too weak. You are neither of those things. The flail will work for you, but it will draw on your strength; until you are trained to use it properly, it could kill you. Marsum built it to kill those who wielded it." His words wove around me, and in part of my brain, I knew it was a spell, but it felt good. Like he was telling me things I'd known but forgotten and desperately needed to hear.

He stared up at me. "You must face your fears and learn to trust again. Fight what seems impossible. Take your place in your pride as the alpha you are. Be the warrior your father raised you to be, Zamira of the Bright Pride. Zamira, the queen of the lions."

The words echoed and reverberated through me

like a gong. I couldn't even come up with a response, though I could think of one. I blinked and I was sitting there on Balder all by myself, shivering, staring at nothing.

A scream of a single word echoed through the air. My name on Maks's lips.

"*Zamira!*"

"Shit!" The warlock was forgotten as I spun Balder and drove him forward.

I might as well have booted him with all my strength while screaming at the top of my lungs. He plunged forward, snow spraying up around us as he dug in for traction, racing toward the sounds of cries and the snarl of a much larger, predatory animal.

Please don't let it be the Wolf, please let it just be some forest brown bear, an oversized rabbit with sharp teeth . . . anything but the White Wolf.

My seat came loose, and for just a second, I thought I was going to go flying backward over Balder's ass. I grabbed at his mane, tangling my fingers through the long steel-gray threads, catching myself before I tumbled to the snow. I was off balance for more than the powerful animal under me. The warlock and now Maks screaming my name had unglued some sense of self-preservation I held to.

Lila swept toward us, her eyes wide. "The Wolf! It's on Maks!"

I grimaced and settled into the saddle as the

horse beneath me plowed through the snow like it was nothing. His long legs ate up the ground, and Maks's shouts grew louder with each step we took.

The pitiful light of morning broke through the evergreen tops as we rounded a copse of trees. The scene in front of me was hard to comprehend at first. Maks was standing, and he held a short knife out in front of him, pointing it at his attacker. Where the hell was his gun?

They were two hundred yards from us, far enough out that anyone else wouldn't be able to see the details on Maks. But with my eyes, I could see him clearly. The wound in his leg, the wide blue eyes, the sweat as it rolled down his face.

"I'll be honest, I thought we'd dodged him since he took out Steve," I growled.

The White Wolf approached Maks snarling, his belly dragging in the snow. He was stalking him, ramping up the fear. That was the only reason he was taking his time. He was so focused on Maks, he'd not even noticed us yet.

Balder dug at the ground with one hoof.

"Easy." I put a hand on his neck but he was having none of it. He plunged forward and whinnied at the Wolf, drawing the big canine's attention to us. The Wolf lifted his head and narrowed his eyes in our direction.

As if to prove his point, Balder went up on his

back legs and pawed at the air, screaming as horses do before they fight one another. His call was a challenge if I ever heard one.

Something in that sound pierced the fear that had started to claw its way up my spine. Smaller I might be, weaker I might be, but I was not alone in this. I was from the Bright Pride, and I was going to save Maks's ass from the White Wolf. I had to, no one else was here to save any of us.

Merlin's words echoed through my head over and over.

Take your place in your pride as the alpha you are. Be the warrior your father raised you to be, Zamira of the Bright Pride. Zamira, the queen of the lions.

Queen of the Lions . . . I straightened in the saddle, confidence like I'd not felt in years tripping along my spine.

The Wolf still hadn't moved from his stance other than to swivel his head in our direction, waiting to see what we would do.

Maks took a few more steps backward, using the distraction to give himself distance between himself and his attacker.

I grabbed the flail from its place in my back loop and let it out until I held only the end of the handle; the wood heated my palm immediately. Merlin had said it was more than it seemed, just like me, and that it was dangerous, but something told me that I would need a magical weapon if I was to face a magical White Wolf.

I drew a deep breath and let it out before I spoke. There was a twist in my gut. I was going to die, but at least I'd die doing something my dad would be proud of. I was going to die with some sort of honor as I fought to protect someone else. The only question was, would it be the flail that killed me, or the Wolf?

"Lila, get Maks out of here, and help him get Darcy," I said. So much for Maks being the one to not make it. That thought made my lips twist upward, the irony not lost on me.

She snapped her wings in the air, cracking it. "You need me here, to back you up."

I dropped Balder's reins, but touched his neck, signaling him to wait on my command and he calmed. "He needs you more. Get him out of here." I couldn't say goodbye because I had a feeling Lila wouldn't leave me if she understood what was really happening.

The little dragon was loyal to me as if we'd been riding together for years.

Balder pawed at the ground with one front foot, and then the other, churning up the snow and ice. More than once he flicked his head at the Wolf. Still challenging him. Why he would be so damn insistent on fighting a wolf was beyond me.

Time to take the plunge.

"Wolf, how you feeling? Like dying today? I've always wanted a wolf skin cloak to lie on the floor at home," I called out to him. If I didn't have his attention before, I had it now. Insults, I was good at those at the very least. "Come, come, you forward and unable worms." I smiled to myself. *Taming of the Shrew*, that was always a good one for insults.

"You . . . fucking cat. You dare come into my territory and *challenge* me?" A deep growl rumbled past those big teeth. He turned his attention from Maks fully, and started toward us. Shit, he was big. With him slunk down in the snow in stalking mode, I didn't realize he was taller than Balder. Which meant he was over six feet at the shoulder.

"Dare? I mean, I can't help it. You're obviously dumb as they come, even for a canine. Shitting in your own backyard. Wait, do you eat shit? I hear dogs do that. Disgusting. Your breath is no doubt bad enough to kill me on its own." I fired the words off at him, keeping his eyes trained on us as Lila swooped low over Maks and got him moving to safety. He tried to turn around and I caught his eyes. I shook my head and mouthed a single word.

Darcy.

"I'm going to rip you apart," the Wolf snarled.

"Big talk for a Chihuahua." I smiled at him and started to swing the flail in a loop, twisting my wrist for a snap of speed at the end. I'd used one once before in a training session, but it had been forty pounds and a bitch to get going. This flail whipped around faster and faster, almost like the momentum fed itself. That was what I got for using a magic weapon. The heat emanating from it curled tighter around my fingers, clamping them to the handle.

This was about to get ugly.

There was a moment where the world seemed to pause, where the sun stopped moving above the trees, where the Wolf tensed and the horse under me did the same. My heart slowed, and then we launched at one another.

The Wolf drove toward us, and the horse under me matched his movement without any cue from me. We were going in for a head-on collision, but that wasn't what I wanted. I needed Balder to move to the left at the last second so I could use the flail as a lance.

Our only hope was that the combined speed of the horse, the power of the weapon, and the sheer force of the blow would knock the Wolf on his ass. I wasn't holding my breath.

I held myself upright as I swung the flail faster and faster, breathing through the motion as I tried to time things. Impossible, this was impossible and stupid but I couldn't stop. I could still see Maks's eyes, the blue of them full of the determination not to back down.

A human worth saving, who would have thought it?

The distance between us closed. A part of my brain said my father would be ecstatic that I was living out his fantasy of being like one of the knights of the Round Table. That I was jousting with a fucking wolf the size of my horse.

The other part knew he would have wanted to protect me, thinking I was not capable because of my size.

The Wolf crouched in his next stride, muscles bunching and mouth gaping, canines dripping with saliva. This was it, the moment of impact. I drove my right heel into the Balder's side, sending him to the left. The Wolf was already in the air, leaping for us in a space that we had been only a second before. With a yell, I swung the flail upward, into the Wolf's belly with every ounce of strength I had.

This was a literal flail of hope if ever there was one.

The snow churned up around us as the impact of the flail's two spiked metal balls drove into the White Wolf's belly. The crunch of multiple bones and the tear of flesh as it opened, ripping wide, shocked me. Blood sprayed outward, coating the snow in a perfect slash of red. I stared, stunned at the damage the weapon had done. The moment slowed and I saw the blood on the spiked balls disappear, soaked into the metal still attached to the white pelt. Oh, that could not be good.

What the hell just happened there?

Time sped back up.

Balder plunged forward in the snow, then kicked out with both back feet and a flick of his tail. I saw the flash of the hooves as they connected with the Wolf's jaw, heard the snap of bone for a second time, and hope flared inside my chest. We were going to do this, we were going to take this big dumb dog down and then we'd all go home and have tea and crumpets in front of a nice warm fire while we recounted the heroic tale to all our friends.

Yeah, I wasn't that big of a fool.

The spikes of the flail stuck deep in the Wolf's hide, and I tried to let go. I really did. But the weapon was having none of it. The spikes stuck in the Wolf's skin and I was yanked from the saddle as the carnivore rolled away from us, away from Balder's hooves. I flew through the air, pulled by my grip on the handle of my weapon, or rather its grip on me.

The Wolf rolled away, landing on his side with me falling to the snow in front of his belly, my hand still tight on the wooden handle. I yanked it hard and nothing happened. I finally dared to dive in, put my boot against the Wolf's belly and jerked the handle for all I was worth. The spikes came free with a popping sound of flesh letting go of the silver tips.

Once more the blood on them soaked into the metal and this time the heat coursed through my arm at rapid speed.

The Wolf groaned and I stumbled back more than a few feet. He turned his head toward me, blood coating his teeth as he snarled.

"You can't kill me, pussy."

"I'm sure as shit going to try," I said as I took another step back and then another and another. I made myself spin the flail again, turning it 'round and 'round. Thank the goddess it was light in my hands or I'd have been done in already by the weight of it.

"Balder, go to Maks!"

He kept on running, heading straight for where Lila struggled with Maks. He slid to a stop, dropped to his knees and Maks pulled himself into the saddle.

The three of them would survive. The three of them would get to Darcy.

I spun back to face the Wolf as the sound of hoof beats faded into the forest.

"You're a fool. That man you think is *human* played you." The Wolf spit the words at me, the snow flecking with his blood.

I blew out a breath, not liking that he was right. "Nah, he's going to meet up with me later. Laugh as we talk about you losing control of your bladder." I pointed at the yellow stain in the snow behind him.

His ears flattened to his skull and the bare skin on

the one side of his face tightened, pulling at the edge of his eye. At some point, his face had been burned clean of the white fur that covered the rest of his body, and the scars were red, new and very angry. Darcy had done the burning of his face. I was sure of it, and I would finish what she'd started as best I could.

"You know, that's really not a good look for you. I'm betting a golden lion did that, a girl a little bigger than me with a thing for fire bombs and amazing accuracy?" I grinned at him, giddy with the knowledge that I wasn't making it out of here. There was a freedom in knowing you were going to die.

Prepare yourself, my father's voice trickled through me.

I slowly lowered the flail, laying it in the snow. My father *had* prepared me for this moment, as he'd done with Bryce. I felt with a surety I couldn't deny that I would not walk away from this battle.

I reached for the two kukris I carried. "I raise the blades of my father."

"What are you doing? You cannot kill me with those tiny blades. They are nothing." The Wolf clawed at the snow, worming his body toward me.

Memories of long-ago training surged through me and with them came the words I'd tried so hard to forget. "I will face death and laugh as it comes for me." I twisted the blades around once, settling them against my forearm. I put one foot behind me, bracing my body for the impact that was going to come in about three seconds. I'd seen Bryce train with this move a hundred times, taking the blow of a bigger animal, another lion usually to practice, to learn how to roll with the weight of the other creature. The Wolf was double that big at least, even if I was nowhere near the size of my brother. There was no other choice. It was do the dance of death and pray I could at least die with dignity. More than I'd been living with, I knew now. The bitter, angry Zamira was not someone I liked all that much.

"You're going to die," he snarled as he steadied himself, pushing to his feet.

"Then I will die with honor." I whispered the final words, feeling the weight of them on the tip of my tongue, my eyes blurring with tears even though I wasn't sad. I wasn't scared. I just . . . felt this moment like I'd been preparing for it my whole life, which was ridiculous. Stupid. I was never going to be trained for battle like my brother, not when my mighty shifted shape was a damn house cat.

All my thoughts fled as the Wolf launched at me, his mouth and front paws reaching for me. I bent backward, going into a limbo with the flexibility only a cat had, as he sailed above me. I drove the two kukri blades upward and the Wolf's momentum opened him up like nothing else I could have done. A spray of hot blood splashed across my face and I closed my eyes against the sensation, against the taste of his life's blood on my lips as I peeled him open like a ripe piece of fruit.

I fell backward, unable to keep myself in that limbo for long. The snow caught me and I waited for the Wolf to spin and be on me, to snap my head off with a single bite. Blinking through the blood, I stared up at the clouded sky and the snowflakes that fell, melting as they touched my wet, warm skin. I rolled to the side and peeked up over the edge of the snow. The Wolf lay on his belly, his back legs sticking straight out behind him. His body unmoving.

I pushed to my feet and carefully made my way around the side of the big canine. As I reached his head, his eyes rolled to me.

"The Ice Witch will kill you." He grinned at me, blood flowed out over his blue gums and tongue and a whoosh of air rushed from him.

I picked up my flail, flinching at the heat in the handle, and stepped back. "Not before I finish you off, dog breath."

I brought the flail down hard on his head, shattering his skull with a resounding, sickening crunch that echoed through the still winter landscape.

The last of the air that slid out of him was not just plain old air, though. It spun and danced into a whirlwind that picked up speed until a figure stood—ethereal and transparent—in front of me.

A woman, a crown of bones and diamonds on her head, and in the center of the bones sat a giant blue sapphire. She wore a dress of blood red and her lips were rouged to match. She was pretty in a harsh way. More than that was the power emanating from her. I had no doubt I was staring at the Ice Witch, the Queen of Pojhola.

Her eyes narrowed on me and I found myself glaring back, a low rumble escaping me. Like a pissed off kitty cat.

"Leave my family alone, bitch," I snarled, the words flowing before I thought better of them.

She smiled, but there wasn't an ounce of kindness behind it. A gust of wind snapped between us, blowing the image into the clouds. I watched the sparkling air as it moved north against the wind.

"Yeah, that's not normal at all," I muttered.

I made myself bend and wipe my blades on the Wolf's pelt, then tucked them away. Using the snow, I scrubbed the worst of the blood off my face and cloak, rubbed the flail into the snow to rid it of the hair and blood but it was already clean. Like it had never been used. Well, that was handy. At least the cloak I wore was red. Shock was setting in. There were no two ways about it. I needed to find Lila,

Balder, and Maks and Batman, and get something warm into my belly.

I glanced at the steam rolling off the blood in the snow and I almost considered it. I shook my head against the rise of nausea that caught me off guard. Nope, that was not going to go well if I let my mind wander into drinking the Wolf's blood to stay warm. Time to go.

Time to find my friends and get our asses through the next chunk of territory and hope to hell it went better than this one.

At least, that was the plan. The flail against my back heated suddenly, like a red-hot poker laid across my back. I screamed and went to my knees as the pain lanced any cohesive thought I had in my brain.

CHAPTER TWELVE

"**Y**ou know," Merlin said softly, "she did much better than even I thought." He touched the sphere that floated in front of him and Flora. She'd created it, though he could have. He'd told her that he'd been feeling lazy, which she believed. He couldn't tell her yet just how dangerous it was, his coming here.

His companion snorted.

"Well, she certainly did better than that fool, Steve. I practically gave him a map of how to get by the three guardians, and he just ignored me. In fact, he told me to go flounce myself!" She shook her head. "You knew he'd be like that, didn't you? You knew he'd fail no matter what help he was given."

Merlin smiled. "He's a typical beta lion, thinking

he can muscle his way through everything. This is going to take a bit more finesse than crash and smash."

The sphere twisted and turned, showing Zamira in the snow, passed out.

The flail was working its magic on her, and there wasn't a damn thing he could do about it. His jaw ticked. "She will have to figure out this part herself if she is to conquer the flail and make it her own."

"Not possible." Flora added softly, "I know you liked her. I know you wanted her to win for you, but now you can find someone else to help us. Someone with a little strength at least."

That was just it, there was no one else to help do what had to be done. Even though the oracle had told them it would take two desert-born creatures to take down the wall amongst other things, he knew it had to be Zamira.

If not for the flail, she was otherwise unharmed from her encounter with the White Wolf. Which was impressive in itself.

"I'm surprised she's not hurt more," Flora said. "I mean, how did she know how to kill him?"

He was quiet for a moment, thinking on how to best word his response. "The long and short is she was trained alongside her brother. While her brother is probably the one that would do the best, as he is a blend of Steve's size and power and Zamira's cunning and determination, he is beyond help."

"Pity." Flora reached up and touched the sphere and the picture shifted to show Steve strapped in chains next to two females. All were stripped nearly naked, shivering and in various states of distress. "You didn't tell Zamira that her rival was taken too, did you?"

"I'm not that big of an idiot." Merlin shook his head even though he'd done that very thing. Kiara was no longer her rival, and it showed Zamira's strength that she would help the woman who'd bedded her—at the time—husband. Well, the *two* women who had bedded her at-the-time husband. "She'll find out soon enough."

Flora gave a soft little hum. "What now?"

"You go ahead and see if you can help Steve." Merlin grinned at her. "And I will continue to help my player."

"Within the rules, no magic, correct?" She pointed at him. He crossed a finger over his heart.

"I always play by the rules, Flora."

She rolled her eyes. "That's a load of bullshit if I ever heard it."

Except that all their lives depended on Merlin holding to his word this time. If the emperor caught wind of Merlin . . . there would be no saving any of them. His eyes swept back to the sphere. "Perhaps.

But in this case, you have my word. I want her to succeed, which means I have to play by the rules."

He touched the crystal ball and Zamira in the snow came back into view. She had it in her. He just needed to figure out how to show her that her strength was truly there.

CHAPTER THIRTEEN

The pain scorching through me was a burning torch, a brand of flames that had been jammed against my spine and set my body on fire.

Bits and pieces of my life flashed before me, my childhood in the desert, the Oasis, the pain of losing my family, the Stockyards, my friends there, and the kiss with Maks. All of it pooled around me and I knew this was somehow the payment I had to give for the taking the flail's help.

For using its strength.

Now it would take mine.

There was a flicker of something moving in the snow, a figure that swayed toward me, her smile a mirror of my own, her eyes a mirror of my own.

My mother crouched in front of me.

"Oh, my girl, you have taken the hardest path again, haven't you?" Her hand reached out and brushed along my face, tender and soothing.

"Mom," I whispered, "help me."

"You're dying, Zamira," she said softly. "I do not know how to stop it. But you would be with me then. Safe."

I blinked back tears that slid off the tips of my eyelashes. I loved my mom, but I'd never known her, not really. She'd died when I was so young that the memories I had were nothing more than the stories my father and brother had given me of her. The snow around me melted as the heat increased under my skin, spreading outward through my limbs.

My mother stayed there, watching me, pain in her eyes. "Zamira, you're fighting it."

"I have to," I whispered. "I'm not ready to die yet."

Her smile was gentle, showing only the tips of her canines. "I was like you, Zamira. Too small, a shifter that was not quite a lion. But your father saw my value and my strength. You must find your own."

I stared at her, understanding flowing through me. I was like my mother. And my father had loved her anyway despite her size, despite the fact that she wasn't the powerhouse she could have been.

"Flail." I managed only that one word, the rest stolen from me on the pain that rocked through me.

"Yes. It will draw your life force when you use it." She brushed a hand over my cheek again, cupping my face.

"Stop it," I whispered as my heart began to pound, alternating between being violently fast and slowing to a near collapse.

"Let it go," she said. "You must let it go."

I rolled my eyes to where my hand clutched the wooden haft. My fingers were white with tension as they gripped the weapon. I drew a breath and willed my fingers to loosen, to let go even a little bit.

I thought of Darcy depending on me. One finger relaxed.

I thought of Bryce waiting on me to come home. Another finger.

Of Lila. A third.

Of Ish. A fourth.

My ring finger remained glued to the handle. A fifth, I needed a fifth person that I cared for—Maks.

My finger flew off the handle and I rolled away from the weapon, staring at it in the snow as if it had come to life.

I scrambled up to my feet, swayed and fell to my knees. I felt like I'd not eaten in a week as I raced through the desert. My skin was parched, thin, and dehydrated. I swallowed hard and made myself scoop up snow and shove it in my mouth. Not the best thing to do, but it was all I had.

There beside me sat the flail, seemingly harmless if you discounted the weapon itself. "You can just stay there in the snow, you fucking piece of shit weapon!" Let someone else use it, die on its point . . . I pushed slowly back to my feet, but I'd only taken a few stumbling, exhausted steps before I slowed. I couldn't leave the stupid thing behind. It was too damn dangerous. What if a child found it and played with it? Could the innocent one die from such evil?

Groaning, I turned, but it wasn't there in the snow anymore. Fear flickered through me and I reached up to find the handle of the flail sticking above my shoulder, ready once more.

It belongs to you now, my mother's voice whispered.

"Awesome, just fucking awesome that a psychotic weapon that wants to kill me likes me enough to just attach itself to my back like a damn cactus." I clenched my hands at my sides in part because I wanted to grab the flail and chuck it off my shoulder, but I also did not want to touch it.

Which meant it was just going to have to stay there. Forever.

I stumbled through the snow, following Balder's hoof prints through the trees. It wasn't long before hoof beats reached my ears. Only it wasn't Balder, but the other horse, Batman.

He snorted and danced as he got close to me, his eyes rolling as his nostrils flared. "I know, I stink like blood and wolf. But the big bad wolf is gone." I held a hand out to him and he slowly drew close enough to where I could grab hold of his reins.

I pulled myself, groaning, onto the saddle and urged him forward, following Balder's prints in the snow.

They were headed straight north which was no good. We needed time to figure out how we were going to get past the next guardian. I knew enough to know that our luck would run out sooner rather than later. That's just how it worked. I couldn't use the flail again, that just wasn't going to happen.

Not if I wanted to make it all the way to Darcy.

As I rode, I scanned the ground. Here and there were scarlet droplets in the snow.

"He's hurt," I said to myself. But I'd already known that. However, if it was bad enough that he hadn't stopped to fix it, just how bad was it?

Batman snorted and I took it for a question.

"No, I'm wrong. It's not enough blood for it to be too bad, I think. Enough to slow him down though." I grimaced. Slowing him down would mean slowing us down. Not that I was in tickety boo shape myself at the moment.

One of my last conversations with Darcy rolled through me.

We'd been outside the Stockyards, watching the few humans that remained on the outskirts try to harvest food in the wasteland. There had been two children in their number, and they'd been thin enough that their eyes had a hollowness to them. That had twisted in my gut like an impaled knife, so I'd offered to help them.

Darcy snorted and pulled her long blond hair into a high pony tail as we walked to the humans. "Remind me again why we are helping a bunch of humans who're going to die anyway? I need to make sure you really want to do this."

I grabbed the shovel and bucket for gathering the root vegetables. I didn't want to look at her. She'd admitted to sleeping with Steve while we'd been married, admitted she'd been drunk and it had been a mistake, but still . . . she was my best friend. I didn't understand how she could have done it.

"Because," I said. Weakness was not something I could afford to show, not even to Darcy. Especially not right now.

"Not an answer," she countered. "I want you to say it out loud."

Sand gods, I did not want to say it, but she was right. "Because my father would have helped them. Because protecting the weak was what he did. What we all did."

"Yeah, that's what I thought. And where did helping people get your father?" Her voice softened. "You need to think like a proper supe, Zamira. Not like the bleeding heart that your father was. His softness got your family killed, wiped out. He got all *of us wiped out."*

I hated that she was right, but I also felt in the core of

*my being that I couldn't just walk away. Not when I'd
promised my father so long ago to try to help those who
needed a hand.*

*"I know," I said. "I know I'll probably get myself killed.
But that's why you're here, to save my ass, right?"*

*She snorted and flicked the back of my head with her
fingers. "True enough."*

I smiled as the memory faded, but the smile
didn't last as I spied a body on the ground ahead of
us. Balder's reins were tangled in a tree branch. Lila
shrieked and shot in and out at large black shapes
hopping toward Maks's body, which happened to be
face down in the snow. Eight big dark carrion birds
edged toward him, their beaks open; a low clicking
sound emanated from their throats. I moved as if to
grab the flail before I really thought about it, then
paused. That was not a good idea, and it hadn't been
mine. It was like my hand had been drawn straight to
it. Yeah, that was not good.

I flexed my fingers and reached under my leg to
grab the shotgun from the sheath. I smiled. "Chicken
for dinner tonight?"

Lila's eyes shot to me. "I hate these birds. I don't
want to eat them."

"I got it. Out of my way," I said.

The eight carrion eaters circled Maks's body.
They were oversized like everything else in this
world, strong, and well fed. Which did not bode well

for Maks. I was going to have to move fast or they would fly off with all two hundred-plus pounds of him.

I lifted the gun and aimed down the sights. "Bugger off, you shit heads."

They launched themselves not at me, but at the man on the ground, going for their defenseless prey. I booted Batman forward, and pulled the trigger as we galloped toward them.

The bird closest to us spun its head my way, like an owl rather than a vulture, a split second before the first slug hit right between the eyes. The skull exploded, sending out a spray of blood and bone. I twisted to the side and pulled the trigger a second time into the next bird before it could launch itself at me. Bones crunched as it was sent flying, end over end, to crash into a tree twenty feet away with a rather satisfying thud and a poof of black feathers. I put my left heel to Batman, spinning him in place as I aimed at the third one. The bird launched straight at me, talons outstretched, and damned if he wasn't big enough that he could have picked me up and carried me away by himself. Lila whimpered above me.

"Kill them all, Zam!"

I pulled the trigger, and the bird's middle opened, flesh and feathers everywhere. Three down, five to go, and one more shot in the gun.

I kept the momentum going, grabbed a kukri

blade and threw it at the fourth bird. The blade sang through the air with a sharp whistle as it cut straight through the bird's neck, perfectly beheading it. The blade sank into the ground beside Maks and I screamed at him.

"Maks, little help here!"

Four down, four to go. The odds were not in my favor because I didn't dare pull the flail off my back no matter that it warmed considerably as I fought. Much as it could tip the scales in my favor, after seeing what it did to me for killing the White Wolf I wasn't about to take the chance.

I swung the gun around and pointed it at the bird going straight for Maks's prone form. The boom of the gun rattled the ice in the trees above us, and a few icicles dangled precariously like miniature guillotines ready to drop.

I was at Maks's feet, my breath coming in a slight pant. I got off Batman so I could stand over Maks. Three left. One knife and the gun as a stick.

Lila was above me. "You've got this, Zam."

I didn't have the breath in me to ask why she wasn't using her acid. That would have been helpful.

The three birds surrounded us easily, spreading their wings. I crouched over Maks. Fighting in the snow was no easy trick.

"I said, bugger *off*." I threw the words out as a challenge. The last three birds were the biggest and they came at me in a group. Smart, did I forget to mention that the carrion birds on this side of the wall were creepy smart too? They'd seen their buddies go down, and now they would take me on together.

I braced myself, yanking one of the kukri blades out, the curved edge catching the reflective light off the snow. A weapon in each hand was the best I could do.

"Hang on, Lila. This is about to get rough." I snapped my hand up that held the kukri blade, but the bird never reached the edge of it.

A swirl of a fur-lined cloak and a man holding a long sword as he stepped out from behind the birds shocked me. The sword made no noise as it cut through the two birds closest to him, downing them in an instant. The last bird spun and leapt into the air. I threw my second blade at it, catching it midflight. The final bird screamed and fell, plummeting to the earth with a thud that belied its size.

"Hello again, Zamira." A voice I knew and was beginning to dread curled through the air. I turned slowly and found myself facing Merlin yet again, the sword still in his hand, blood dripping from it along with a few black feathers.

This was the third time I'd faced him. Third time's the charm and all that jazz, was that how it was going to work with him?

"Seriously? Are you following behind like a lost

puppy?" I was still trying to catch my wind, and the words were breathier than I would have liked.

He smiled. "I saw you were in trouble, and came to help. That's the polite thing to do, isn't it?"

"Supes don't help strangers. You're giving yourself away," I said.

"You were helping him." He pointed to the still face-down Maks.

"That's different. He's my friend." I went to Maks. I pulled a glove off and put my fingers against his neck. Alive, but his heart was slowing with the cold and whatever injury he'd sustained. Fear sliced through me. I needed to get him warm and stitch him up. "Thanks for your help, but I've got to get him somewhere warm."

"I can help with that. You can stay the night. Again. Though, I'm impressed that you are his friend. Truly." He grinned, then the grin slipped. "I cannot use magic, so we have to do this the old-fashioned way." He bent down and pulled Maks up and onto his shoulder with a grunt. "Damn it, he's a big brute. You sure you don't want to just let him die?"

Lila dropped to my shoulder.

"Can we trust him?" she asked quietly.

"He's got Maks. We have to follow him for now, but no, I don't trust him," I replied. I grabbed the reins of the two horses, retrieved my knives and settled in behind Merlin.

"You and your little dragon, Lila, are an interesting pair. Zamira, did you know you are well known amongst the supes?" Merlin asked.

I frowned. "No. Why would I be well known?"

"You have a penchant for trying to help the underdogs. That does not go unnoticed in places where it is common practice to eat or be eaten. There are rumors of a woman on a horse who will help those that are hurting if she can." His brown eyes were—if I was reading him right—amused.

"You find that funny?" I twisted around to check behind us for more carrion birds. They were known to fly in flocks as big as thirty. Thirty and I'd be forced to use the flail again.

"Well, if I don't laugh, then perhaps I will end up sitting and crying. Life is shitty, Zamira. It's what you make of the shit that tells me who you really are."

"Riddles," Lila grumbled.

I didn't say anything because his words echoed something my father had told me when I was a girl.

"Zamira, you take this shit here. It stinks, you want to get rid of it, right?" he kicked at the pile of manure in front of him, "but maybe you can use it. To grow your food, to light your fires and keep you warm, to keep the darkness at bay. Shit isn't all bad; it just stinks."

I shook my head to clear the past. More than ever before the memories of my family and life in the desert pressed in on me from all sides. Why now?

Something to do with the warlock? I suspected that was the case. I gritted my teeth against the anger.

We walked a few hours, just into the edge of the night. I checked the stars when I could, marking our progress and general placement. North, we'd gone north, which at least took us closer to the next guardian's territory.

"Do you not have questions for me?" Merlin asked as we walked.

I snorted. "Would anything you tell me be the truth?"

"How did you know who she is?" Lila piped up.

"I knew her father," Merlin replied. "Many years ago, before he came to the desert to find more people like him."

He could be telling the truth, but my coloring alone gave me away as a desert-born. If you discounted my green cat eyes, and pale skin. I favored my father there.

"Why are you still helping me?" I asked.

"I told you, it is in my best interest."

Merlin turned his head and lifted both eyebrows. I frowned.

"What do you mean by your best interest exactly?" Now that the questions had started, they lined up to pour out my mouth.

He smiled and then slowed his steps. "Wait a moment, ah, here we are." He stopped in front of a small hut built in the center of four large evergreen trees. Their branches hung low over the roof, giving it not only extra protection from the weather, but a nice camouflage. Not unlike the last shack. Only this one had leg traps hanging off it and a weathered look that made me think it was older than the first.

He moved easily with Maks's body on his shoulder like it was nothing despite the grumbling he'd done earlier. The door opened and firelight bloomed, welcoming us forward. Lila groaned as a wash of heat rolled out the door. "Just for a few hours," she whispered.

I nodded. "Do not agree to anything he offers," I warned her.

"Got it." She was off my shoulder in a flash and through the door.

I followed more slowly, looking around. At the back of the house was a pen with a small shelter. I put in both horses, and again, there was food and warm mash for them. They dug in, and I left them there to rest, though I didn't take all their tack off, just loosened it.

I stepped over the threshold of the small hut and the warmth enveloped me. The door shut on its own with a click and I just stood there, snow melting off my boots and long cloak. The heat sunk into me, making me sleepy within seconds. Not good, not good at all.

I drew in a breath, and the smell of meat cooking assaulted my nose. Garlic, onions, and . . . cheese? The groan that slipped out of me was not my fault. Cheese had not been on my menu for years, and I loved it.

"Go ahead. Eat. You owe me nothing." The warlock waved a hand at the table to my left. I turned to see food laid out like a damn banquet.

I made myself hold still. "Maks first."

"Ah, I'll stitch him up. Not that he deserves it." That last bit was muttered and I was pretty sure I wasn't supposed to have heard him. The warlock spread a hand over Maks's foot and calf and it was then that I saw the full damage the White Wolf had inflicted. His foot had been mauled, but even I could see it wasn't broken. Thank the sand gods for that. My hacka paste might have even done it, but I kind of wanted to see what Merlin could do. Surely he'd use his magic this time. A tingle of apprehension flickered through me.

"Can you really heal him?" I took a step toward Maks. If he was the warlock he said he was, then maybe he could help Bryce?

"I can, though it will not be as fast as if I used my magic." The warlock didn't look at me. "He will owe me something, but you do not."

While that last bit was good, about me not owing

him anything, the rest was questionable. "Why can't you use your magic on him?"

"There is someone looking for me. Even a trickle of my magic on the wind could let them know I'm here. And that would not be good for any of us." He finally looked at me, his dark brown eyes serious.

I suspected he was full of shit and this was his way of covering the fact that he had no real magic, which made me think perhaps he was just a delusional mage believing he was a delusional back-country supe. So what if he had a weird Merlin complex? He was in fact helping us survive and that was fine by me. I was not so proud that I would turn my back on what he offered.

I went to the table, thinking about Bryce. There was no point in asking the warlock about helping my brother. It was obvious there was no skill in his hands if he had to rely on hacka paste, the same as the rest of us. I sat and picked up the hunk of white, creamy cheese that all but called for me to stuff it in my mouth. I put it to my lips and took a bite. The cheese seemed to melt on my tongue, like a rich butter. I might have groaned, but I'll admit to nothing.

While I ate—slowly, savoring each bite—I looked around the small place. Four walls, two beds, one on either side of the room. An open fireplace humming with heat, and a door beside the fireplace that led out. Just like the last place, really, only a little bigger with a few more creature comforts.

"Why are you really here?" I mumbled around my third piece of cheese. This one had some sort of herb spice in it. Caraway seeds maybe?

"Well," he paused in his stitching and seemed to think things through before he spoke again. "A friend and I have something of a bet going. We each chose someone we believed in and are doing what we can to help them in their respective goals."

My mouth all but dried up, despite the flavors. Instincts kicked in. "You mean Steve, don't you?"

His head snapped around and his eyes narrowed. "How could you know that?"

"I'm a good guesser." A veritable pain in the ass trait if you asked my brother. It was my ability to guess what was happening that had landed me in the middle of the Oasis when the Jinn had come.

I shook my head, clearing it of that memory before it could take hold. What the hell was going on? For years, the memories had been faded and dull, like black and white photographs. Now, they were bubbling up around every corner.

His hands left Maks and the glow of the hacka paste on fire around the wound faded. "Yes, my companion is trying to help Steve. She believes he is the one who will stop the Ice Witch. I've put my money on another horse." His brown eyes came back to me.

Another horse. Like I was in a race and he thought I'd win?

I burst out laughing. "Shit, you are about to be sorely mistaken. I hope you didn't bet anything amazing on me."

I popped another piece of cheese in my mouth, still grinning. "I'm the runt, Merlin. Just like Lila here." She gave a little wave with one wing tip as she bit into a slice of meat. "I have my place in this world, and it isn't as a hero. A savior. Or as a wall breaker." Damn it, where had that last bit come from? My father and the memories were spilling up through me after years of suppressing them.

I wanted to bite those words back and swallow them whole, but it was too late. It had slipped out.

Merlin smiled at me. "That is exactly what you are, Zamira the Reckless. A Wall Breaker."

CHAPTER FOURTEEN

I hadn't heard the words "Wall Breaker" since Bryce and I had escaped the desert, Ish saving us, the Jinn chasing us, fear along my spine, the last of my family wiped out. And now here I was, the one saying them.

Before Merlin could get another word in, I stood and walked to the door. I needed to breathe. I needed the fresh air of the winter ice to clear my mind and the memories that suddenly seemed to be at the surface of my skin.

I lifted my hand to grab the door—or tried to. The knob was gone and the door was nothing but a flat slab of wood. My jaw ticked and anger sliced through the confusion that had caught hold of me. "Let me out now. I do not do well with being caged."

"Of course, you don't. Trust me when I say I am

taking a massive chance using even that small amount of magic in order to get you to stay." He lowered himself into a chair next to the so-still body of Maks. "You are a desert cat, and they don't like being tied up, held down, chained, caged, whatever it is you want to call it. That is why your father tried to face the Jinn, isn't it? So that cage he was in—no matter how big it was—would be opened."

I could feel the blood drain from my face. "How do you know about that?"

He ignored my question. "He tried to take on the most powerful guardian of the southern wall and he *failed*. Then the Jinn went after your family, cut them all down like stalks of wheat. The blood stained the sands, their dying cries filled the air and fed the Jinn's power for years."

His words were like a gong inside my head and suddenly I was no longer in a shack in the middle of the northern climes but back in the desert. Filled with a child's beliefs that I knew now were wrong.

I ran across the golden sand, the sun at my back, playing with my older brother. Or, at least, I was playing; he was just trying to avoid me. I grinned and ran faster, leaping and jumping as if that would propel me closer to his back end. He was a shifter, a bright lion of the southern desert as were all my family members. Lions with eyes of gold, we were the natural protectors of the supernaturals here from the wildly unpredictable Jinn that had been set to guard this section of the wall.

Then there was me. I ran on four paws too, but smaller paws. A mere house cat to my family's massive counterparts —and jet black from the top of my head to the tip of my tail. A part of me knew it was not good, that there was something broken in me, weak. But my father didn't point it out. He said I would find a way to make my size work for me. Like right now. I knew something was up, could feel it on the hot wind, and I aimed to figure out what it was.

I hurled myself forward, using the last bit of my energy, and landed on my brother's rump, digging all four sets of my claws into his hide to hang on. He roared and spun, his mouth open wide enough that he could have eaten me in one bite. But he couldn't reach me. He wasn't flexible enough.

"Zam, get the hell off my ass!" he roared, spinning and bucking in an attempt to loosen my hold.

I grinned at him and stuck my tongue out. "No, take me with you!"

"It's a meeting with the Jinn. You can't come," he snarled.

I unhooked my claws and slid down his back leg to the sand. So that's what it was. Getting my brother mad was the best way to get the truth out of him. "I'm coming, one way or another."

"No," he growled as he trotted away, his footprints deep in the loose sand. I hurried after him, determined not to give up. At thirteen, I knew my mind and I was not easily ignored despite my size.

Bryce didn't slow his steady pace, but he forgot that I didn't sink like he did into the sand.

As he climbed a sand dune, he glanced back at me. "It's on the other side in the Oasis. You need to stay low and hide if you're coming in. It's just a talk tonight; if it goes well, then . . . our world will change."

I grinned and bobbed my head. The light of the day had faded and dusk fell around us, giving me the ability to hide within his shadow as he crept down the hill. My father ruled the bright lions, if ruling was even the right word. He led them. He was the pride's leader and protector. He oversaw the other prides that ranged around us. Bryce would soon follow in his footsteps.

Bryce quietly filled me in. The Jinn had requested a parlay, to meet with the strongest of the bright lions. To speak with them of peace. If it happened, Bryce was right, our world would change completely. No more raids, no more losing those we loved to anything more than a natural death, no more fear for the Jinn in the night. The possibility filled me with hope.

I'd never seen a Jinn before. I'd heard they were fearsome, deadly, and cruel. That they had no love for peace but preferred to make war. Those were the truths I'd been raised with. So even in that moment, I wondered why they would ask for peace.

I crept across the sand through the Oasis where the meeting was to take place, the evening sun dropping slowly but giving me cover. I kept to the shadows, my dark body and small size hiding me well.

Parlays were always held near water in the desert, a sign of peace. For without water, the desert would take you faster than any wound or enemy.

The undergrowth was a perfect cover for me and the foliage barely shifted as I made my way to where the spring-fed pool bubbled. Under the cover of thick leaves, I watched as Bryce joined my father and the others of our pride. I knew all twenty of them by name, knew that they fought to protect us and keep us safe. I lay down and put my head on my paws, waiting, nothing moving but my eyes and the tips of my ears.

The bright lions, and our pride of the same name worked to keep all supernaturals safe from the Jinn. They had learned to hide from those who would kill and rule us, fighting only when necessary and working as a pride to take the more powerful supernaturals down. The Jinn were normally creatures of solitude, and so they could be fended off with enough of our pride working together.

The light around us disappeared completely as the sun finally dipped below the horizon. I watched as my father stood waiting, still as a statue.

Bryce moved up beside him. "Do you think he will come?"

He . . . the Jinn that everyone feared the most. Marsum. His name meant pain, and he seemed to take it like a calling he would not shirk.

The lions of my pride barely moved as they waited. Patience was taught at a young age—both for hunting and for reprimanding one another. Silence fell over the Oasis, the birds of the night going still, and a heavy mist crawled over the water like a living thing. I clamped my mouth shut and just stared at what I knew in my belly was the Jinn's arrival.

Only it wasn't just Marsum.

Seven Jinn flowed into existence. They looked like men after a fashion, if larger than the average man. They seemed to float above the ground, the mist spilling out around them and making it look like they had no legs. But Bryce claimed he'd injured a Jinn once, slashing its legs.

Now, I wasn't so sure he'd been telling the truth. My eyes shot to my father. He hadn't moved.

"Marsum. You came to speak of a peace accord. Yet you bring all your friends," my father said, his voice a deep rumble.

Marsum flowed toward him. His body was the biggest of the Jinn, broad across the chest and belly, but far from fat. He was thick all over but his face was surprisingly pleasant. Soft, like a child's that had never seen the sun. It was his voice, though, that struck me, melodic and singsong and lovely.

"Ahh, Dirk. You came, and you brought your friends. Why could I not bring mine?" He smiled and his face stretched with it.

"What is this peace accord you wish to discuss?" my

father asked, still not moving from his position at the water's edge.

"The offer is simple. We are the rulers here, not you. We were set in place by the emperor to hold this wall, not you."

"We do not want to hold the wall," Bryce snarled.

"We are aware of that," Marsum drawled. He brushed his hands over his body and stared down at the lions. "Which is why we asked you to be here. There have been too many problems. We would like to rectify that now. No more fighting."

He snapped his fingers and the other Jinn floated forward, surrounding the members of my pride, of my family. My skin prickled with warning.

"Kill them," Marsum said.

The Jinn flew at the lions, and my family reacted with speed and violence that had been honed in the desert for generations. I stared, unable to move. Knowing that I would be of no help.

Or would I?

The battle raged with the roars of my pride, and they would not go down easily. But what if I could get to Marsum? He was the leader; if he was killed or injured, perhaps the others would falter. I was small enough, I could leap on his back and bite through his neck. That's what I believed. That's what I'd been trained to believe I could do.

I shot out of from under the cover of the bushes and raced around the edge of the battle. I kept my eyes locked on my prey, ignoring the cries as my pride went down, one by one, their pain echoing through me. Blood sprayed across my face, blinding me for a split instant before it cleared once more. Marsum had his back to me and he'd lowered himself closer to the ground. I took a breath, bunched my muscles and leapt straight up, easily taking ten feet in height in that one bound. I landed on the back of his neck and dug my claws in. He screamed and I went straight for his vertebrae. My teeth sunk in and he roared with anger.

I think I heard Bryce. I think he called my name. "Zamira, no!"

But this was my family. I wasn't going to let them go down without any effort to help them. We were a pride. We lived together, we would die together.

I bit harder and shook my head, doing all I could to snap his spine to kill him. I knew that it would be the only way, even at that young age, that Marsum would just keep coming. He had to die.

A hand dropped onto my back and I was torn from my prey, hissing and spitting, slashing at the air with my claws extended. "I'll kill you. I'll kill you!" I screeched the words as a strange sort of mania spilled over me.

Because I knew this was the end. I was dead. He'd kill me now. Marsum drew me close to his face, so he was just out of reach of my claws. "You . . . belong to this pride?"

"Let her go!" Bryce snarled and then there was a horrific crunch. I twisted around as he fell, a Jinn on top of him. A Jinn who held a spear that had been driven deep into my brother's back, snapping his spine. Dropping him instantly.

His eyes were still on mine, even as the light faded from them.

My big brother, my hero, my protector. I lost my mind screeching and flailing, twisting around to bite Marsum's wrist, slashing at him with my back feet. He flung me away with a snarl, out into the deep water of the Oasis where I sunk to the bottom.

With a ragged breath, I pulled myself out of a memory I'd not revisited in years. "Why . . . would you do that to me?"

"To remind you of who you are. To remind you that you are not weak the way you've been allowed to believe, that the fight inside you is a burning ember ready to be flamed to life once more." Merlin hadn't moved.

Lila flew in front of me, back and forth in her version of pacing. I held a hand up, swaying where I stood.

"I know who I am." I breathed the words out.

He smiled. "I'm not so sure you do anymore. But that's what I'm here for."

"What do you mean she doesn't know who she is?" Lila snapped. "She's Zamira, and she's a good supe. There is nothing else she needs."

Merlin continued to smile. "You have it in you to bring this wall down, Zamira. It is in your blood to be a protector, the same as your family. I would like to point you in that direction."

Lila snorted. "She's cursed, you know that?"

"Yes, I do," he said, his face sobering. "And that is why she is the perfect supernatural to take on this challenge. Everyone underestimates you, don't they? You have many strikes against you." He lifted his hands and began ticking off his fingers with each point. "You're a woman, you're small in both forms, your shifting ability is to a mere house cat, you have no magical abilities as far as I can tell, and you've been cursed by the Jinn. All these things are held against you which allows you to be ignored to a degree. But I believe they could also be your greatest strengths."

I stared at him hard, my opinion of him shifting and changing as he spoke. There had been no magic in his hands, but there was something in his words that was moving me in a direction I wasn't sure I liked. "You really are the Merlin who made the wall?"

He tipped his head to one side. "Yes. And as I believe I've mentioned, I'm trying to rectify what I did in the past. I can't do it on my own. The spell holding the wall together locks me out from doing anything to bring it down directly." His eyes dipped, looking away from me. There were lies in with the truth he was tossing around.

I snorted. "Sucks to be you, huh?" I needed to

find ground that I felt safe on again. Sarcastic, snarky, stronger than him ground. Because the memory he'd forced me to relive had rocked me along with his assessment of my abilities. I wasn't the strongest supe out there. I wasn't even close. That was not news to me. But the idea that I could be strong enough to do the impossible . . . I won't lie, that drew me. To be the hero for once was a pull I couldn't deny.

"No more than it sucks to be the last living dark lion from your mother's line, cursed by the Jinn, and set to wandering the world alone." His words were as sharp as any knife.

"She is not alone. She has Maks," Lila said. "And she has me."

"Ah, yes, Lila the Gnat. That is what the other dragons call you, isn't it?" He lifted an eyebrow at her. She flew to my shoulder and hissed at him. He went on. "Cast out because of your size. Because you have no flame to call your own, because like Zamira here," he stood and went to the table and picked a few things to eat, I don't even know what because his words had me so mesmerized, "you are considered weak. Small. Female. Terrible combination in the supe world, isn't it? Especially as the daughter of someone important." I wasn't sure if that last bit was about me or Lila.

She cringed with each word until her head was

tucked under her wing. "You trying to be an asshole, or does it just come naturally?" I said.

"Pointing out that you two are very much alike. Driven to be strong, but not given the tools as others have been." His eyes softened. "I knew a girl not long ago. She was dying and she took on becoming a supernatural in order to save her life. She hated it. Hated being a 'super duper' as she called it."

"Well, that's a stupid name for us to start with," Lila muttered. I put a hand over her head to shut her up because this story of Merlin's felt important. Like a scent in the air that would lead to food, water, or safety.

"What about her?" I asked.

"She finally embraced what she was, learned to use it to her advantage and managed to take down a wall." His eyes went to mine. "I believe you have that potential in you, Zamira. I would not be here if I didn't."

His words tugged at me, made me want to believe them. Made me want to think it was possible. That I could be the hero my father had wanted me to be.

I snorted. "You are as big a fool as your namesake. There are no walls down."

"There were more places that had supernaturals than here. For a long time, the world believed you all resided here. But it became known that they had spread, like a virus."

"We are not a virus!" Lila snapped, her head snaking around.

He held his hands up, palms out. "No. I agree. But the humans have always been afraid of what they don't understand. That is nothing new." He frowned as he popped a chunk of cheese into his mouth and chewed.

I stared at him, his words nothing but lies to my ears. "You're going to help Maks?"

"I already have." Merlin nodded, speaking around a mouthful of cheese.

I looked at the door, then back to Maks. "Then we go. Darcy is waiting for us."

"Ahh, but don't you want to know what Maks is?" Merlin grinned, cheese stuck in his teeth here and there.

"He's human," Lila said. "Even I can tell that. I can smell the normal on him."

Laughter flowed out of Merlin. "Fine. Fine. Tell yourselves that. I think it will be a fun surprise when the truth finally comes out."

His laughter seemed to stir Maks.

I moved sideways to stand next to him. "Maks, you ready to go?"

"Where are we?" he mumbled as he wobbled to a sitting position. I looked at his leg, and made myself run a hand over the calf and ankle, checking for the wound that had looked like it would cost him his foot. He flinched under my touch and I gritted my teeth while Merlin continued to laugh softly at me. At us.

"Can you stand?" I held a hand out, but Maks didn't take it.

He pushed himself up and then took a step, then another and another, testing his balance. "Let's go." He glanced at Merlin with something akin to . . . hatred. But what did he have to hate Merlin for? He'd just saved Maks's life, and leg.

Just what in the sand dunes of hell was going on here?

CHAPTER FIFTEEN

Merlin watched us leave the shack, gather the horses, and take off at a trot, but he said nothing more. It was the weight of his eyes that I couldn't shake. He didn't have to say anything really, because his smile said it all. He'd stirred shit up, just the way warlocks had been stirring shit up for a thousand years. He'd made me relive memories I thought were dead. He'd made me question the truth from both my companions and wonder if I could be strong enough to change the world.

That last bit was the most ridiculous of them all.

Wasn't it?

The sun was low and we would have to find another place to stay, to hold off the night's killing chill. But where to stay, was the question.

No. That wasn't the question. The question really

was about what Merlin had said, if it was true, if it was false. Did it matter? No, we were going after Darcy and that was what mattered. The Jinn were coming for her, and I would not let that happen to someone I loved, not again.

Which brought up another question.

"Do you love her?" I blurted the question at Maks, suddenly needing to know if that was really why he was here. Or if it was something else, the way Merlin was implying.

He startled in his saddle like I'd smacked him in the head rather than asked a question. "Love who?"

I stared hard at him, frowning because his reaction set off warning lights inside my head. "Darcy. Do you love her? Is that why you're helping me get her back?"

And it was only in that moment I realized that a question so important should have been asked a long time ago. In fact, it was a question that had started to form many times but I'd never managed to spit it out, like it slid away from me when I went to ask. Water through my fingers. I frowned, wondering if my brain was addled by the cold. Or if something else had been holding me back.

"I . . . care for Darcy." His skin flushed and he wouldn't make eye contact. "She's a friend and she was kind to me, which was more than most in the Stockyards."

Right, of course, she was. Darcy was nice to everyone. A little too nice in some areas.

"Why are you asking me this now?"

Lila answered before I could say anything. "Because you kissed her, and she's wondering if it was just the plum liquor or real feelings." She drawled the words along with a jaw-cracking yawn. Horror flickered through me like a bolt of lightning, and it made Balder jig sideways under me.

"No, that . . . *that* is not why. I'm asking because you could have died back there. You're human, but you're facing pretty much the worst conditions you could face for a woman who even if you *were* an item, you weren't for very long. So . . . I assumed that means you love her." I cleared my throat. "I mean, she's like a sister to me. I couldn't live with myself if I didn't try to get her out of there. And Bryce said you had a thing for her, but you've not talked about her at all while we've been on the move."

Maks shrugged his shoulders. "Maybe I have my own reasons for wanting to be here."

That was not good. Whatever trust I'd started to put in him slid away at a rapid rate. Yeah, that shit wasn't going to fly. "Like what?"

"None of your business," he said softly.

I wrestled with the implications of his words. He wasn't here for Darcy, which meant he might abandon helping me at any point and potentially at an important crisis where I really needed him. "Okay, are you going to fuck off on me—I mean us—in the middle of a fight?"

"What? No, of course not." He shook his head. "I'm going to see you to the Witch's castle."

"And then what?" Lila flew up between us and landed on the ridge of Batman's neck so she could stare at Maks, her jeweled eyes narrowed to slits that seemed to be shooting daggers at the human. "What are you going to do then?"

Thank you, Lila, I thought.

Maks's jawline twitched. "There is a boat that leaves once a month from the bay at Pojhola that goes around the northern part of the magic, far out into the ocean. It goes to the human side of the wall to pick up supplies. I plan to be on it."

I blinked a few times as his words sunk in. "You mean, you're escaping. You're leaving."

"Yes." He rolled his shoulders. "I . . . you said it yourself. I don't belong here. I'll only cause more harm than good if I stay. I know that."

I blew out a slow breath, not liking the tightness in my chest, or the way my emotions were reacting to his lies. I'd never asked before. This was on me to have been the one to make him tell the truth. Pull it together, Zam.

"But you'll help me get Darcy out?" I asked him again.

"I'll help you get to the castle, that was the goal all along. I will be no good to you once you are there. Too weak, too big and hard to hide, right?"

I nodded, not liking the tug on my sentiments that I thought were somewhat dead when it came to men. "Then I'll help you get to your boat after we get Darcy if I can. Deal?"

He turned to face me, confusion racing over his features. "Why would you do that?"

I shrugged and managed a smile. "Maybe you're not the stupid, useless human I once thought. And you're right, you'll die if you stay here. That would be . . . a pity."

Maks laughed softly but there was something in that laughter that was forced. "Pretty words like that, I'll think you're trying to get in my pants."

I urged Balder to move faster because of the embarrassment that flooded my body and lit my face with a heat that should have had steam rolling off me. He was leaving, and that was for the best all the way around. This weird infatuation was nothing more than proof that I was ready to move on, that Steve no longer had a hold on me.

Lila and Maks laughed at me as I rode ahead of them. Not leaving them behind like I'd done before, just putting a bit of space between us to hide what was a probably a bright red face that would have nothing to do with the cold.

I thought about Darcy as I rode ahead of them, my head space my own for the first time in what felt like forever. I'd been worrying about taking Maks with me, then trying to survive the dragons, the cold, and deal with Merlin, the White Wolf, and all of that had pushed Darcy aside in a way.

No matter what happened, she and I would be friends. I realized that somewhere in this journey, I'd finally forgiven her for what happened between her and Steve. I'd never forget, but the forgiveness felt good.

And it was as if the thoughts of my friend coming to the surface brought me to the scene of the crime where she'd been stolen away.

Ahead of me was the outcropping of a cave partially covered by snow, the opening just big enough to slide a person through. That wasn't what drew my eyes, though, despite it being a place we could hunker down for the night.

No, it was the horses that had been hung by their back legs from the upper branches of the trees, their gear still on, the clank and jangle of bits of metal like a morbid set of wind chimes calling us to them. Richard's and Leo's horses.

Maks caught up to me. "What the hell did this?"

"The White Bear," I said softly, as if by naming the creature we'd somehow call him to us. The White Wolf I knew more about, the Bear not so much.

Mostly because so few got past the Wolf. "Lila, do you know much about the Bear?"

"He's bigger than the Wolf, and he's known to do this, store his meat in the trees for later consumption." She shivered as she crawled inside my hood. "And he can change shape, so he might be a bear, or he might be something else depending on his mood and who he's facing in battle. He became a dragon once, according to my father."

"Wonderful," I drawled as I hopped off Balder's back and headed for the small opening of the cave. Just what we needed, another dragon.

"Wait, you can't be serious? We aren't staying here in a friggin' food locker. We aren't," Maks spluttered.

I pulled a blade and used it to knock the snow down that covered the opening until it was just big enough to get the horses through. "We *will* die of exposure if we don't get in here. We don't know when the White Bear will come back. Could be weeks. And could be that he wouldn't think to come back here at all, that the horses hanging in the trees would scare travelers off."

"We can find somewhere else," he said, but there was no real conviction in his voice. There was nowhere else to find this close to when the temperatures were going to start dropping once more.

"You start a fire, we'll find some food." I handed Balder's reins to Maks and crooked my finger at Lila.

No one argued, but then again, it was cold and only going to get colder.

I pulled my hood over my head and settled into a crouched walk as I made my way through the trees around the forest. I could have climbed the tree that held the horses and taken meat from them, but we weren't that bad off. I'd cared for those horses, fed and groomed them, trained them. I couldn't make myself eat them unless there was no other choice.

"Lila, can you drive some smaller game to me, do you think?"

"As long as I can get back into your hood after." She shivered. "I don't like this cold place. It feels as though death is stalking us at every turn."

"I don't like it either, but we're almost there," I admitted. "And yes, you can get back in my hood after."

She crawled up and out of the warm space. With a rush of her wings, and using her back feet to push off on my chest, she sent me stumbling back as she launched into the air. I settled in between two trees that held a small amount of cover for me, waiting for the game.

I concentrated on my breath, slowing it, hearing my father in my ear as he whispered to me from beyond the grave. Damn Merlin, and his meddling with my memories.

"You are the predator, but a predator with a mind. A

heart. A soul. Do not let the chaos take you, Zamira. You are better than that. You are not a creature of madness. But of thought and intelligence. Kill when you must, to feed yourself, to protect those you love, but for no other reason."

I pulled the two curved blades from my thighs. I could throw them and hit a bullseye at thirty feet. But rabbits were sketchy little things that moved like lightning in a bottle when they were running scared.

A tiny thump sounded in front of me, like the crack of leather on leather. Lila's wings snapping through the air to drive the smaller creatures and let me know that they were on their way.

Two solid white bunnies bounded toward me. I stood and cocked my right arm back, and threw the first. My kukri spun end over end in a flash of light before pinning the first rabbit to the frozen ground. The second rabbit dove to the side and I moved with it, throwing the second blade and catching it in mid-hop. Both were dead before I lowered my hands.

There was a prickle of sensation, like I was being watched. I turned my head ever so slightly and caught the flicker of a dark shadow behind me, studying me. The Witch's shadow then . . . which would lead the White Bear to the cave.

This was not good, and I had to do something about it now if we were going to survive the night. Indecision began to rattle its way through me, pushing me one way and then another. I had to find a way to dodge the shadow if we were going to make it all the way to Darcy. And the only thought I had on how to do that was not one I liked.

I went to the first rabbit and ran a hand over the thick winter pelt. They'd been eating well, that was good. "Thank you." I whispered the words then pressed two fingers to my lips and then to the rabbit's head. I repeated the gesture with the second rabbit, thanking it. I would have a few more minutes before I had to actually decide how to handle the shadow.

Lila flew down from the branches and hopped along the ground toward me. "Oh, two! You got them both!"

I made myself smile up at her and then skinned the rabbits quickly, flicking the still-hot innards into the air for her. She gulped them down happily, her belly swelling until it brushed along the ground and left a trail in the snow as she walked. I let the plan form slowly on how I would best the shadow figure tracking me. Or at least, the beginnings of a plan. Though I wasn't sure how good it was, it could possibly give us a chance to keep the White Bear at bay long enough that we could slip by unnoticed.

I couldn't afford to be indecisive any longer. My father was right, hesitation killed faster than just about anything else.

"Goddess, I'm not going to be able to fly for a

week." Lila licked her chops as she spoke, her tongue as black as the night around us.

I rolled my eyes. "You just want a free ride under my hood."

"Well, that doesn't hurt either." She grinned up at me, blinking several times.

We quickly went back to the cave together. I handed the rabbits to Maks and then dug around in my pack for the two collapsible buckets I carried. The most expensive material out there because it was so hard to find, they were made of plastic, and were perfect for gathering water for the horses.

"I've got something I have to do," I said as I pulled the buckets out.

"What?" Lila whipped around to look at me. Maks didn't ask anything, didn't say anything as he skewered the rabbits, his face only mildly green with the task. His eyes, though, spoke volumes.

Be careful.

"I'll tell you when I get back." I shooed her toward the fire and left the cave, heading east, toward the sound of rushing water. This river, if we followed it upstream, would take us to the bay and the bay was where the Ice Witch's castle stood.

I hurried along, head down as I faced the whipping wind. My spine tickled as though something had touched me. I didn't look back, just kept moving until I came to the edge of the river. The shadow was far bolder with me on my own.

My plan was a solid one, good in theory, at least. But I didn't like it. Spirits only followed those who were alive. If I could make the spirit think I was dead, then it would no longer follow me. This would be slick like camel butter if I pulled it off.

I went to my knees in the snow at the edge of the frozen river with the bucket in my hand. Under the ice, the water moved and swirled. I pulled the flail from my back, and the handle warmed as before. I swallowed hard. I wasn't using it to hurt someone, so here's hoping it didn't try and suck the life out of me again.

I swung it once, driving it into the ice. The river water exploded upward with the force of the weapon, spraying me with the wicked cold droplets. I gasped, and the handle cooled.

I stared at the water a long time. Going for a dunk in this could kill me in a matter of minutes. And that's assuming I didn't get swept downstream. I grimaced. "Stupid, it was a stupid plan." For a moment, I'd thought I could play dead, make the shadow think I was not worth following. But the cold of the water changed my mind as it splashed across my face.

I sighed, knowing that the flip-flop decision was no better than hesitating in some ways.

"I might as well get water while I'm here," I muttered to myself.

I put the bucket in, careful not to lean too far over the edge. Now that I'd decided I was not going for a swim, I had no desire to fall in accidently.

The thing was, I didn't get a choice as to how far I leaned.

Something shoved me from behind, headfirst into the slow-moving, frigid water.

"Shit!" That was all I managed before I went under, my clothing and weapons dragging me deep, the current spinning me away from the opening I'd created, downstream as I'd feared under the ice.

I swam to the surface of the ice, my face pressed against it in time to see Merlin standing there. Merlin! That fucking warlock had pushed me in!

Behind him was the shadow figure that had been dogging me, and they left together.

There was no time to think about what that meant to me, what I would do if I ever saw Merlin again, or if he'd been playing me all along. Right then, I had to figure out how the fuck to get out of the water.

And fast. My limbs slowed with each passing second as my muscles stiffened, and my lungs began to burn from holding my breath. I reached first for my kukri blades. I grabbed one and used it to hook into the ice, stopping my downstream flow. I grabbed the other and did the same, driving the tips into the ice, dragging myself back to the opening inch by inch. Bubbles slid from my mouth, spurts of air escaped me in hopes I would breathe in a big gulp very soon.

Hand over hand, I pulled myself upstream while the water worked to drag me down in more ways than one.

The water spilled into my nose, my mouth, and ears. I swam with all my might for the surface, breaking through with a gasp. I looked around for the Jinn, but they were gone, as if they had never been there in the first place.

But my family, the strongest of my pride were there on the banks of the water, their bodies still. My eyes found my father and Bryce first, their golden coats sticking out clearly against the greenery of the Oasis. A coppery tang of blood and death blew in the breeze, coating the inside of my mouth with death. A panicked cry slid from me as I swam toward the shore, frantic to get to them. Why had the Jinn left me alive? Why had he tossed me into the water instead of snapping my neck like they'd done to all the others?

Those were the thoughts that I focused on as I swam because I didn't want to think about what I was going to find on the white sand. I already knew, but I didn't want to let my mind go there. Even when I saw the dark red stains pooled around the bodies, even when I saw the pink flesh opened through the thick golden pelts, the weapons and blades that stuck out of their bodies, I didn't want to think about it. I ran to my father first, ran and slid to a stop, spraying sand pebbles all over his face. His tongue stuck out through his massive teeth as if he'd lain down in mid-roar.

"Papa," I whispered, patting at his face with my too-small paws. "Papa."

He didn't answer me.

Bryce did.

"Zam . . ." He groaned my name and I leapt up, searching for him.

"Bryce, where are you?" I was all turned around, my mind breaking under the strain of the death in front of me. I should have been able to smell him but my nose was coated with the scent of blood and death. I could smell nothing else.

A low groan pulled me forward and I found myself tripping and stumbling over bodies, limbs no longer attached, bits and pieces of viscera I tried not to see to get to my brother.

He was on his belly, his back legs stuck out at a strange angle and his head twisted nearly all the way around. Broken spine. I knew it—our father had trained me in that much, recognizing wounds and injuries.

I crouched by Bryce's head and allowed myself to shift back into my human form. I leaned over him, my hands shaking as I cupped his large face. "Bryce, don't leave me."

"Warn others," he breathed out, a gurgling of air slipping in between the words. "Go. They need you."

I bent my head to touch his, breathing in as he breathed out his last. I wanted nothing more than to stay and hold him, to hold him and Father before their bodies cooled so I could pretend for a little while that they were alive.

But Bryce was right, the rest of the prides in our valley had no idea an attack was coming and I could warn them. I let him go, and let the change flow over me again until I was once more nothing more than a common house cat.

I raced across the sands to our home, the one place the Jinn had never dared come because of the strength of our pride. My breath came in ragged gulps, and the closer I got to the valley between the rocks, the more my fears coalesced into reality. Smoke reached out to me, and in the smoke was the death of my life as I knew it.

I topped the last rise that looked down on our small village. The homes were burning down to the last one. Like the Oasis, bodies were strewn everywhere in chunks and out of order, bits and pieces mismatched as they'd been torn from their owners. Not unlike a child playing at war taking the limbs off its toy shoulders.

Standing amongst the bodies was the same Jinn who'd grabbed me, Marsum. Something in my young mind snapped, breaking against the strain of seeing those I loved slaughtered. My family, my friends, my whole world destroyed for what? Because we protected those who needed our help, because we guarded the lesser supes from the Jinn's cruelty.

Without a sound, I raced down the slope, skidding and sliding, tumbling the last few feet head over tail. Laughter greeted me, but I didn't care. I'd never been so angry in my *life. I'd never felt so completely out of control of who and what I was.*

"Look at this one, all fierce and puffed up," Marsum drawled.

"A house cat? How is she a house cat when her family lines were bright lion?" That second voice was younger and sounded ill. "Let her go, Father. She's a child. This wasn't what you told us was happening."

I didn't look for him, the younger one. No, I kept my eyes locked on Marsum as I streaked across the blood-soaked sand. Marsum lifted a foot as if he'd kick me, and I dodged one way, deking him out and using the misdirection to leap at him, claws extended, mouth open, tiny fangs bared.

Only he was faster than me, impossibly faster. His hand shot out and he grabbed right under my front legs, his hand wrapping around my chest like a vise. I twisted and turned, shrieking at him as I fought to get free. To kill him.

He laughed at me, laughed and laughed, and that sound burned into my mind. "Look at her, still fighting. Pity she wasn't a true lion, she'd be worth killing then. As it is, I think letting her live will be far more painful, don't you think, son?"

I slowed my movements until I was doing nothing but staring at his face, shock freezing me. He had long black hair twisted into dreadlocks that seemed to have a life of their own, moving and turning even though there was no wind. His eyes were the color of the sand, but lifeless, dull. Cruel, thin lips, a sharp nose and sharper chin finished off his face, leaving nothing to the imagination in terms of his personality.

"You aren't going to kill me?" I couldn't help the horror from bleeding into my words. In death, I would be reunited with my father and mother, with Bryce. We would be together at least.

The Jinn stared down at me, a slow, wicked smile sliding over his lips. "I'm going to curse you, cat. That disaster will follow your life, that you will find nothing but sorrow and disappointment, within every endeavor you take on. They will all be nothing short of a catastrophe." He laughed and then looked over his shoulder at someone I couldn't see. "Don't you find that funny? Cat-atstrophe? Get it?"

His companion didn't answer and Marsum turned back to me. "To clarify, I won't be killing you. I only have the authority to kill bright lions from all the prides today, of which you are not." He threw me for the second time. I hit the ground hard and flipped over three times before I came to rest on my belly. The change slid over me without me wanting it, but I couldn't help it. Too much pain, too much heartache for such a small cat to take. My tiny body couldn't hold all the grief and pain inside.

I stood slowly, my skirt billowing around my legs as they trembled. The Jinn and those like him turned their backs on me and flowed out of the village.

"I'll kill you!" I screamed after him. "One day, I'll kill you!"

He waved a hand at me, dismissing me, not even bothering to turn around or answer me. That was how little he thought of me and he was right, I was nothing.

At the edge of the village he and his companion slipped away, disappearing, and I was left with the bodies of all those I'd known and loved. Alone in a desert of death.

My knife slid through open air and I grabbed the edge of the ice, pulling my face out from under it. I choked and gasped, spit water out and managed to get myself to the edge of the river.

Shaking so hard my teeth rattled, I crawled out of the water and back the way I'd come. There was no one to watch me struggle to stand, fighting to survive this time. I was on my own again.

Or so I thought.

CHAPTER SIXTEEN

"Zam!" Maks's voice cut through the brutal cold that had caught hold of me, the last vestiges of the river trying to drown me as my body froze into a solid block of ice in the open air. He grabbed my arms and tried to get me to move faster. "What happened?"

"Pushed . . . in . . . Merlin . . . did . . . it," I stuttered the words and went to my knees, unable to fight the cold any longer.

"Son of a bitch, this is my fault," he growled as he picked me up with ease, and carried me back to the cave.

The fire was going, and that was about all I could see. My eyelashes had frozen during the distance between the river and the cave.

"Zam, I have to strip you down. Do you understand?" Maks pulled at my clothing, yanking the mostly frozen material from me. It pulled on my skin in places, already sticking to me. I bobbed my head and tried to help him but my hands were a fumbling mess. He pushed them away.

"Just let me." Maks had my clothes off quicker than I'd have been able to. "Lila, get more wood from the back of the cave. We need to warm her up quickly."

"On it."

And I stood there—barely—unable to do more than shake with nothing left to me but my necklace which felt like a veritable ice block against my skin. Maks stripped off his wet shirt and pants and I just stared. Damn it, he was nicely put together. I might have said it out loud, I'm not sure.

"Come here, we need our body heat to fight off the cold, to get some warmth back into you." He took my hand and helped me to lie down on a blanket as close to the fire as it could get.

He all but pushed me to the floor and the warmth of the fire was nice, but it got better. Maks tucked in behind me, his body like a fire of its own, like the desert sands in midsummer. I closed my eyes as the heat began to bring feeling back to my body. The hurt of the ice leaving me made me grit my teeth but I knew it would fade. Lila came back with wood and dropped it on the fire, then she came around to curl up on top of my hip, perched there, watching me.

"Is she going to be okay?" she whispered. I tried to smile for her but my face hurt.

"She just needs to get warm." Maks's arms were around me and I didn't fight it. He was better than me, not caring that I was a supe and helping me anyway.

My shivering slowed and the heat began to work magic on me, drawing a heavy sigh from me.

"Zam, I need you to talk to me," Maks said. "Are you sure Merlin pushed you in?"

I drew a breath which pushed my back against him. I wanted nothing more than to close my eyes and sleep while I could, but Maks was right. We needed to talk about what happened out there.

"Someone pushed me," I said. "When I looked up through the ice I saw Merlin and the shadow that the Ice Witch set to watch me." I blinked a few times. "I'd been wondering if there was a way to lose the shadow. Then we'd be able to slip past the next two guardians easier."

I turned so I could look at Maks. "Why did you say it was your fault?"

"Merlin doesn't like me," he said. "He doesn't want me to escape. He thinks I should stay on this side of the wall."

I frowned. "What would it matter to him that you

266

escape?" *You're human, aren't you?* I *almost* said. But something held me back. It was ridiculous. Of course, he was human. He smelled as human as he could. Merlin was just playing games with my head.

Maks shook his head and my breath caught. "Look, he thinks you're helping me, which means he won't want to help you."

It was my turn to shake my head. "That makes no sense. Why would he have healed your leg then? Why would he have given us a place to stay in that first snowstorm?" Which made me wonder if Merlin really had pushed me in after all? But if he hadn't, he'd seen me go under and just watched me go.

Lila cleared her voice. "I think he did push you in."

I turned my head toward her. "You do?"

"The shadow that's been following you makes it hard for us to escape notice. Merlin said he wanted to help you find Darcy—amongst other things—so what if this was a way to help us? A shadow wouldn't follow someone they thought was dead, would they?"

I found myself nodding, albeit with some reluctance. "I was thinking along the same lines when I was pushed. That if I could somehow make the shadow think I was dead, it would leave me alone and we'd be free of its eyes."

"Then Merlin must think highly of you. To try to kill you, and assume you wouldn't die." Maks's words had more than a heavy dose of biting sarcasm in them. He pulled his arm off me and I grabbed it.

"Look, don't take this the wrong way, but you aren't going anywhere. I'm still cold." Little bit of a lie there, but we would both be warmer if we stayed together. In the most platonic of ways, of course.

He slid his arm around my middle and we lay there while the fire crackled. Sleep crawled over us, lulled by the soft sounds of the horses, the fire, and each other's breathing.

A few hours went by and I woke with my back to the fire, one arm around Maks's middle and the other pinned between us. I blinked a few times to clear the sleep from my eyes. Maks was still sound asleep. My belly rumbled and demanded I pay attention. The fire needed tending and I needed food. I moved to shift Maks's arm off me.

He mumbled in his sleep, tightening his hold, his fingers splayed over my lower back, pressing me to him. "No, Zam is mine."

My eyebrows shot up and I tried again to slide out of his embrace. Not that I wanted to, not really, he was warm and smelled good. Amongst other things. He pulled me against his chest and buried his face into my loose curls, breathing in deeply before he relaxed again, but didn't loosen his hold on me. I could have woken him, but wasn't sure I could handle staring him in the face while we were both pretty much naked and he'd just made a strong declaration in his sleep.

There was only one thing to do. I walked through the doorway between two legs and four and let the shift take me. As a house cat, I slipped out from under the blankets and went to where my clothes were just barely dried. Grimacing, I shifted back to my human form and put the still-damp, cold clothes on.

I knew they would warm and dry on me faster and we needed that. Speed. Because now there was no one watching our movements and we had a very short window of time to take advantage of it.

I moved quickly, getting the fire going, setting the second rabbit over it and then tending to the horses. I took my second collapsible bucket and filled it with snow and set it by the flames. While it was a slower way to collect water, at least I would survive if someone pushed me head-first into it.

Lila woke first, stretched her wings and tail straight out while cracking a yawn. "Are we going?"

"Soon, I think." I tipped my head, listening to the wind outside the cave. The cold wasn't as bad as the night before. I wondered if it was because the Ice Witch thought I was dead. Was it possible? Regardless, it was time to get going. Again, the choice would be unexpected if there was anyone watching for us still. No one in their right mind started out in a snowstorm.

I went to Maks and tapped him on the back of his leg with the tip of my boot. Because . . . space between us was going to be essential. Likely his whole "Zam is mine" had been a weird dream, but he was going to leave when we got Darcy back. And I'd lost enough people I loved to not willingly add another to the list. Not that I loved him, but I knew how my heart worked. I fell hard and fast when things felt right, and then I would be in trouble.

"I'm awake." Maks sat up as he scrubbed a hand through his dirty blond hair. The blanket fell into a puddle in his lap. I turned away to keep from staring at his chiseled chest and abs. I grabbed his clothes by the fire and tossed them back to him.

"Get dressed. We'll eat and ride out as soon as the horses have had a drink and something to eat too."

He nodded and didn't fight me on my plan. Resigned, that was how the energy off him felt to me, though it took me a bit to pin the emotion down. Like he couldn't escape. But I would help him do that too.

I ignored the twang around my heart. Yeah, it was time for Maks to go before I fell too much deeper into those baby blues.

Apparently, Maks hadn't eaten the night before. Or maybe he'd been avoiding eating rabbit after his first experience. We ate quickly and he managed to keep the rabbit down. Then again, this time wasn't partially raw like the first go-around.

Lila was still full of the innards she'd gotten the night before and shook her head when I offered her a rabbit leg.

"I'll explode if I eat any more," she said. "And nobody wants that."

Maks snorted. "Acid everywhere?"

"Something along those lines." She flashed him a grin that had a devilish edge to it. "Also, you talk in your sleep, Maks."

I froze in midmotion of putting Balder's saddle on and dared a look at Maks. Who also looked frozen and more than a little horrified.

"What did I say?" The words seemed to be strangled out of him.

Lila preened, running her tiny claws over her wings, massaging them. "You reeeally want to know?"

"Yes." That was not strangled; that was a hard word from him, about as definitive as I'd ever heard him.

Lila sighed. "It was really sweet, if you think about it. Don't you think, *Zam?*"

"Didn't hear a thing," I said as I cinched the saddle on. I had to stop this, we didn't need any more embarrassment, but Lila seemed bent on it. "We need to move, you two."

Maks was up, his clothing, boots and weapons all on in a flash. "Agreed."

She swept around in front of us, her eyes darting from me to Maks and back again. "Come on. Don't either of you want to know?"

"No," we said in unison.

She pouted. "Damn it. Please?"

I just shook my head. "Not the time for this, Lila."

Her pout went deeper but she kept her mouth shut. Thank the sand gods for that much.

When we stepped out of the cave, the night still held tightly to the sky, but it had cleared enough that there was light from the moon as the clouds moved about.

"We go hard to get through the White Bear's territory. The White Raven holds sway the closest to the castle," I said as we rode out. The horses' breath came out in big billowing streams as though they were filled with fire.

"Then?" Maks asked.

"We leave the horses behind and go in on foot. The Raven will be watching from above; we'll be able to avoid her easier that way."

"Her?" Lila curled herself around my neck. "Are you sure the White Raven is a girl?"

"From what I know." I shrugged. "Doesn't really

matter. We know less about her than we do about the White Bear."

"Unless she has eggs," Maks said. "Eggs would make her meaner, like the dragons."

Lila bobbed her head. "Oh, I never thought of that."

Goddess of the desert, please let there be no eggs involved.

We rode through the remainder of the night with nothing more than the cold to keep us company.

More than once, Maks twisted in his saddle to watch our trail. "Wait here," he finally said, "I think something is stalking us."

He spun Batman around and urged him back the way we'd come. Which was stupid because if anyone would have noticed us being followed, it would be me, the one with the extra sensory abilities. Then again, I was focused on how we were going to slip into the castle and get Darcy out. I didn't know the schematics of the castle—Steve had those.

We'd never found Kiara's horse, but that would still be our best bet. Dead, we'd be able to track the scent if I could find the original kill site. But that would mean back tracking into the Wolf's territory and I could feel time ticking by faster with each moment. I reached up to touch my ring, my talisman.

The only thing that kept my curse from coming into full effect.

It was gone.

I opened my mouth to tell Lila we had to go back, we had to search for the lion's head ring. Without it, we were opening ourselves to a disaster of proportions we'd not yet seen. We'd all die. Horribly. In the worst way possible.

I spun in my saddle to see Batman and Maks racing toward us. All the sound I'd blocked out in my hyper-focused panicked state came roaring back in a flood. The bellow of the massive White Bear as it galloped toward us, the thunder of Batman's hooves, Maks shouting at me to run.

I booted Balder in the sides and he leapt forward so hard, my hood swept back. My hair streamed out behind me, and for just a moment, I thought about using the flail on the Bear like I'd used it on the Wolf. Except it would probably kill me this time. And Balder didn't seem at all interested in facing the big carnivore coming hard at us.

This was bad. The curse seemed to curl around me, the power of it driving spikes of heat through my skin and Marsum's laughter spilled around me. Like he knew I'd finally succumb to his curse.

"What do we do?" Lila screeched the question as she clung to my shoulder. I wasn't entirely sure myself.

"We'll outrun him!" I yelled, though I didn't think we'd have a chance. A thump snapped my head around in time to see the Bear ripping a tree out by the roots and throwing it. At us.

"Oh, fuck," I whispered. "Right, go right!"

Maks and Batman peeled to the right, as I pressed Balder to the left. The tree slammed down where we'd been only a moment before, just missing us.

The snow sprayed up around it, sending a shower of ice chunks, rock, splinters, and earth into the air.

"Trespassers!" the White Bear roared and was once more right behind us. Balder scooted forward, tucking his ass under himself to keep from the swipe of the monstrous paw that cut through the air.

"So much for slipping by," Lila screamed.

I couldn't argue with that. "Fuck off, Bear!" I yelled over my shoulder. The curse tightened, like a noose. I wanted to live; the curse would bring me to my death.

"You killed the Wolf!" he roared back.

"He deserved it! He was an asshole with bad breath!"

Maybe that wasn't the best thing to say, but it was the truth. And if I was going to die, I was going to go down swinging.

I twisted around in the saddle. The White Bear was, of course, right on us; every etched scar in his face down to the broken and sheared canines were clearly visible. Behind him, though . . . Maks and

Batman were coming up fast. Maks had the shotgun up.

The one with the grenade launcher.

There was a thump in the air and then the projectile shot straight toward the Bear's back. It went off, the explosion mimicking the tree being thrown at us, only it was flesh and bone instead of tree trunk and stones splattering against us.

"How come I don't think that will save us?" Lila asked as we slowed and turned to face where the Bear lay in the snow. His yellowed coat seemed sickly against the white of the snow. He lifted his head, black eyes finding me.

"My queen will have you yet, cat. There is no escaping me," he snarled. I blinked. He didn't want to kill us, he wanted to capture us.

And an idea formed that I knew was quite possibly my worst yet. An idea that almost felt like it wasn't my own.

Hesitation killed.

Which meant I had nothing to do but put it into play.

If I was cursed and the curse worked against what I wanted . . . then maybe I had to change what I wanted.

CHAPTER SEVENTEEN

I was gambling our lives on an idea that had bloomed in mid-panic, in a near-death situation where probably it would have been better to think this through. The curse on me was nearly twenty years old and I'd never considered trying to use it to my advantage before. I hadn't had to because I'd always worn the ring Ish had given me, the ring that kept the curse at bay. But now I could feel it wrapping around me, the heat of the desert within it as it sunk into my skin ready to fuck up my life and kill me for good. Depending on what I wanted to do. So, I would just have to change what I wanted. At least . . . that was the theory in my head.

"Yeah, you think so, do you? You think you can catch me, you big fatty pants? You look like you stole your dad's fur costume and put it on, slopping around in it. All saggy in the ass." I slid off Balder's back and turned him away, slapping him on the rump. He ran around to Maks and Batman, snorting and tossing his mane.

Maks held the shotgun up, aiming at the Bear, and I held up both hands to stop him as I shook my head.

Goddess, this was stupid. I knew it was, which only made me surer that it was what I needed to do. If I was set to fail everything as Marsum had cursed me, then I would set myself not to survive this encounter. I would go in, believing, wanting to die. "I want to die," I whispered. The curse tightened on me, nearly strangling me as it constricted my entire body. I fought to breathe through it and then it began to ease.

Calm fell over me in a way I didn't know possible. I was going to die, but my friends would live. I pulled the flail from my back and began to swing it. If I was going down, there was nothing to fear in the power of the weapon. "Come for me then, if you are going to kill me. Let's get on with it."

The Bear roared, spittle flying from his flapping lips, spraying the snow in front of him with flecks of blood and snot. He launched toward me, the ground rumbling and shaking my legs as he thundered my way. I held my ground to the last second, breathing through the adrenaline. It was almost like I wasn't in control of my body, which was dumb, but that's how it felt. The curse seemed to slide into my limbs.

I wanted to die.

Something seemed to twist me out of his way and I snapped the flail toward his head with everything I had. The spiked metal balls slammed into his skull with a crack that sent a reverberation all the way down my arm, through my shoulder and back.

The curse had done that. Not me.

The Bear went down onto his front knees which put him at Balder's height. "Cat, I'll kill you now. My mistress will thank me."

"That's the plan, right?" I yanked the handle, freeing the spikes from his skull. He roared and swiped at me with a paw. The weapon heated against my skin, not unlike the curse curling over my body. Time, I had time yet before it sucked my life away.

I leapt up and forward, landing on his back. I swung the flail fast and hard, driving it down into . . . well, I was going to say the wound that Maks had made with the grenade, only there was no wound. It had healed already.

Underneath me, the white fur shimmered and rippled and the space I stood on shrunk to the point that there was nothing to stand on. I dodged sideways, rolling in the snow, coming up with the flail spinning fast again.

The Bear had turned into a man, a big man,

bigger than any I'd known since I was a child. He was big like a lion shifter big.

I want to die. The curse swept through me again in a rush.

I missed him completely with the swinging flail, and spun around with the momentum of the move. The Bear, now a man, lay on the snow, panting. Golden-haired, broad-shouldered, and when he lifted his eyes—a lion's golden eyes—I stumbled back and would have dropped the weapon if it had not taken me in its hold. "No, it's not possible."

"Daughter." My father held his hand up to me and I couldn't stop staring at him, at the blood soaking his skin and hair, at the desert sands around us, the cries of the dying and the taste of smoke on the back of my tongue. I blinked a few times. No, we couldn't be back in the desert. That wasn't any more possible than this truly being my father. My father was dead. Wasn't he? Confusion rocked me and I put a hand to my head. Where was I?

He pushed to his feet, wobbled and went to one knee, a hand around his middle, blood pouring through his fingers. "Daughter, please, help me. We can escape."

My father was dead. I knew he was. But this was so real, like I could reach out and touch him. Like he would hold me one last time. But it wasn't him, I knew that. "I can't." But I couldn't move either. His words and the image of the desert, of him injured again had frozen my feet to the forest floor.

"You can help me, come here, *daughter*." There was a snap of demand in his words that the cat in me wanted to obey, that the many losses of fights I'd had tried to remind me that I was supposed to be submissive. Not dominant, not alpha. I should lower my head and do as I was told.

Like I did for Bryce.

Like I did for Ish.

Like I wanted to do for Maks.

I shook where I stood, wobbled and took a step forward. He held one hand out to me, a hand I knew, that had wrapped my injuries as a child and held me close when I'd cried for my mother I'd never known. A hand that had *never* been raised to me in anger, though I'd given its owner enough cause to beat me senseless more than once. Father would never hurt me. I was his girl.

The spell he wove grew tighter around me and I buckled under it.

Someone shouted my name, tiny claws dug into my shoulder and a mouth jammed in my ear.

"Zam, don't! He's stealing your memories and using them against you!" Tiny teeth cut into the edge of my ear, the pain slicing through the hold the Bear had on me.

I drew a breath a split second before my fingers

touched his. I forced my head up and looked him in the eyes, made myself stand up under an alpha's gaze. Made myself feel the weight of it, and the disapproval of what I was.

He stared right back, his mouth twisted in anger.

His eyes full of hatred.

My father had never looked at me like that.

I yanked a kukri blade from its sheath and jammed it into his eye in a single fluid motion that took less than the beat of my heart from one pulse to the next. No hesitation. The tip of the kukri buried deep and I rode him backward as he roared. I pushed off, jamming the blade in until I could feel the back of his skull scraping against the tip.

His body gave a jerk, a spasm, and I pulled the knife out, rolling to the side. I stayed in a crouch, breathing hard as I stared at the prone form of my father who was not my father. I had to still fight the desire to go to him, to let him hold me. He hadn't shifted back into a bear form. Was this his true shape then?

No, that wasn't possible.

He stirred, his body making a twisted snow angel, splattered with blood. Groaning, he rolled to his hands and knees, blood and white fluid spilling from the gouged-out eyeball.

"Bitch," he gurgled as he lifted his head to face me, shocking the shit out of me. How was he not dead? His one eye was wild with fury, pain, and I stared him down.

"Not a bitch," I growled. "That's *queen* to you."

He roared, his whole body tensing as the sound rolled from him. I opened my mouth and screamed right back at him, the two cries clashing in the air. He'd impersonated my father, and tried to make me bend to his will. Tried to make me submit by using my nature against me.

This Bear was going to be turned into a rug.

"The flail!" Maks yelled from the other side of the Bear. "Use the flail!"

The Bear—still in human form—twisted around to face Maks. They clashed as Maks raised the shotgun and pulled the trigger. The blast from the weapon rocked the Bear-man guardian back, slamming him in the chest, but didn't drop him.

I dove forward as the two men's fighting intensified.

"Help Maks!" I yelled up at Lila as I scrambled to prepare myself. To die, I wanted to die. The flail warmed and I could have sworn it was happy. I ran toward the fight in time to see Lila cut between Maks and the Bear-man. A hand shot out and grabbed her around the waist.

She screamed, a howl that made my skin crawl with fear for her. I didn't slow down, but instead sped up, spinning the flail for all I was worth once more.

I want to die.

"This way, bastard!" I yelled at him. He turned, Lila still in his hand. He was shifting back to his bear form. I could see the energy spike around him. I swung the flail right at his head. There was a moment where the shock in his eyes would have made me laugh. Like he couldn't believe what was happening.

Then the two spiked balls slammed into the side of his head. The first one hit his cheek and the front of his face, the second hit over his ear and directly onto his skull. A loud crack of bone, like the snapping of an ancient tree branch seemed to throw us all back. More like there had been an explosion versus a simple blow to the head. I sailed through the air, the flail's handle still in my grip. I hit the ground, rolled and was back on my feet in a crouch, waiting for the Bear-man to get up.

His form was unmoving on the snow. But he hadn't moved the first time I'd hurt him either. Lila winged down to me and landed on my shoulder.

"You okay?" I asked without looking at her.

"Bruised, but dragons are hard to break. Even when they're small."

I nodded and took a creeping step forward, then another and another.

Maks was doing the same from the other side. He put a finger to his lips. I wanted to roll my eyes because, let's be honest, either the Bear would hear us or he wouldn't no matter how careful we were.

Maks's hair was mussed. Blood was on his face and he was limping, but otherwise, he seemed okay. At least he'd fared far better than when we'd dealt with the White Wolf.

I leaned over the Bear-man looking for signs that he was dead. Like dead, dead.

His hands shot up at me. One wrapped around my neck in a vise grip that instantly cut off my air supply, blood supply, and ability to think. I reached for the hands around mine as I got my feet under me and kicked at him, nailing him in the ribs.

"I might die, but you'll die too, bitch." At least, I think that's what he said. There was a pounding in my ears that I was fairly certain was my heart about to explode. I fought his grip but it was unbending, unending. Spots danced in front of my eyes as I bucked against him. But even I knew my efforts were dwindling, weakening. There was a roar of fury and pain and the hold on me tightened further. My fingers slid off the handle of the flail.

And then just like that, it was gone, the fingers slipping from my neck.

I fell to the ground, half on and half off his chest. I lifted my head to see Maks standing in front of me, his hand on the wooden haft of the flail, the two balls buried in the head of the guardian, splitting it like a ripe melon. My eyes were fuzzy from lack of blood, but I was sure, for just a moment, Maks was floating, like a vengeful spirit come to life, his eyes blazing with anger and his body shaking with adrenaline.

"Maks, let go," I whispered. There was no way he'd survive the flail drawing on his energy and life force.

And then there was nothing but blackness as my eyes closed and I slumped all the way to the frozen ground.

I don't really know how long I was out, but I caught bits and pieces of conversation between Lila and Maks.

"I can't believe the acid didn't work on that Bear," Lila murmured.

Someone tightened their hold on me. "It's okay, Lila. None of us knew what we were getting into there. And we've got farther yet to go."

"What do you mean?"

"The Ice Witch has an army, Lila. You know that, you said they killed dragon fledglings for their armor. She doesn't just depend on the guardians out here. The army she has is wild ice goblins for the most part. Few people know about that last line of defense.

Never mind what else she might have in the castle guarding her. She's no fool."

"How do you know this?"

"I know a lot," he said softly.

I twisted to sit up and I realized I was in Maks's arms, astride Batman. I blinked a few times, so close to Maks's face that I could see the individual whiskers of the stubble growing in. When had he shaved last? I wasn't even sure I'd ever seen him shave. Part of my head knew that the ideas roaming through my skull were a scattered mix because of the fight. The other part thought it was perfectly logical. Which was stupid, of course.

"You have whiskers." I reached up and touched his cheek. Maks looked down at me with both eyebrows raised.

"I think we need to worry about more than my unshaven face."

I shrugged or what passed for a shrug in his arms. "I kinda like it."

Lila snickered. "Careful, or I'll remember that I saw you two kissing."

Maks's arms stiffened around me, and I leaned my head against him. "That was just a dream, Lila. Humans and supes don't mix well. I would never do that. And Maks likes Darcy, if I recall."

He didn't relax. In fact, he tensed further. There was something I needed to ask him about. Something to do with the flail, but my brain would not give me the words I needed.

"We need to dismount, and stash the horses. We're close enough to the White Raven's territory that we need to think about more stealth. We should go in on foot from here out. Like you planned," Maks said.

Another male voice piped up. "I can help with that."

We both twisted to see Merlin standing in the snow not more than twenty feet away. Fury coursed through me so hot, it burned away any residual shock and dumbness from the fight. I scrambled out of Maks's arms and dropped to the snow, hissing all the while. Balder and Batman danced sideways away from me.

"You son of a camel! You tried to kill me. Are you back to *try* and finish me? Because if I'm right, you can't use magic, which means I'm about to kick your ass!" I started toward him, wishing I could shift into a lion so I could bite his face off. If he thought I'd go down easily, he was dead wrong.

He rolled his eyes. "I was *not* trying to kill you. You yourself had the thought that you needed to get rid of the shadow attached to you. I just helped that along. Ah, I see your *human* is still with you. That's a bit of a surprise."

"You helped her by pushing her into the river,

under the ice?" Maks snapped. "That's a crock of shit if ever I heard one, *mage*."

Merlin gave Maks a tight, strange smile that I would almost have pegged as condescending, but it was there and gone in a flash. "The shadow spirit no longer follows her, which means the queen has lost her eyes on you. For the moment, at least. And don't be rude, boy. You should know when one of your betters is talking to you, and that they shouldn't be interrupted."

I stared at him, wanting to call him all sorts of names, but the reality was . . . I hadn't felt the eyes of the shadow figure on me since the river. But I'd also lost my ring. Whatever was between him and Maks would have to wait.

Lila flapped between us. "Are you sure, though? She didn't actually die."

The warlock rolled his eyes. "The spirit had only to take his attention from her for a short time and then I helped him along. Sent him back to the haunt he came from."

"Why?" Maks threw the question down like a challenge. "Why are you really helping us?"

"Oh, I'm not helping you, *human*." Merlin drawled that last word and I wondered just what he was getting at. "I'm helping Zamira. She has a rescue to perform. A jewel to steal. A wall to break."

"Tell me Darcy is still alive," I blurted out before I could think better of it.

Merlin nodded. "She is, but she's starting to give up hope, and with that, her strength wanes. And the Jinn are only hours away now. You have to hurry."

Maks made a strangled sound. "Hours?"

Merlin gave him a nasty smile. "Yes, hours."

Maks stepped between us. "You're trying to get us all killed."

"Well, not Zamira," Merlin said softly. "You, on the other hand . . ."

"Wait!" I put both hands into the air, my voice echoing between the four of us. "Stop it, both of you idiots. I don't know what's between you and I really don't care." I wobbled a little where I stood. "Here's the deal. Merlin, you stash the horses for us on the banks of the river, a mile away from the castle on the far side of the river. Maks, you, me and Lila are going in as soon as the sun drops. We need the cover."

"I'm not going with you into the castle. I only said I'd get you to the castle itself," Maks said. Which was totally opposite of what he'd just said only minutes before. Then he'd said we needed to stash the horses and find a way into the castle. As if he'd been coming with me. But no, the more I thought about it, he'd not ever explicitly said he'd go in with me. With us.

And now?

Not so much, apparently.

The curse twisted around me and again I thought I could hear Marsum's laughter against my skin, heating it, cursing me further.

One companion gone now. Because I'd wanted him with me.

Damn my cursed life.

I twisted around and looked at him, shock settling into me. Of course, he was close enough, he could go now. He could escape, go back to the human world and forget we were trapped here. Just like the humans always did. Anger spilled through the hurt like water through the desert, finding the smallest cracks in my armor.

"Right then. Off, you fuck," I said and turned my back on him, choosing not to think about the stab of pain in the region of my heart. It was better this way that he left now, better that I not get any more attached to him.

"And just how is that going to go?" Merlin said softly. "You don't have a map."

My jaw ticked. "I saw the map back at the Stock-yards. I was studying it as I study all my resources." Goddess, I wondered if they could tell I was lying. I had no map. The only map had been with Kiara and Steve. And now there was zero time to go back, find Kiara's horse, her saddlebags, and hope the map was there.

Hours, Darcy had hours to live, hours before the Jinn showed up.

Merlin arched an eyebrow and his lips twitched as though he held back a smile. "Sure thing, Zamira. Off you go then. Rescue your friends."

I took a step, then another and another. Lila dropped her head and whispered to me, "You don't really know how we're doing this, do you?"

I shook my head.

"I could scout," she offered.

I shook my head again. "We need the cover of the trees. The White Raven will see us otherwise."

There was only one way I was going to slip in and that was in my smaller form. For the first time in years, shame didn't follow the prep for shifting. It caught me off guard. Maybe it had to do with seeing my mother, of knowing that she had strength in being tiny too. Or maybe it had something to do with Maks liking me. Maks not minding my smaller form.

Nope, nope. I was not going there.

Maks was no longer part of my life.

End of that chapter of my story.

I dashed the one tear that fell from each eye before it froze to my skin.

CHAPTER EIGHTEEN

I didn't even wait to get to the trees before I stepped through the doorway in my mind that took me from two legs to four. My weapons and clothes worked themselves into a collar around my neck, bigger than I'd ever had before. But then that could be the flail's doing. It was only then I realized it was still with me, reattaching itself to my back like it belonged there.

I swallowed hard. Why hadn't it taken Maks down?

Lila dropped to the ground and trotted alongside me, keeping up easily.

"I can't believe Maks just abandoned us," she said.

"You said it yourself," I flicked my ears trying to pick up on the sounds of anything that might do us harm, "he's a boil."

"A toad," she whispered, and I thought perhaps her voice hitched. "But I kinda liked that toad."

"Yeah. Me too. For a human, he wasn't so bad. But he's better off leaving now and not ending up on the end of an ice goblin's spear," I said. But I didn't slow. We had just ducked under the canopy of the trees when the shush of feathered wings above us dropped me to my belly. I flattened on the ground and burrowed under the snow. With a grumble, Lila followed suit.

Let her find us, I thought, and the curse tightened, then relaxed.

I peered up through a break in the snow to see the shadow of a bird float above the treetops. Sure, the Ice Witch might not have a shadow attached to me anymore, but we *did* just kill her Bear.

That had to give her at least a place to start when it came to tracking us. I breathed out slowly as the shadow faded.

Lila burrowed out first. "You know, we have killed the first two guardians. Why not just take out the White Raven and then we can go in clean?"

"Because." I shook my coat to shed the loose snow and then broke into a trot.

"That's not really an answer," she said. "Because why?"

"Because that White Raven is not just any raven.

Because that Raven is known to scoop people up and climb through the clouds where she tears their bodies apart so it rains blood. She's like facing a dragon, Lila, and I can't do that. Neither can you." I glanced at Lila. "There are rumors that she eats dragon fledglings. That the dragons would eat her if they could but never are able to catch her. That there is some power holding the dragons out of her territory."

Lila shook her head, but not before I saw her eyes dart to the side. "No, I never heard that. There is nothing holding the dragons out of her territory." Her words sounded off to me, like something she was saying by rote.

I frowned. "Lila, what aren't you telling me?"

"Nothing."

A lie. I stopped moving, turned and looked at her. "Lila, *what aren't you telling me?*"

Her head lowered and she swayed from side to side. "I can't tell you. I'm bound by my family's oaths which means this is not something I can even say. Seriously, I can't even speak it."

I closed my eyes. "Are you actually here to help me?"

"Yes, but . . . I miss my family, and you said you were scouting their grounds. And if they know that the first two guardians are gone, that I helped kill them, they might let me come home. I love being with you, Zam, I do. But . . . the chance that I could go home is too much," she whispered. I opened my eyes to see her staring back at me with something akin to hope blended with sorrow.

Maks had left me.

Lila wanted to leave me.

Merlin tried to kill me.

With friends like these, I didn't need to worry about enemies. I lifted my lips into a snarl. "Go then, go back to your family, Lila." The words were not hard as I intended, but full of fatigue, mixed with a sorrow that I didn't want to think too much about.

The curse on me flexed and I knew it was slowly tearing my life apart. Just like it had been waiting years to do.

I took off, racing through the snow, my light body not even breaking the top crust. There would be no tracks to follow, which would help. I tried to keep my mind focused on what was ahead, that I would find Darcy and everything would be okay. We'd get out, we'd go home, we'd laugh about this trip like we always did when we told our stories of our hunts and thefts.

She'd know I finally forgave her, and we could be like we were before stupid Steve.

Only it felt like there would be no laughter this time, only tears, like the curse would finally be the end of us all. I ran as fast as I could through the sparse forest, keeping to the shadows on instinct alone. And that was about all that saved me.

An arrow slammed into the ground right in front of me, spraying snow up in my face. I caught a glimmer of sparkling blue and silver material attached to the back of it right before the material shot toward me, like a living rope seeking me out. A catch arrow.

I blinked and dodged to the right as a chorus of howls went up through the night air. The blue and silver cord slid across my back and tightened but not fast enough. I turned on the speed.

Maks hadn't lied about the Ice Witch's goblin army, and part of my brain bucked against that. Only because how could he—a human—possibly know more about the Ice Witch than us? How could he know about the flail, that it would kill the White Bear, and how could the flail leave him untouched when it had almost drained my life? How could he be all those things . . . unless he wasn't human.

The interactions with Merlin made sense in that context.

Maks wasn't human, but . . . if he wasn't human, what was he?

Another arrow cut across my path and buried into the tree to my right. The same blue and silver cord shot out from it and I dove to the left, right under the feet of a freaking ice goblin.

I blinked up at him, took a single look, and then shot between his legs. His ears were black, frozen, and dead with the cold, same with his nose and lips, eyes of silvery white, and dressed in rabbit furs and dragon scales if the smell was any indication.

"Get that fucking cat. I want pussy for dinner!" he roared after me. I grimaced and bolted, doing what I could to stay ahead. But as soon as I thought that, the way ahead of me closed off, a wall of goblins.

I curse you that nothing you do will go right, that you will always end your choices in disaster. Marsum's words cut through to me and I let out a breath. The same thing I'd done with the White Bear, I had to do it here too. I had to do it to live.

I had to try and get caught.

I slid to a stop and sat back on my haunches, though it went against every instinct. There was no time to hesitate, none at all. "Okay, take me then. I give up. I want to be captured."

The goblins all looked at one another like they weren't sure what game I was playing. Adrenaline pounded through me and I knew that I had to hold my ground if I wanted to get caught. I had to believe it completely. Or it wouldn't work. I lay down in the snow and rolled onto my back as fear cut through me in that vulnerable, submissive position.

"Come on then. I'm here. Take me."

"She's playing a game. Be careful. What magic could she have?" a goblin growled.

I rolled back to my belly so I could see who was speaking. "No, I'm not playing any games. You want to eat me, I want to die. Or be caught, whichever you like."

The words seemed to stick to the roof of my mouth. But the goblins didn't come forward. I stood and took a step toward them, doing my best to give them soft kitten eyes. "Seriously, *take* me."

They backed up farther. One nocked an arrow and his buddy put a six-fingered hand on his arm. "Don't . . . something is wrong with her. Maybe she's sick—contagious."

The group of ice goblins covered in weapons and body parts that didn't belong to them took a collective step back, then another and another.

"Come on, I *want* you to eat me." The words sounded so dirty, and I had to struggle not to let the near-hysterical laugh bubble out of me. I mean, who the hell wanted a goblin to eat them in any way, shape, form or . . . anything? Nobody in their right mind.

I mentally wanted to reach for the necklace, the ring of my father's that had protected me for so long, but of course, it wasn't there. That was the whole issue.

I took a few steps toward the goblins, and they promptly broke rank and scattered ahead of me. I turned and looked over my shoulder, sure that there would be a dragon behind me, fooling me into thinking that little old me was the reason behind their fear.

Nope, not a single breath of dragon wing behind me.

I took off as fast as I could, taking advantage of the goblins' weird fear of me. Score one for the cursed kitty cat.

As I ran, I kept my ears pricked and swiveling for any sounds that would give any more goblins away, but they were gone, as if they'd never been there.

The trees around me thinned further until they were so scattered, I had to run to each one to hold to any sort of cover. With a grimace, I slid to a stop at the last tree. Ahead of me was the castle of the Ice Witch and it was one big, bad, ugly looking fortress. This was no princess castle with winding spires and gilded turrets glittering in gold and silver. The palace was a square black block on top of other black blocks, on top of other dark squares, and it sat on top of an outcropping that looked out toward the open sea on one side and the massive river that flowed around it like a natural moat.

And of course, that moat was what I had to cross. Hundred feet or more of flowing icy river. Being this close to the sea, the salt intake kept the river from freezing over like the southern part of it which was a . . . "Son of a bitch." I hadn't taken that into account. I'd thought I'd be able to just truck across it. No problemo. La-dee-fucking-da.

I bit my lower lip, a growl slipping out of me as I stared at the water, listening to it gurgle and flow.

"Come on, let's get back to the castle. Queenie ain't going to be happy we left the cat out there."

"Nah, that wasn't the one she wanted. She said it was a lion shifter to look for. That was a damn pussy cat. Black to boot, not even gold like the others."

The goblins' voices called out to each other and I crept through the snow toward them. Fifty feet up river they stood on the bank, a boat bobbing along still tied to the shore.

I swallowed hard. "Curse, you'd better be a real fucking thing and not crap out on me in the middle of this."

A curse meant to destroy my life, and now I was banking on it to help me save those I loved.

The irony was not lost on me.

I crouched against the tree closest to the bobbing boat as half a dozen ice goblins climbed into it. I waited until they pushed off, as they started across the river with long poles and oars. I drew a slow breath in, out, and then bolted forward.

At the edge of the water, my paws touched the

ice-cold death that would take me and I leapt into the air, sailing over to the left of the boat, deliberately trying to miss it. Deliberately trying to hit the water.

The boat veered suddenly and was under me. I landed on the prow and balanced there. I grinned at the goblins as they stared at me. "Hiya, boys, did you miss me?"

They roared and scrambled to get away from me, two of them going overboard. This was ridiculous, but I would take it. "Come on, I thought you wanted to eat me?" I couldn't help the grin this time. The ridiculousness of it all was just too much. Giddy, I was giddy with adrenaline.

The remaining four managed to pull themselves together and formed something of a barricade against me, spears and swords out. Shaking. Their weapons were shaking as I sat balanced on the edge of the boat.

"You know, we're going to end up in the ocean. I think that's a good thing," I said, pushing my cursed ability just a little further. What would that fucker Marsum say if he knew I was using his curse to actually help me succeed?

That thought sent a shiver down my spine and my fur raised so I was a black puff ball. The goblins blinked as if waking from a deep sleep. As if . . . they realized that I was indeed worth killing. What had I done?

Marsum's laughter tickled the edges of my ears again, like he knew and had changed the curse accordingly.

"Get her," the lead goblin snarled. "Now!"

Ah, fuck, that's what I got for being cocky. We spun sideways in the boat, and I looked to the shore. We were about twenty feet off solid ground. I blew out a breath and leapt off the prow with all I had. I covered over half the twenty feet before I hit the water, sliding under the waves. No ice covering my head was about the only positive I could come up with. Arrows flashed through the water around me and I swam as if I could set myself up for being hit.

I came up for air, gasping, waterlogged and swimming for all I was worth, not for the shore but for the ocean. Stupid, it was stupid but the curse kicked in again, and a weird twisting current swept me up onto the shore in a splash. I scrambled forward, running before I thought of anything else, my fur dripping wet.

The goblins were still in the river and trying to get to shore after me—at least, if their cursing and the splash of their oars were any indication. There were no trees to hide behind, no cover for me other than the dark of the night.

That would have to be enough to get me to the

edge of the castle. Though looking at the slick stone sides of it, with no apparent doors other than the drawbridge, it wasn't like I had a way in. I slid to a stop and looked back at the goblins as they finally reached the shore.

I dropped to my belly and wormed under the snow, cursing the cold water as it froze my fur. But the snow helped to soak up some of the moisture, which I would take as a win. I waited, shivering violently as the goblins made their way up the slope. "Come on, boys, you can find me," I whispered. "You can find me."

They turned around and round like they were blind to my tracks and the spot I'd buried myself.

"Fucking cat is a fucking ghost. Come on, it's cold and I want to warm my belly before we report to Maggi." The leader made a waving motion with his hand and they fell into line, trekking right past my measly hiding spot. The fourth in line stepped on my tail and I bit back the howl that bubbled up my throat. As it was, as soon as they were ahead of me, I slipped out and stepped into line with them.

Not one of them looked back. I held onto the thought that I wanted to be discovered, that I wanted to be caught. And they stoically led me all the way along a path that was barely visible, to a section of the castle wall that looked like every other part. The lead goblin used the tip of his sword to place a complicated knock against the stones. The wall fell inward—a hidden door—and the goblins trudged inside.

I took a breath.

This was it.

I shot in with them, into the castle of the Ice Witch.

CHAPTER NINETEEN

The Ice Witch's castle was no warmer inside than outside. In fact, I would have sworn the temperature dropped at least another ten degrees, crystalizing the tips of my still-damp fur. The four goblins ahead of me took a left at the first intersection and I paused to think about where to go next.

I was in, but I still had to find the dungeons. I would guess on them being low. A part of me wanted to shift back to my two-legged form, but I knew I was safer like this. Small and easier to hide in the shadows with my pitch-black fur.

I frowned. If I wanted my curse to work for me, then I needed to find a way to word things in my mind. I worked it through a few times before I whispered it out loud. "The last place I want to find is the dungeon. I mean the absolute last place. Worst place ever, who the fuck would want to be in the dungeon?"

Nothing happened. I screwed up my nose to try again and caught a whiff of something I knew almost as well as I knew my own smell.

The scent of lions. They were mingled together, but I could pick out the threads of those I knew. Steve, Darcy, and even Kiara. But there was a fourth lion I didn't know.

I held it in my mouth and tasted it to decipher how old the scent was. A day at best for that fourth one, but he—and it *was* a he—was not known to me at all. It didn't matter, I would get them all out.

I crept along the edge of the stone wall, my breath puffing in front of my face, following the smell of lion. Maybe it was good that Lila and Maks had abandoned me.

It hit me like a ton of bricks that the curse had done that too. Taken away my support.

Left me alone, and in that, had helped me get further toward my goal.

And it was right about then the entire plan, the whole rescue Darcy and get the fuck out, went right to shit.

Cue the curse in full effect in three . . . two . . . one . . .

Screams erupted ahead of me, filling the walls with the horrible sounds of blood in throats, of fear and pain. The blast of a gunshot that echoed against the stone walls.

And above it all was a voice I didn't expect for one second.

"Damn it, where are you, Zam?"

Maks had come back.

I shot down the hall like a bullet from a gun, careening off the corners as I slid around them, my claws scrabbling for purchase on the stone, and then finally skidded to a stop. Maks stood in the middle of a large room, goblin bodies around him— in what was a freaking bloodbath. He had his shotgun in one hand and a short knife in the other. His hair was mussed and his eyes wild. I let the shift take me back to two legs because, let's be honest, it wasn't like we were slipping by at this point.

"Maks, what are you doing here?" I took one step, then another. "I thought you were escaping?"

"Changed my mind." He lowered the shotgun. "We need to get to the dungeon."

"I'm working on that," I said, and he shook his head.

"This way."

He turned on his heel and led me away from the big room and down a hall to a set of stairs. Something blocked his way; he pulled the gun and the boom of it echoed back to me. I clapped my hands over my ears.

"Maks, this is going to draw the Witch's attention!"

"I know." He looked back at me and there was a glimmer in his eyes. "This is the best I can do for you, Zamira the Reckless. I'm sorry, for everything, and this is the best I can do to make it better. The dungeon is down there," he pointed to a set of stairs. "There's an escape door as well on the southern wall. It opens onto the cliff, but you can do it. All of you can do it."

His jaw ticked and his eyes raked over me, as if this were . . . the last time he'd see me.

"Maks, you're human, you can't—"

"I'm *not* human, Zam. I'm not. I lied to you. I thought . . . I thought I could escape my past, but you kept showing me that my past was something I had to try to rectify." He shook his head, grabbed me and landed a hard kiss on my mouth, catching me off guard. He let go of me and I stared at him.

"Maks."

"Now go. We don't have a lot of time."

The best he could do for me? What the hell was he talking about? He spread his fingers out, palm to the ground, and a black mist curled up around him, covering him wholly. So, he was a supe, a mage, and suddenly things made sense in our journey that hadn't before. For now, I would take his word and get to my friends. But what Maks didn't know was that friends were hard for me to come by, and I wasn't about to let him down either.

"I'll be back for you," I whispered.

I turned and ran for the stairs, leapt down them ten or more at a time, grabbed at the walls to keep my balance until I was at the very bottom, crouched and searching the shadows. The smell of lion was strong, but so was the scent of something else.

Something dark and full of blood, something that didn't like daylight all that much.

"Well, well. Do we have a new friend to chain up today?"

The voice was drawling, and had such a thick accent, I could barely make out what he was saying.

"Vamp?" I asked.

"You betcha, little lion," he growled and then he launched at me from the darkness.

A blur, he was just a blur of arms extended, white fangs, and glittering blue eyes. For a moment, I thought it was the dead vamp from the graveyard, but no, this one's face was not so lovely.

He was fast, but I was no slouch in the reflex department. I spun to the side and drove my knee up, catching him in the solar plexus. With him caught on my knee, I pulled my blades and rammed one into the back of his neck, and the other somewhere in the kidney region of his back.

"Ah, fuck. You want me to hurt you?" he growled

and promptly threw me off. I slammed into the stone wall, my head cracking against it, the flail's handle digging into my spine. I groaned and slid to the floor. The flail . . . the handle was wooden. I pulled it from my back and the vamp laughed at me. I was going to take a chance that using the wrong end wouldn't hurt me as much.

"Fancy weapon, but we're in too small of a space to use it. But by all means, go ahead and try." He grinned and I realized he'd not even bothered to take the two knives out of his back. Either he was supremely lazy, or he was truly not affected by them. Which was impressive considering the fact they were supposed to work only on supes.

He took a step and I rolled the flail once, twisting it so the spiked balls clicked against one another. His eyes flicked to them and then back to me. "You don't have the balls."

"Actually," I spun it harder, feeling the momentum build, "I believe I do. I have two metal ones with spikes on them."

He snarled and lunged forward which made sense. The closer he was to me, the safer he'd be from the metal end of the flail.

I dropped to one knee and braced with my foot against the wall behind me. I used the momentum of the spiked balls to spin the handle around, pointed end up, spiked balls jammed into the ground for bracing as the vamp ended his jump on top of me.

"Ah, fuck!" he roared as the wooden handle slid through his chest, heart, and out his back.

Blood poured around the weapon and down over my face. I closed my eyes and turned my head as I threw his body to the side. He slid off the handle with a sucking pop that made me turn up my lips.

There was no time to be squeamish though. Not here.

Not now. The handle warmed against my skin.

I braced myself, but the blood didn't soak into the wood. The handle was not cursed like the metal spikes. I grinned. "Hell, yeah."

I bent over the vamp, getting a good whiff of him as I frisked him, looking for the keys. That was the scent that I'd caught earlier and couldn't quite pin down. I snorted to clear my nostrils just as my fingers touched the cool metal of the keys attached to the back of his belt. I pulled the large ring with a single key on it up, but it was snagged on the belt. Using one of my knives I pulled from his back, I cut the leather strap he'd tied it on with. With both blades in their sheaths, flail covered in vamp blood and key in hand, I headed deeper into the dungeon.

My nose was coated with the scent of blood and I couldn't smell anything beyond it. I was going to have to settle for old-fashioned detective work.

"Darcy, where the fuck are you?" I called out.

There was a groan at the far end of the dungeon and then a voice I could have done without hearing.

"Zam, thank the goddess you're here! Get us out!" Steve struggled against chains by the sounds of things. I passed by his cell—well, his and Kiara's— gave them a shrug and kept on walking.

"What the actual fuck? You can't leave us here!" he roared and the chains rattled again. He was right, I wouldn't leave him there, nor would I leave Kiara, but I'd let them think I would for a minute or two. That was the least they deserved, fuckers.

There was no fourth lion, though I could still smell him. A fourth lion I didn't know? But he'd escaped, that much had to be true, because there was no body.

I reached Darcy's cell. Her body was pinned to the wall and her head hung low, her blond hair dirty and tangled. "Hang on, Darcy," I whispered as I put the key in the lock.

"I'm so sorry for everything. For Steve," she whispered.

"Water under the bridge." I grinned at her and she shook her head.

"Trap, it's a trap. The queen wants you for Marsum." She spoke as though she had done a fair amount of screaming. I hurried to her and lifted her head. Bite marks were scattered around her neck and chest from the vamp. Anger burned bright in my belly. This was why she was so weak, she'd been fed on.

"I should have made him suffer," I said. "Burned him alive." I got the key into her manacles. They popped open and she slid to her knees. I swept my thick cloak off and put it over her shoulders. She needed the warmth more than I did right then. "Come on, let's get you out."

I helped her to the door and she kept on muttering about a trap. But that could mean anything. Especially when she was this far gone. I chose to ignore the fact she knew the Jinn were on their way.

I went to Steve and Kiara's cell next and opened the door, then flipped the key to them. "Hurry up, I'm not waiting for you." I helped Darcy along the hall, heading toward the southern side as Maks had said.

I ran my hands over the wall, looking for an edge, a lip, anything.

The longer I looked, the more the panic set in. If we couldn't find the door, we'd have to go back the way I'd come, and I wasn't sure that was the best idea I'd ever had.

Steve and Kiara caught up to me. "What are you doing?" she asked first.

"There's a door here. It leads to the cliff and you

can shimmy down. Cross the river and wait with the horses."

Kiara blinked at me, those big gold eyes of hers so uncertain. "What about you?"

"I have a friend I can't leave behind," I said.

A moment later, Steve gave a grunt. "Here. I found it."

The door slid open, and only because he had the muscles to push it. A burst of fresh winter wind cut through the dungeon and it was only then I realized just how stifling the air was. I breathed it in as did the other three.

"Kiara, help Darcy." I handed my friend off to the younger lion shifter.

Darcy shook her head and her eyes finally focused on mine. "Don't go. Come with us. It's a trap, the Jinn . . ."

"Then it will buy you time, my friend." I gave her a quick hug. "I'm not much good for anything else but doing that. When you get home . . . tell Bryce I'm sorry I've been such a fuck-up. And he loves you. So . . . don't tell him I told you."

Her arm was weak around me, her sob deep. "No." But Kiara was stronger and she pulled her away. Steve stood on the edge of the doorway.

"I still hate you. But thanks," he said.

I turned my back on him, because really, what was I supposed to say to shit like that?

"Get them home safe, Steve."

"What about the jewel?" he growled. "Ish needs it."

I bobbed my head. "I'll get it if I can."

Fuck, I was putting only a little strain on myself. Save Maks, find the sapphire in the Ice Witch's crown. No problem, right?

Right.

I ran back the way I'd come, once more taking the stairs several at a time as I fought to think of another way to get my curse to work for me. How was I going to spin this?

"The last thing I need is to find Maks," I whispered as I ran. "Don't find Maks. He's trouble and that means it's going to be a trap, just like Darcy said."

There was a moment, a pause where I could almost feel the Jinn's power on my skin, like the heat of the desert sun as it cut through the sky and then it clicked into place, pushing me up and to the left. Toward Maks.

I might be a weak-ass kitty cat, but I had a weapon no one ever expected.

A curse that was turning out to be a fucking magic genie that only obeyed me.

CHAPTER TWENTY

Merlin tapped the crystal ball in front of him, a smile on his lips. "Flora, look. She's going back up to get that little shit, Maks."

"Why are you grinning then?" Flora leaned over him and he dared to slip an arm around her waist. She didn't stiffen or pull away from him, which was a decided improvement over the last time he tried to touch her. He rubbed his other hand along his jaw—Flora had a mean left hook.

"She's using the curse to help her, and we know it will take two creatures of the desert to take the wall down. That's what the oracle said. I thought it would be Steve and Zamira, but perhaps . . . perhaps, it will be Maks the oracle meant." He leaned closer so he could see the details in Zamira's face—the fierce determination that lined her mouth and the fire in her eyes that blazed with green light. As a lion, she would have conquered the Jinn on her own . . . it was no wonder they cursed her. Not once but twice. The first curse had come at her birth . . . but she didn't know about that one. Her brother did.

He wondered if Bryce would ever tell her the truth.

Zamira paused at the top of the steps and plastered herself to the wall as a troop of ice goblins raced by.

"You mean she's actually using the curse to help her? Oh, goddess, that is going to piss Marsum off." Flora frowned and gave a shiver. "That we don't need. He's already trying to wake the emperor."

"No, we don't need that at all." Merlin glanced at her and tightened his arm a very small amount. As if giving comfort. Which he was, of course. "But I don't think Maks will be reporting to anyone any time soon. He's trying to escape."

"Any idea who or what he really is?" Flora tapped the crystal ball and it shifted to show Maks facing off with the Ice Witch.

Merlin let out a slow breath. "I have my suspicions, but they don't fit with what I know of his kind. Assuming his kind is even what he is."

"Riddles, you know I hate them," Flora grumped and, merciful heavens, she leaned into him a little, a sigh slipping past those luscious lips of hers. "Just like I hate games, Merlin."

She pushed his arm off her waist. "What are we going to do?"

"At this point, there is nothing we can do," he said. "She's on her own now. If she can take down the Ice Witch, or at least dethrone her, then there is a chance the wall will begin to crumble."

Flora gave a nod and turned her attention back to the crystal ball. The real issue was far larger than Merlin was letting on. Flora would be pissed as a wet hen if she figured out that taking the Ice Witch on was only the first part of breaking the wall. The first part and the least dangerous.

He sighed. "You can do this, little cat. You have to or we're all doomed and the emperor will wake."

The minute the emperor woke and found the world he'd built between the Western and Eastern Walls was crumbling, there would be hell to pay in the most literal of senses.

CHAPTER TWENTY-ONE

I crouched in the shadows of the hall. The Ice Witch's castle was about as cold as her name, and without my thick cloak, the sweat had begun to freeze on my skin even though I was burning energy at a rapid pace.

For a moment, I wished Lila was with me. Stupid, but true. I'd let the little dragon become part of my circle and I missed her weight on my shoulder and her voice above me. The speed at which I'd let her and Maks into my life told me everything. I wanted to trust those around me. But it wasn't a good idea and this was not the time to be missing Lila, I needed to focus. Maks had come to find me and that was worth something more than a friendship cast aside. The thing was, I kept looking around for her, as if she would show up and announce she'd been kidding. That she had been wrong to leave.

Straight across from me was a pair of double doors that had been locked from the outside with a bar, and when I say a bar I mean a *big fucking bar*. The chunk of wood probably weighed three hundred pounds and was easily twelve feet long. And I had to get through it to reach Maks.

To get to the Ice Witch.

Merlin's words came back to me about getting the jewel. Steve's words about getting the jewel. *There's still time to get the stone while you're at it.*

I sucked the inside of my lower lip and bit down on the skin. "Don't get cocky," I whispered as I skulked across the hallway, looking each direction for more goblins. They seemed to have all buggered off. Which seemed strange considering the attack was coming from the inside.

A woman's scream of absolute fury ripped through the air, making the hair on the back of my neck stand on end.

I ran toward the doors and got the bar on my shoulder. I was not a lion shifter, and I didn't have their strength. But Maks was in trouble. I drew a big breath, put my hands under the bar and lifted with my legs and arms. The bar shifted upward not quite to the top of the hook holding it in.

"Come on, you fucker!" I growled the words as I

fought with the three-hundred-pound chunk of wood. My legs began to shake, my arms were already there, vibrating as the weight pressed down on me.

"Little help?" a voice called from the open window across from me.

I dropped the wooden bar with a boom back into the hooks.

Lila sat in the window, right on the ledge.

I didn't waste time on pleasantries. "Don't just sit there, Maks is in trouble."

Lila shot over to the bar and I set myself up again. "On three," I said. "One, two—"

Another scream echoed from inside the room, only this time it was Maks, his voice torn with pain.

We pushed together, lifting the bar high enough to slip it over the bars that held it on. It fell to the floor with a crash and before I could even catch my breath I pushed on the big door, shoving it open.

I needn't have worried about catching my breath. The scene in front of me did it all on its own. Maks was on his knees, his dirty blond head bowed, hands flat on the stone, blood pooling around him as it dripped from his face. The Ice Witch stood over him, a long staff in her hand. The top of the staff glowed with a blue sapphire that drew my eyes even over the blood on the floor. I knew . . . that was the stone we needed. But not unless I could get Maks out first.

"Hey, bitch witch, we need to have a chat. Woman

to woman, as it were." I snapped the words out as I grabbed the flail from my back, my decision made. I would use it, and that would be that. My skin crawled with anticipation as she turned her gaze on me.

"Ah, so the littlest lion arrives at last." She smiled as she spoke and turned fully toward me, ignoring Maks. He didn't move from his position as though perhaps he was frozen there.

I made myself smile. "Listen. Here's the deal. Me and my friends are going to leave, and you're going to let us."

Her tall form swayed with her laughter. "And what makes you think I would do that?"

"I'll kill you if you don't." I continued to smile and it became a real smile the more I spoke. "Because I've already killed your Wolf and your Bear, so really, how bad can you be if a little old me could do that? Perhaps you're just full of shit, not all that ice power everyone seems to think you're full of." The words were unstoppable and I could see the rage lighting up her features which only pushed me harder. "I mean, come on. Ice? Cold? Easily defensible. Get a coat. Light a fire. Wolf? Kill it with a cat. Bear? Push it over on its fat ass like a turtle on its back. I mean even your White Raven was easy to avoid by merely staying close to a tree, and your ice goblins were fucking pitiful. Like little children scared of the dark."

From above me Lila was whispering fast. "No, don't make her angry, that's not a good idea."

But it was the only idea I had. "You see, the thing is, I don't want to leave. I like it here. I'm never leaving. I'm going to stay here and you're going to let me. This is going to be my home, and you're going to allow it."

Her eyes slid to a narrow slit. "You are cursed."

"Well, yes, that's fairly common knowledge." I began spinning the flail, feeling the sparse weight of it, feeling the handle warm against my skin. Using the metal spikes was going to suck the life right out of me.

Her grin caught me off guard. "And if I remove the curse from you? What then?"

Oh shit. Time to think fast.

"You can't. Only a Jinn could remove this curse," I said.

She waved a hand at Maks. "Excellent, then, that I have a Jinn in my thrall."

Nothing else could have stopped me in my tracks like those words. I railed against them internally while I spoke like a normal supe not breaking inside. Not thinking of the man who'd held me against the cold, the man my heart had stumbled for.

"No, Maks is not a Jinn." He'd kissed me goodbye, he cared for me, he fought to help me survive. No Jinn would have helped a lion shifter like that.

"He is. He was trying to escape, but he needed my permission. The dragons already denied him, and, of course, his own father would never let him go." She slid back to him and ran a hand into his hair, grabbing a handful of it. "Isn't that right, *Maks*?"

His eyes swept to mine. "Zamira, this isn't how it looks."

The urge to vomit rolled through me so strong, I could barely hang onto standing upright. "I swore I'd help you escape this wall," I said softly. "And *I,* at least, keep to my word." He hadn't come back for me at all. He'd come to speak to the witch, to beg her for safe passage.

"Remove the curse from her, Jinn."

"I can't," he said. "It would kill her to remove it now."

The Ice Witch laughed. "Perfect then. I said remove it, *slave!*"

Maks's head bowed to the ground and he shook all over, fighting whatever spell held him. Lila shot forward but the Ice Witch flicked her fingers at the tiny dragon and a shot of ice slammed into her form, sending her tumbling over and over through the air until she hammered against the wall.

I had to do something and fast, or we were all going to die. "You're a fucking coward."

The Ice Witch spun to face me. "You are a fool."

"A coward and a weak-willed witch who has others

do her dirty work. You can't even kill me by yourself. You have to use a Jinn to do it? What kind of witch are you? A weak, silly girl who found a spell book, I bet. I bet you didn't even come from a long line of witches. At least, I've got that going for me. I might not look like a lion, but I've got the blood in my veins to prove it."

"Then we shall see that blood," she screeched like a fucking banshee and came at me, the air around us icing over so fast, it took my breath away. I would only get one shot at this, of that I was sure. I ran toward her, spinning the flail fast and hard, prepping to spin it into her.

She had to believe I was going to use it for this to work.

And at the last second, I jumped, and shifted in midair. Her eyes widened as I landed on her face, biting and scratching, going for her eyes as the room dropped into sub-zero temperatures. Her blood tasted like fire and death, but I didn't quit. I clawed and bit, and for a moment, I was back in the desert and it was Marsum, the Jinn who'd cursed me, under my claws and fangs. Tears leaked from my eyes as I found a strength and speed in my tiny body I'd never known. I was still nothing more than a house cat.

But I fought like a lion who'd lost her mind, a lion whose pride was in danger of being wiped out.

The queen's scream lit the air, but I didn't slow. I

went for her jugular as her hand dropped onto my back. I bit in as she grabbed me, her fingers digging into my soft sides and pressing on my rib cage threatening to crush me, to break through to my heart. The vein pulsed under my tiny teeth and I held her there. If I pulled her vein apart there would be no healing it. Whatever added strength came with carrying the flail gave me that understanding. My bite, tiny as it was, was deadlier than any spell.

"Zamira," she whispered my name with as much hatred as she seemed capable of, "this is a draw. You cannot survive, and you have me in a checkmate. I am no fool. I know the power the flail gives you even in this form, but it will drain you of your life here, as it would if you stood with it in your hand."

I didn't dare let go because the second I did . . . I would be done for.

With a snarl, she tightened her fingers again and I clenched my teeth over the vein, blood trickling past my lips.

"I will speak for her," Lila said, though her voice was broken and laced with pain, which only sent my fury higher. A growl slid out of me while Lila spoke. "Let the three of us go, give us the jewel, and we will let you live."

"Never." The Ice Witch growled the word.

"Then you will die. I see it in every line of Zamira's body. She is committed to this, ready to die to stop you so Maks and I will live." She choked on those words. "Even if we don't deserve it. She is better than us. She will protect us with her body and life. Her loyalty is true."

I flexed my front claws in the Ice Witch's shoulders and my back claws against her arm. I wanted so badly to bite through, to see her life spill out around her. For imprisoning Darcy to give her to the Jinn, and then for hurting Lila . . . and maybe even a little for hurting Maks. She was ready to kill us. She'd been drawing us in to trap us and I didn't understand it, but really, I didn't need to.

The sound of a horn blasted through the air, a horn that made my hair stand on end, a horn from the worst of my childhood memories, of the Oasis and my family being wiped out.

Maks let out a low groan. "The Jinn are nearly here, Zam."

"I will kill her now." The Ice Witch shouted the words though they cost her my fangs digging in deeper. But her hands didn't move. I could feel her waiting . . . for something, but I didn't know what she could possibly want to wait on. And for that alone I held still, waiting with her for the unknown moment.

Lila let out a tiny roar. "NO!"

There was a whoosh of wings and then Lila was flapping in the Ice Witch's face, snarling and snapping her teeth, but still the hands holding me didn't lessen or tighten further. What the fuck was she waiting for? The Jinn? I didn't think that was it at all. What was I waiting for?

Anticipation tightened around us in a strange net.

"Enough!" she roared and once more Lila was thrown back. "I thought my sister would come for you," the Ice Witch whispered. "But I was wrong. She does not care for you as she claimed. In that, we are the same." Slowly she lifted her hands from me. I let her go and dropped to the floor, shifting so I landed in a two-legged crouch.

I had the flail in my hand and I snapped it forward, curling the twin spiked balls around the bottom of the Ice Witch's staff and yanking it toward me. It skittered across the floor, the sapphire striking the ground which sent a ripple of energy blowing out around us. The Ice Witch stumbled back and Maks was released from whatever spell had been holding him down.

He rolled to the side with a groan, his body shaking as the cold seemed to take hold of him. The Ice Witch stared hard at me and her body seemed to fold in on itself. "You are no safer now than you were. You might have my staff, but there are others who come to take my place." Her eyes were sharp and they reminded me of something I couldn't quite put my finger on. "You are to be the death of this world, Zamira the Reckless. I've seen it. I tried to stop it, but you are . . . not what I expected. However, you will not escape the Jinn. They know you are here now."

She took a step, then another and another toward the wide-open balcony. I watched her go as she stepped up to the edge and then . . . did a complete and total nose dive. I ran—limped really, with a hand clutched to my bruised ribs—to stare down as she fell in a fluttering array of her white dress, and then she shimmered and feathered wings spread out around her.

The Ice Witch was a shifter. An owl, snowy white, flew away from the castle.

The silence battered at my ears as loud as any battle. I slowly turned to see Maks standing behind me. His eyes were still the pretty blue they had been before.

"Jinn." I threw the word at him like a curse. He nodded.

"I am."

"Not the time," Lila barked at us. "Like, really, really not the time. You know how the Ice Witch said others were coming? She wasn't kidding." She winged toward me and then landed on the side railing. "There. Do you see them coming? They'll kill us all. I'm sorry. I thought they would take me back."

I looked into the dark night, the edge of the horizon turning pink with the rising sun. Black shapes winged toward us, flame curling out around their mouths as they came for their prize, as their enemy was driven from her home. As if the Jinn weren't enough, we had dragons to contend with too.

I blew out a breath. "Then we run."

CHAPTER TWENTY-TWO

There were no words I could give to Maks right then even if we could have sat around and had a discussion regarding his lying to me about being a Jinn. Or just why Lila had thought her family would forgive her or how the hell she'd gotten all the way to her family and back to the castle so fast.

Later, the questions would have to come later.

We bolted down the stairs and ran for the main set of doors. I clutched the staff in one hand and the flail in the other but they threw my balance off. With a growl, I jammed the flail into the back sheath and took the staff in both hands.

I slid to a stop and snapped the staff across my knee so that I only had twelve inches of length to deal with instead of six feet.

I almost tossed it up to Lila to carry, but hesitated at the last second. She shook her head, sorrow in those jeweled eyes of her. "Don't give it to me. I would be bound to carry it to the dragons. Even in exile, I am still a dragon and they will always come first no matter what I want." Her words were full of sorrow. "It is in my blood, Zam. I can't help it."

I ground my teeth and clutched the wood. I didn't even bother to look at Maks. There was no way he was getting it from me.

Out the front doors we ran as the first dragons came into view. Below them and to the south was a growing glowing golden aura that could be only one thing. Maks grabbed my arm. "The Jinn, they will kill us all."

"Fast as you can!" Lila shouted. "The dragons are here for the hold and the jewel. They won't bother with us if we get out of range."

I wasn't so sure that would hold true for the Jinn too. I could almost feel their eyes turning to me. A daughter of an alpha, a princess of the desert prides.

Shit. Fuck. Damn.

The stairs leaving the castle were almost vertical, but I didn't slow. I raced down them letting gravity take hold of me. A burst of bright red and orange flame erupted over our heads followed by a roar that rattled the inside of my brain.

I didn't look back to see if Maks was with me, I

didn't need to. I could feel his presence now and I wondered how he'd hid what he was from me so well. How had he hid it from Ish? Or Bryce, who'd fought the Jinn so many times? From Steve or Darcy? Or was he letting me in now that I knew?

Goddess, I'd *kissed* him, almost gone to *bed* with him! I stumbled on the next step and a hand shot out and grabbed my arm, steadying me from a straight out fall to the bottom. Which would have slowed us up more than I wanted to think about.

I jerked my arm from him and kept my eyes forward. A Jinn. He was a fucking Jinn! Another roar above us and Lila screamed.

"DUCK!"

I didn't think it could get any worse, but I was wrong. It could. There was the screech of a rather large, rather angry bird.

The Ice Witch had left her Raven behind, and I had a feeling she knew who had the jewel.

I dropped, the wings brushed to either side of us, and there was no time to think through what my instincts were screaming at me to do. I leapt with all my might, pushing off the stairs and into the air toward the White Raven's back.

The Raven would track us, bring the Jinn right to our doorstep. Which meant the only way we had a snowball's chance in the bowels of the desert of surviving was if we killed the Raven.

I landed on the back end of the bird, dragging her down a bit with my weight. She shot into the air and I clutched at the feathers with my fingertips, dangling from her body while Maks yelled for me below.

To let go. That he would catch me.

Another time I would have snorted, but I was saving my breath for what I had to do.

My friends were depending on me. And maybe I couldn't fully trust them, but they could trust me.

I worked the words through my head that would reverse the curse. I did not want to hurt the Raven. I wanted the bird to live a long, long life.

She flattened out and I realized we were so high above the ground that I could no longer see the specks of Maks and Lila.

"You are a fool to challenge us," the White Raven cawed into the wind, her wings flapping as though she had no concern in the world. I pulled the flail from my back.

"Probably you're right about that. My friends betrayed me. My husband betrayed me. I've lived my life under the assumption that I'm not capable, that I'm too weak to be of any use. Yet here I am, still standing. Or flying, as the case may be."

She tipped her head so one large dark eye peered at me, intelligence flickering through it. "You are not what I expected."

"Well, I'll be honest," the cold wind pulled at my hair and I suppressed a shiver, "I wasn't really expecting a long conversation up here."

She cawed and I thought it might have been a laugh. "If you'd killed the Ice Witch, I would have been free. As it is, I must follow her commands."

She barrel rolled without any warning and I fell to the side, stopping my fall only by thinking I wanted to fall. Her clawed talon shot out and grabbed me in midair. The Raven squawked in surprise.

"What spell is this?"

"A freaky-assed one of the Jinn's. I don't suppose you'll let me go knowing that the curse on me will reflect on you and I can guarantee you'll die? I don't suppose you'd just fly off and not help the Jinn?"

Her grip on me tightened and I held my breath. Fighting I was good at, negotiating not so much.

"I'll give you the flail of Marsum if you let me go and swear you won't follow," I said.

"On the souls of my ancestors, I swear it."

This was too good to be true. I lifted the flail and stuck it out so she could take it in her other talon. The second she grabbed it, she let me go, cawing, laughing at my stupidity.

Oh, I really should have worded that better.

I dropped through the sparse clouds, the icy wind battering at me as the sounds of the dragons below grew louder.

Maks had said he'd catch me.

Lila had said she'd catch me.

I closed my eyes. Not thinking of anything, not wanting to be caught, not wanting to die, just floating in a state of near nothing.

A roar right in my ear snapped my eyes open as a dragon swept in and caught me in his talons when I was only fifty feet from the ground. I yanked a kukri blade out and drove it deep into the scales.

He flung me away and I shifted in midair. Maybe I wouldn't hurt as bad if I hit in my cat form.

"I got ya!" Lila swept in from the side and caught my hurtling form, but she was not any bigger than me and we were suddenly spinning through the air. Slower, but still headed for the ground.

"Lila, drop me!" I screamed.

"No, you're my friend!"

And then we were both caught in something black and inky, a mist that belonged to a Jinn.

I blinked and Maks was there, crouched on the stairs, his hands held out, and from them poured the mist that had caught us.

A Jinn had saved me.

A cry went up to the south, and I spun. The rest of the Jinn had taken note.

"Look out!" cried Lila. This time I heeded her warning a little better.

I flattened myself to the stairs and the brush of

wingtips made me hold my breath. I stared up at the enormous black dragon that looked back at us, predatory hunger in his eyes. He opened his mouth and the curl of flames licked over blackened teeth. I didn't wait for Lila to suggest I move my ass. I shot down the stairs, so close to them now that they brushed my belly fur.

There was a grunt behind me and then Maks was at my side . . . as a caracal. His blue eyes were the same, but the rest of him was a forty-pound cat with black tipped ears and a tawny hide.

I knew the Jinn could shapeshift. I'd just never seen it. Suddenly there were pieces of our journey that made sense. The moment that Batman had kept up with Balder, how the horses had run much farther than they should have, well past exhaustion, how he'd stopped to lift his hand to the dragon that first time as if to fire off a spell, his animosity with Merlin. It all fit.

Side by side, we raced down the last of the stairs with Lila close above us. "Hurry, across the river you have to go, the horses are waiting for you there as Merlin said they would be."

Something in her words slowed me. "Wait, you're coming too."

"No. They'll come for you harder now that they know I'm alive and with you." She stalled out above us. "I'll do what I can to lead them away. I thought . .

. I thought by telling them that the Ice Witch was going to be overthrown they would let me back in, but . . . I was wrong. They hate me still and everything I represent." She glanced over her shoulder at the biggest dragon, the solid black one now perched at the top of the castle. "That one there . . . he hates me more than all the rest and will hunt for me now because I've escaped so many times. I must go. Thank you for being my friend, Zam. I'm sorry I wasn't a better friend to you."

Before I could say anything, she shot off to the south and east. I called after her but she didn't turn.

Which left me alone with Maks.

"I must go too," he said, shifting back to his human form. "The Jinn will hunt you for the same reason the dragons would hunt you with Lila riding at your side."

I still couldn't look him straight in the face, but our horses—check that, *my horses*—waited for us.

"Then go, Jinn. Be with your real friends." I had nothing else for him. There was nothing else to say.

I bolted across a tiny footbridge and lifted my nose. The smell of Balder and Batman was faint but there and I ran toward them. And then got a whiff of goblins.

I turned on the speed, leaving Maks behind, leaving all the questions I had behind. I was pissed enough that when I rounded the copse of trees that hid the two horses and saw the goblins trying alternately to stab them and mount them while they reared and fought to keep clear of the fucking little monsters, I may have lost what was left of my cool.

I shifted while still running which means I basically appeared out of nowhere, screaming bloody murder, a kukri blade in one hand and the Ice Witch's sapphire in the other. I hit the goblin closest to me with the knife so hard, I sent him twenty feet into the air. He landed with a lifeless thud. They scattered and I stood, shaking and breathing hard enough that I wasn't sure it was a good idea to approach the two horses. They on the other hand had no such qualms. The two horses trotted to me, both sticking their noses into my belly, demanding attention. I breathed in and out slowly, trying not to think about everything that had happened. About how messed up my life had become in such a short time.

I made myself pull my extra cloak from my saddlebag and slid it on. It smelled like Maks, of the desert and the hot sun, and I knew now why he smelled like that—because he was born and bred there, the same as me. As much as I wanted to rip it off and toss it to the ground, I also didn't want to freeze. I slid my knife into its sheath and strapped the sapphire still on the staff to my chest under the cloak.

What I didn't realize was that Maks had caught

up to me. I turned to see him standing there, sorrow in his eyes.

"Go where you need to go, Jinn." I reached for Batman's reins and tucked them into my hand. Maks was no longer a caracal, but a man once more. A Jinn, I reminded myself. Not human at all.

"Will you not even let me explain, Zam?" His blue eyes were earnest and part of me did want him to explain. But I'd heard that line before.

"You mean like Steve explained why he couldn't help himself? That he just *had* to fuck Kiara? You want to explain why you—a Jinn—have been using me to escape your family? You think you're the only one who wants to escape them? You think the rest of us wouldn't like to get away?" I might have been yelling, but at that point it all bubbled over. A mess of words and hurt. "I've been lied to enough in my life, thank you very much." I started to turn away when he held up a flashing silver chain.

"I took this from you, Zamira, so you could see that the curse laid on you could be used for good." He sighed. "You're stronger than any of the Jinn want to believe."

I grabbed the chain that held my father's ring on it, the etched lion's face that sometimes seemed to wink up at me. The ring Ish had given me to help me no longer be the curse I was on everyone else. He'd taken it from me when he'd stripped me at the river. That was the only time it could have happened.

"And what, were you sent to kill me then?"

"No, I was sent to kill Steve and Bryce," he said. "I took the job but—"

"Enough!" I roared the word at him, unable to stand any more of his lies. "Enough," I said softer.

I tugged on Batman to follow me and Balder, but he jerked his head and snatched the reins from me. He walked over to the Jinn and put his head down, asking for a touch from him.

I couldn't stop Maks from taking the horse, and I didn't want to kill him. I mean, I did. But I didn't.

So, I did the best I could. I turned my back on him and urged Balder into a gallop. I had to find Darcy, Steve, and Kiara. And why hadn't they waited at the horses for me? Once we found them . . . what then? Would I tell Steve who Maks really was?

Part of me wanted to, the other part was torn and wanted so badly to believe that Maks wasn't the absolute asshole that every other Jinn was. Which was stupid, and childish. Stupid. I looked back only once to see that Maks was not behind me. Which was good, and hurt me more than I cared to admit. I rode hard, the sounds of the dragons taking their place in the north echoing through the air around us, announcing their arrival.

I found the three lion shifters two miles south of

the castle. They were all in lion form, but Darcy was slower than the other two and they were not waiting for her to keep up. I slid from the saddle as I drew beside her dulled tawny form. She stumbled in the snow, her reserves so low, I could count every rib and vertebrae. For her to shift back she would use the last of her energy, but it had to be done. Balder was strong, but he couldn't carry a full-grown lion.

"Darcy, shift." I gave the command and she did without question as if I were truly her alpha. She stood in the cold snow shivering, buck naked, and I stripped down, giving her my warm clothes one piece at a time. I had no others left, and quite frankly this was better for multiple reasons. Steve and Kiara hadn't done more than glance back at us, which meant they hadn't noticed I had the sapphire. And in my smaller form, I could hide both myself and the jewel. Lick my wounds as it were.

As soon as all my clothes were off, naked but for my weapons and the necklace back in place, the ring dangling between my breasts, I helped Darcy into the saddle and then shifted.

What would she say when she found out that Maks was a Jinn? That she'd been kind to him and he'd used us?

A tiny part of my brain said he had come back to help me, so that said something, didn't it? Except that his coming back had only been to get permission to leave, to escape the wall.

Darcy settled onto Balder and I leapt up, crawling into the back of the hood and clinging to her.

She reached up and touched my head. "Thank you, Zam. You saved us. You saved us all."

Only she was wrong, I hadn't saved us all. Lila was still out there, and I essentially let the enemy go, sent him on his way with one of our best horses and more information about us than the Jinn had ever had before.

So they could come for us, unaware in the dead of the night, and finish what they'd started so many years ago.

I closed my eyes and shuddered. There would be time to decide if that was going to happen or not. Until then, it was just one foot—or paw—in front of the other until we were home again.

The journey back to the Caspian Sea took two weeks. We had to keep it that long to avoid running into the Jinn if they turned and headed south. Kiara and Steve did the hunting, and for the first time in my life, I stayed in my cat form for more than a few hours. Steve and Kiara poked fun at me, but I ignored them. I'd done more in this form than they'd managed in their big-ass lion forms and I wasn't about to forget it, or let them forget it. Each day the hours of light stretched longer and the temperature rose. Mind you, it didn't turn into the heat of the desert, but it warmed above freezing which was a bonus.

We went wide around the Dragon's Ground now that we had the extra time, avoiding the virtual death trap waiting for us there. And without my curse actively working, the trip was straightforward.

I found myself staring at the tall trees just dusted with fresh snow as we turned east, away from Dragon's Ground. My heart ached as I thought of Lila, of where she'd gone, and if she was even still alive. I tucked my nose against Darcy's neck. I knew what it was to want your family to love you. I didn't blame her for what she'd done, not in the least. I just didn't want her to suffer for it.

"What is it?" she whispered, her voice and throat still raw from the chains that had held her for weeks on end.

"Lila. She . . . she left to protect us and I'm worried about her."

Darcy pulled Balder to a stop. "Do you want to go find her?"

I blinked up at my friend. "I do, but I don't know where to start. And . . . she is worried that the dragons will seek her out, that they will kill us if we try to help her." I'd told her about Lila's part in my journey already so she knew the bond that was there.

Darcy frowned. "She seems to be awfully important for someone so disliked. Is it possible there was more to her than she let on?"

She had a very good point. If Lila had just been a nobody, why would any of the dragons care if she was alive still? What was really going on? I thought back to what Merlin had said about us both, about being daughters of important males, of the alphas. Was that why she was so hated?

"We'll get you home first," I said. "Then I'll figure out how to help Lila."

That awful twisting in my gut, that had started when Lila left us, eased. I would find her, even if it took me years. I was good at finding jewels, and Lila was, if nothing else, one of the best treasures I'd ever stumbled on.

When the first glimmer of the Caspian Sea came into view, Steve let out a roar that echoed through the air, Kiara joining him.

There were a few answering bellows, and he glanced over his golden shoulder. "What, no welcoming home roar, Zam?"

"You're a dirty bastard," Darcy growled. "You're lucky she let you out of that cage at all."

"That's not how I remember it, is it? Kiara, how do you remember it? Weren't you and I the ones to rescue Darcy and Zam?" He glanced at his mate and she bobbed her head, and wouldn't meet my gaze. But I didn't care. I had the sapphire, which meant everything Steve said would be negated the second I handed it to Ish.

"Let them go ahead, I want to talk to you anyway," I said quietly so only Darcy heard me.

She held Balder back as the two lions raced toward the Stockyards that was our home. But it didn't feel like a homecoming, not to me. For the first time, I didn't want to walk through those doors.

I hopped off Darcy's shoulder and landed on the front pommel of the saddle. There had been something I'd been thinking about for the last two weeks, and no matter how I looked at it, there was only one real answer. I drew a breath before I spoke. "Let him spin his story. I don't care about that. But . . . the Ice Witch said she thought her sister would come for us. Does that mean Ish is her sister? Because who else would she mean?"

Darcy sucked in a sharp breath. "I have no idea." She glanced at me. "What do you think? I never actually met the Ice Witch. You did."

I didn't move because I'd seen the eyes of the Ice Witch up close. Madness ruled her, power and madness. But the lines of her face. The leanness of her body, they were similar enough to Ish that it was possible. I just didn't know who to trust. Because every damn time I did, I was betrayed.

I swallowed hard but it was Darcy who broke the silence. "Ish is our friend, our mentor, and in some cases, the only mother we've known. I can't believe she would be anything but a good steward of whatever power were to come her way."

I agreed with her.

And I didn't.

Because there had been a moment before I'd left, when I'd seen the fury in Ish when she thought the sapphire would not come back to her, that somehow it was lost. I made myself say the words that were so often dreaded by those around me when they came from my mouth.

"I have an idea."

CHAPTER TWENTY-THREE

In the end, Darcy and I decided to not tell Ish we had the sapphire, to keep it to ourselves. I would gauge Ish's reaction. That was the only way to know what was important to her. Our lives, or the jewels we sought for her.

We rode the rest of the way to the Stockyards and around to the stable. I hopped off Balder's back and ran through his stall and up to the window that led into my room so I could get some clothes. I shifted and stumbled, nausea rolling over me in a wave so intense, I had to go to my knees on the stone-cold floor.

Something was wrong, not with me, but this place. I lifted my head and scented the air . . . lions and blood. That was not a good sign. I scrambled for my clothes, yanking on shirt, pants and boots as fast as I could. I slid my weapons on in their sheaths and put the sapphire under my shirt and tucked it into the back of my belt. Hidden for the moment. I hoped we were wrong about Ish.

I'd never felt the need to walk around covered in my weapons here in the Stockyards before but . . . this homecoming was different . . . dangerous. I touched the necklace for reassurance.

With a deep breath, I reached for the door and let myself into the hall. There was a shout that drew me toward Ish's receiving room, a shout that sounded like Steve crying out in pain.

I didn't run, but I did pick up my pace. Darcy stepped out of the hallway across from me, and we fell into step together.

"Ready?" I glanced at her and she nodded. Her golden eyes were no longer dulled from her confinement, and while she was hardly at her fighting weight, she was no longer completely emaciated.

The main doors to the receiving room rattled suddenly, drawing our eyes to it.

There was a second thud and then the door blasted open. Behind it was not a scene I expected, not at all. Steve and Kiara were laid out on the floor. Ish stood above them, her lean body ramrod straight. "You failed me, lion," she said. Her voice echoed through the room and reverberated into my bones. Steve tried to get up and Ish pointed a finger at him, one that glittered with the stone from the giants.

A wave of power rocked from her hand and slammed into him, pinning him to the floor. He groaned. "Do what you will to me, but let Kiara live."

I stepped into the room and Ish's eyes swept to me and Darcy. "I see . . . you went against what I wanted and you brought your friend back. Did you at least attempt to gather the stone I need?"

I'd never heard her like this, mean and desperate. I glanced at Darcy and knew we were in trouble. "We tried to get the stone, but the Witch flew away with it." I wasn't sure I wanted to ask her if the Ice Witch was her sister right then in the middle of her rage.

I swallowed hard. "I'm sorry."

"*Sorry* does nothing for me," she said. Her words whispered over me like the sands of the desert. Darcy stepped up beside me.

"Ish, we have others we can collect."

"You think you can fight the dragons for their gemstone?" Ish's eyebrows went up.

Darcy bobbed her head. "Send all of us. Steve, Kiara, myself, Zam and one other."

"Bryce," I said. "He can help with the strategy. He's better at that than anyone else."

I knew we were gambling, but what else did we have? Something was wrong with Ish, and we needed distance between her and us. The staff and the sapphire seemed to heat against the skin of my back, reminding me that I could hand it over. That I *should* hand it over. For the first time, I'd be able to prove that Steve was not the hero, that I was strong enough. Even though I was small, I was fierce. A smile tugged at my lips. "We have a friend there, a small dragon."

Ish's eyebrows drew into two sharp slashes. "We do not become friends with the enemy, Zamira. Surely your father taught you that much? Have I not drilled into your skull that we are not like the others?"

Ice seemed to grow like a lump in my belly. "She's an insider we can use. And they have no love for her."

Ish stood over Steve's body and stared down at him. "Kiara will stay with me here. As assurance. And for her delicate state, she shouldn't be running around."

Delicate state, what the hell did she mean? It took me a moment to catch on. If I thought I had a pit of ice in my belly before, it was nothing to the valley that opened inside me. Not that I thought Steve and I would ever be together again, it wasn't like that at all.

More like I realized yet again, I was somehow failing the grade, that a veritable child was able to produce a cub when I couldn't even . . . no, not the time to go there. I clenched my jaw. "Fine. That's fine."

The words were like glass shards to speak, but speak them I did. "But I want to lead the group," I added. "And I need you to say it so Steve will listen to me."

Ish tipped her head to the side. "Kiara, you went with Steve to watch them all for me. Will she be a good leader?"

Oh, hell no.

I made myself turn to look at Kiara, but she kept her eyes locked on Ish's face, her expression giving nothing away. "Steve led us. He freed us from the dungeon no matter what she might say. He is the alpha. He should be the one to lead."

Even though I'd known it was coming, I was still surprised. Still shocked that she could lie straight to Ish's face.

"You're fucking kidding me," Darcy gasped.

I said nothing. I knew how this would go and it really didn't matter.

"Steve will lead you all then. As he has done so well in the past." Ish folded her arms and drummed her fingers along them. "Go then, take what you need. Get me the emerald stone from the dragons to make up for this folly." She turned and then looked back over my shoulder. "But you cannot take Bryce."

"Why?" The single-word question burst out of

me. I had to get my brother away from her, I felt it in my bones.

"Because he's not here," she said. "The rumors of the dragon's healing abilities were too strong and when you were gone for weeks, he didn't believe you would be coming back. He left, heading for Dragon's Ground."

I slowly sank to my knees, unable to believe what I was hearing. Ish had to be wrong, she had to be, because Bryce on his own would never survive.

I reached up to touch the necklace, thinking that perhaps it had fallen off. But the silver lion's head was there, holding my curse at bay. Which meant what was happening had nothing to do with the Jinn.

For just a moment, I wished Maks was there, that I could count on him to be the rock I needed, forgetting what he was. That he'd lied to me. That he was my sworn enemy.

I also took note that Ish didn't even ask about him. She had to believe that he was human and had died on the trip, and . . . she didn't care. That curled a stroke of unease down my spine. Ish was changing.

I didn't like it.

Darcy was speaking to me, Steve barking orders to get out, pack up, and be ready to leave by nightfall. And I knew, I just knew that something bad was going to happen. We never rushed from one job to another, but Ish was pushing us like something was pushing her.

Merlin's words came back to me. The emperor . . . was that what was driving Ish? I stared at her face, trying to read her. Trying to see if there was any fear in the quiver of a muscle, or the twitch of her eyes. But she was motionless, watching us with the predatory gaze of a hunting hawk.

Darcy helped me walk to my room. "We'll find him, Zam. We will."

I wanted to believe her, and a part of me did. I was just certain we would find him in bits and pieces scattered across Dragon's Ground.

"Steve doesn't know about the Jinn coming for us at the castle," I said, feeling the weight of the world crushing on my shoulders. "He doesn't know we'll be riding straight into their path. Bryce could be riding right into their path."

"Then we must convince him," Darcy said. "We have to."

Her unspoken words were between us. We had to, or the last of the Bright Lions of the desert would finally be wiped out by the Jinn.

CHAPTER TWENTY-FOUR

Merlin stared into the crystal ball, tension running through his body as he watched Zamira face down Ish. "She kept the sapphire from her."

"That's good," Flora said softly. "I wasn't sure she would."

The thing was, Merlin wanted Ish to have that stone. But he didn't want Flora to know that, not yet. "She's smart and strong. She just must find her way through the layers that have been laid on her. She barely dodged the Jinn. Barely dodged the Ice Witch's trap to hold her there for them, but she did it. Hell, she even bested the White Raven." He touched the crystal ball, watching as the group scattered, prepping to go back to the Dragon's Ground.

Flora shuddered. "The emperor will know very

soon what is happening. Maggi has gone to try and wake him. I'm sure of it."

Merlin nodded, holding back a shudder of fear. "I agree. She always was a tattletale."

An unexpected roll of premonition washed through him and he spoke before he could catch the words and soften them. "Someone is going to die in the Dragon's Ground, Flora. Someone we need to stay alive."

Her eyes snapped to him. "Are you sure?"

He closed his eyes, seeing the death clearly, seeing the body torn apart by dragons as Zamira sunk to the snow, sorrow breaking her as nothing else could have.

"Yes, goddess help us all, yes."

AFTERWORD

Want more of Zamira, Lila and Maks? Be SURE to get your pre-order freak on now. There is no guarantee that the books will be available on all formats for long periods of time.

Sign up for my newsletter if you want the goods early

NEWSLETTER SIGN UP

Links for Dragon's Ground, Desert Cursed Series Book Two, can be found on my website:

www.shannonmayer.com

If you LOVE the world of Zamira and have missed out, the same world is found in:

Venom and Vanilla
Fangs and Fennel
Hisses and Honey

Which can ALSO be found on my website along with
a metric ton of other books.

www.shannonmayer.com
In case you missed it above ;)

Made in the USA
Middletown, DE
02 April 2018